The Fit Up

A Noble Cause

The Fit Up

A Noble Cause

A.P. Rogers

Matador
9 Priory Business Park,
Wistow Road, Kibworth Beauchamp,
Leicestershire. LE8 0RX
Tel: 0116 279 2299
Email: books@troubador.co.uk
Web: www.troubador.co.uk/matador
Twitter: @matadorbooks

ISBN 978 1800463 561

British Library Cataloguing in Publication Data.
A catalogue record for this book is available from the British Library.

Printed and bound in Great Britain by 4edge Limited
Typeset in 11pt Adobe Garamond Pro by Troubador Publishing Ltd, Leicester, UK

Matador is an imprint of Troubador Publishing Ltd

To Eric

You never doubted my honesty and integrity.
I'm eternally grateful for your calm help and guidance over
the years in seeing the bigger picture.
Thank you Dad.

Contents

PREFACE

The Boomtown Rats didn't like Mondays, but it didn't stop Bob demanding you give him your fucking money for his Ethiopian appeal. Sting wanted his MTV while Mark Knopfler looked at those yo-yos. The days of flares, turn-ups, wide lapels, kipper ties and so on are gone, replaced by 'New Romantic' styles. For the man about town, sharp suits were the order of the day, parallel trousers, thin lapels, narrow ties and smooth leather Italian-looking shoes, plain and pointed, with a low heel.

Whilst programmes such as *The Sweeney* and *The Professionals* had come to an end, others from American shores did their best to fill the void. Michael Mann's *Miami Vice* or later editions of *Starsky and Hutch* provided an alternative portrayal of the boys in blue. It's against this backdrop the book recounts the story of the youngest newly promoted Detective Inspector in the country. He finds himself catapulted into a position of responsibility not only for coming to terms with the hangover of police corruption so prevalent in the sixties and seventies, but also seeking to provide pragmatic solutions to rising crime rates, greeted with a casual indifference by some of his junior officers, and his conscientiousness that higher arrest rates would keep the bosses happy, even if his officers might fall off the wagon at times!

COMMITMENT

Can I trust you? I said, can... I... trust... you? Because if I can't then our conversation is over, finished, never raised again. Now, can I trust you?

Good.

It follows of course that you need to trust me too. I give you my unconditional loyalty, you have that. But more importantly I need to know that whatever you see, whatever you hear, and crucially, whatever you are involved in, I need to know that you have unconditional loyalty to me and dedication to the success of the team.

But if you ever give me cause for concern, then, well let's just leave it at that.

He sat staring at his office door on the other side of his desk. The two commendations, one for bravery, rescuing a mentally ill man from suicide by leaping off a two-hundred-foot pylon, the other for professionalism in a complex theft enquiry, took pride of place on the wall to his right together with his certificate for Freedom of the City of London. The black frames seemed to give them a sense of gravitas commensurate with their importance to him. Two other gold frames contained his qualifications from Hendon as a Detective Officer and a Scenes of Crime Officer. He allowed himself a wry smile as he thought how he had made it into this chair as the youngest Detective Inspector, aged just twenty-nine, in the country.

The early sun burned through the two Georgian windows behind him, and he could tell it was going to be another hot day in late May. But the light beige loose-fitting suit wouldn't be too hot to hold the impending interview, he thought, as he got up to look in his cracked Arsenal mirror hanging beside his closed office door. He adjusted his thin pale blue tie, undoing the top button of his white linen shirt. These were the days of *Miami Vice* on the television, slip-on shoes and no, definitely no socks. He even appeared at Crown Court and gave his evidence not wearing any socks, completing the Don Johnson look, for a bet. *Well,* he thought, *why not? No different to the other games played in not-guilty fights, like getting a particular word or phrase into evidence. Makes it more entertaining than the usual, being told by defence counsel that you're a liar or corrupt.*

He mused, how lucky he was that he hadn't had to go back to uniform to gain promotion, because very few had jumped straight from DS to DI. He was looking at a new recruit for his Central London Pickpocket Squad operating on 'L' Division, part of the Transport Police Division.

I'm interviewing Alan Fish, a young lad recommended by my team as worth giving a go on the squad. Let's see how he answers my questions. If he gets the message, he's in. But if not, I'll kick him into the long grass. Mark my words, this kind of work is sink or swim, and I'm a good swimmer. Let's see if he is too.

"So why do you want to join us?" said DI Bob Trebor, taking a mouthful from his green mug proudly displaying a leaping Jaguar. As was his custom he had with him a junior officer to assist in the interview process. He sat at one end of Bob's desk providing a kind of bridge between the interviewer and interviewee. On this occasion it was Paul Hazel, the officer who had recommended Fish. Opposite Bob sat a young fresh-faced youth somewhere in his early twenties. He knew of Bob's reputation. He sat nervously concocting his answer as he felt the blood drain from his face, his skin colour changed to that of a cheap white envelope. Fish had obviously pushed the boat out, clean-shaven with long but tidy hair swept back to a mullet hanging over his shoulders like Bowie's Ziggy Stardust. By contrast his suit was a quite conservative two-piece dark grey number with a white shirt, reminiscent in Bob's mind of those Jehovah's Witnesses that knock on your door trying to convert you with their latest promotional pamphlets.

With some five years as a uniform PC, Alan Fish was of the opinion that he had more to offer the job. He had a reputation among his peers of being a good thief-taker and investigator, although Bob said he hadn't heard of him.

Didn't know him? Actually that's not true. But I have to maintain this charade of independent view when looking for my new staff. Only an idiot wouldn't do his homework, and believe me, I'm no idiot. Failing to plan is planning to fail. And if I want the best squad with the best results I need to know the form of each of them. This one came to the division under what we call 'a cloud'. He was captured shagging a plonk, aka a WPC, in the back of a Panda car. Well, someone had to go.

The 'Pickpocket' or 'Dip' Squad are 'the Moles', not out of any John le Carré novel, but because in the main, they worked on the Underground of London. They had an enviable reputation among those officers who wanted to work hard and play hard. It only numbered some dozen or so officers consisting of Bob in charge, two Detective Sergeants, the remainder being Detective Constables and a couple of aids to CID. It sometimes inflated in complement when the need arose, say something like Notting Hill Carnival or of course the lead-up to Christmas, or when the South American 'dips' from Chile or Colombia erupt on the landscape of London like an unpleasant rash! Many strived to get on the team. It was a closed shop to those who viewed it selfishly as a good career move; selection for interview with Bob came, many thought, in an unconventional manner. His rationale was that a happy team was a productive and successful team. In other words if each member of the team was content and comfortable working with any other member, a great camaraderie and bond would lead to more success. But you had to be a good thief-taker in the first place. A kind of self-fulfilling prophecy. So to achieve his desire Bob would impress on those working for him that it was they who had the say as to which applicants joined the team. They put forward the nominations as and when vacancies occurred and Bob would interview, but with the proposer present. It worked. It made the squad seem like an exclusive club which many wanted to join. It also produced a degree of envy and vindictive rumour from those who either didn't make the grade or had realised they were inadequate. Jealousy, as Bob observed, is such a wasted emotion!

So where had Fish come from to be caught in the nets of the Dip Squad? It seems he had a past that was, shall we say, a little murky, but by the same token, intriguing. The first four years of his illustrious career had been in north London, or to be more precise, Nam. No not Vietnam. To the uninitiated this meant Tottenham, shortened. During that time he had served his probation, passed his probationary period, got confirmed as a PC, got himself married, and everyone thought, settled. Apart from one dark-haired voluptuous woman police officer, aka WPC, the daughter of a local councillor who took exception to one of the job's rising stars tubbing his daughter. What Fish didn't know was that she had confessed all to Daddy and pledged her undying love for him. Whereas Fish just thought it was regular exercise! Big mistake, because Daddy, who was in the same Masonic Lodge as Tottenham's Chief Superintendent, collared him at the 'Festive Board', the dinner after the lodge meeting, and was reassured that a trap would be sprung to capture the young lovers.

The Royal, to the uninitiated, is a huge Mecca ballroom, which could hold something in the region of 1,500 revellers enjoying either live bands or a disco. Regulars at the venue had been the Dave Clark Five until, as folklore has it, their enthusiastic rendition of 'Bits and Pieces' saw them being banned for stamping their way through the stage and landing in the basement. The ceiling was festooned with thousands of fairy lights and the obligatory giant mirror ball. All round the dance floor, which one had to step down onto, were cheap-looking gold-painted chairs with red velvet cushions, strategically positioned around mock marble tables. To complete the pseudo affluence of the place were about a dozen or so full-sized plastic palm trees scattered around the edge of the dance floor. What an exotic image! Then, as if to make life convenient for the boys in blue, the building was right opposite Tottenham nick. Only some fifty yards from arrest outside to the charge room inside.

"Fish, you're on foot patrol tonight, be outside the Royal at 1am with PC Roberts when they chuck out to prevent public disorder as the 'little treasures' go home," said Sergeant Howard.

"Yes, skipper," he responded.

He thought to himself what splendid irony this was, to be moving on the young bucks as they hung around the exit, just as he had been moved on in earlier years after a night of dancing along with his skinhead mates. Ah, the days of Ben Sherman shirts, Levi 'Sta-Prest' trousers, red braces, and brogues.

"Then team up with WPC Hampton," – the voluptuous beauty – "after your grub at 3am in Panda One."

Play time, he thought, as he confirmed the instruction with his sergeant. She looked across at her lover, and shyly winked at him, without notice of the others on the relief.

"Right then, time is ten to ten, quick cuppa then out you go into the night," said Sergeant Howard as he dismissed the eleven officers of the night duty shift for Tottenham sub-division.

PC Roberts, or Harry, is what in the trade would be called an 'old sweat'. He had about twenty years' service, he'd worked in the West End, he'd done various attachments to vice and crime squads, was well-rounded, and had, some say, a jaundiced attitude to life, particularly those members of the public who had incurred his wrath. He was about forty-five years old, married, two kids in their teens, and lived in a rural area north of Tottenham called 'Coppers Canyon' because so many had found they liked a bit of country life, otherwise known as Cheshunt. Harry was just under six foot with ginger curly hair and a ruddy complexion to his face which gave him an appearance of being constantly angry or out of breath when in reality he had a very relaxed and happy disposition. He was a good journeyman copper, who had no interest in promotion, was robust in his attitude towards young officers senior in rank to him, called a spade a spade, not a shovel.

You get the picture.

At 11.15pm, Roberts, in Panda Two, took a call on the radio to a disturbance at The Royal. He confirmed his attendance as he turned into Chestnut Road to do one circuit of Tottenham's one-way system. Alan amused himself blowing rings into the chilly night air as he walked east along Broad Lanes, having heard Harry's confirmation. In a matter of seconds Harry pulled up alongside him.

"Come on, get in, sounds like there might be a body for you on this one at the Royal."

Fish, ever keen to learn and gain experience from a seasoned and respected copper like Harry, happily jumped into the passenger seat. They parked in the service road and sauntered in, passing through the brass-handled doors, acknowledging the bouncers as they were escorted to the manager's office on the first floor. Harry led the charge and pushed open the door, which had been ajar, and saw the manager sat behind a mock Georgian desk, of the kind you see in that famous black and white photograph of JFK, with his kid playing underneath. Only this time there was no kid – just, to Harry's mind, a curious bloke dressed head to foot in women's clothing, complete with blonde wig, and wearing black tights under a short tartan mini skirt, sat uncomfortably opposite him. Was this some kind of reverential homage to The Bay City Rollers who had recently reformed, probably because they'd run out of money, and were due to play The Royal the following week? *In any event he's not right*, thought Roberts as he looked to the manager for some insight into why he had been called.

Apparently, the transvestite, something of a public rarity, had been cruising around the population of the dance floor looking for a one-night stand, after failing in pulling a punter in the High Road. He had been spotted by one of the floor walker bouncers who, not knowing whether they should thump him or eject him, went for the safe option of taking him to the manager's office. That way they didn't have to make a decision. The manager briefly went over why a man dressed in women's clothing wasn't acceptable in his dance hall. Fish agreed in his mind but couldn't figure out what kind of offence he'd committed.

With a reassuring air, Harry said, "You're nicked, come with me." Without a sound they left the dance hall to a chorus of wolf whistles from the bouncers. He put him in the back of the Panda car for a short ride, round the block, back to the nick, while Al, figuring their latest acquisition wasn't going to cut up rough, wandered across to the nick to await their arrival.

"Sit there," said Harry as he entered the charge room, indicating to his prisoner to occupy the long bench against the wall. Roberts had a brief word with Sergeant Howard, the prisoner was put in cell number three, and having agreed it would be a good arrest for Alan to be involved in, Harry went off to find Fish.

Harry entered the reserve room and said, "Well, Al, there you are, he's banged up, we've just to sort out the script. Do you know what you've got?"

Ordinarily, Judges' Rules allows for officers to confer together and commit to evidence their joint recollection of events and what has been said. But in this situation the 'script' means the officers get together to agree what the evidence is going to be. When, for Harry, the arrested person deserves it, then that's fair enough. In the case of this one, being a social worker, for him, meant he did deserve it. As far as Harry was concerned, you can't have men who are obviously in a position of trust, working with kids, walking around in women's clothing. His view was that he was a liability, and he couldn't have a liability. So sod him, he deserves what he gets.

"You'll be witness to me, cos it has to be an officer in uniform to see the offence and it's got to be corroborated."

"Yeah," said Al, mentally licking his lips with interested excitement. "What's it about then?"

Harry filled him in.

"Can you believe it, I've found out he's a social worker dealing with kids in care. So basically in law he's importuning for an immoral purpose. Heard of it?"

Al shook his head, so Roberts then outlined the plot.

"I've done these before when I was at West End

Central nick doing vice. There are just a couple of things to remember: first, we have to be in uniform to witness the offence being committed, well that's okay. Second, it has to be in a public place."

Harry then went through the evidence. Content with what Harry had outlined, Al returned to the charge room with him where Harry's version of events was related to the sergeant, who without question charged him in his correct name, telling him he would be in custody until the following day to appear at the local Magistrates' Court. They adjourned to the canteen, did their paperwork and committed the evidence to their pocketbooks, while the transvestite made himself comfortable under the one issued blanket, stinking of previous drunks, and the plastic-covered pillow, trying to get some sleep before his appearance the next day.

Inspector Wilkinson, the night duty senior officer, finished chatting up the peroxide-blonde civilian telephonist, summing up in his own mind that she wasn't interested in him, and left the reserve room. Two doors and a short walk later, he found himself in the charge room, where Sergeant Howard was just 'topping and tailing' some paperwork from a couple he charged earlier.

"What's happening to Harry's?"

"Charged him," replied the sergeant. "Appearing tomorrow morning."

Wilkinson, unfazed, simply said, "I know Harry's done this sort of thing before; how's Fish? Any concerns?"

"Don't think so, no. Both seemed happy enough when I charged him, her, it. Whatever. No, no problem, guv."

"Right, after they've had their grub, Harry is to take the dog handler out till booking off. His dog van is off the road with a busted fan belt. And stick Fish with the 'Doris', what's her name again? In Panda One."

"Surprised at you, guv," said the sergeant. "Crumpet like that, how could you forget? It's Norma."

Guv said, "Yes of course." He paused thoughtfully. "Good job her second name isn't Stits," and strolled off into the station yard.

Fish gulped his last mouthful of tea and said, "Right Harry, that's me done, cheers for the body. Are you going to cover the remand tomorrow? I'm a bit tucked up with that hospital appointment as I told you."

Harry responded, "Yeah, no sweat, easy four hours minimum overtime plus two travelling off nights. I'll only be there half an hour, the boys at court will get me on quick."

Al said, "Cheers mate, see you later. I'm out in Panda One with 'Miss Freebody'."

They laughed in unison and went their separate ways. The two lovers met in the police station yard. Norma was driving Panda One, and Al skipped lightly into the front passenger seat as if on air.

Now the Panda car had gone through a number of guises over the years. The reason for this, you would imagine, was to improve the quality of patrol vehicles for the officers to better perform their role. Cobblers! The various police forces using them up and down the country simply bought the ends of lines of vehicles from the variety of car manufacturers. They got them cheap, of course, and the companies got rid of old stock. So it was that, in London, it started with the Morris Minor, then the

British Leyland 1300, then the Allegro, or 'all aggro' as it was often referred to, the Ford Escort and at this time the Vauxhall Astra. When first introduced in the late sixties the idea was to mobilise a number of officers who had previously ridden 'Noddy' motorbikes made by Velocette and by putting them in patrol cars they could not only respond to radio calls for assistance much quicker, they could also convey members of the public to the nick or indeed villains they arrested. Provided, of course, they were willing to behave. Some say the mobilisation isolated the copper on the beat from his public. It also meant male and female officers, if so inclined, let's say hopelessly drawn to each other, could get up to 'naughties' or hanky-panky!

He closed the door, gave a knowing nod to Norma and said, "All right, babe?"

She looked in the rear-view mirror, and seeing she looked presentable, did a three-point turn and drove out of the station yard. He didn't need an answer from her, he knew she loved being with him, and everything that meant. What he didn't know was how she was dressed under the less-than-flattering uniform. She had worn black stockings and suspenders for the past two nights in the hope she might be teamed up with him, without luck. All that regret was quickly forgotten by her as he carefully slipped his hand across her left thigh, reassuringly, unseen by the passing public as she drove to the north end of the ground and his hand went north to her shaven haven. As he did so he recognised the faint outline of a stocking being pulled under strain by a suspender, taut on her firm skin.

"That feels good, anything on your mind?" Norma squirmed, as she increased speed, pulling away from the traffic lights. "Like what you feel? Fancy a trip to heaven? Any ideas?"

Al said, "How about the Tottenham Marshes, the alarm's just gone off at the engineering firm on the service road approaching the marshes."

He took the radio call from the nick, assigning them to it. The marshes were an area of any number of football pitches available for the Sunday football teams and was also the scene of many skid pan antics by night duty officers bored out of their skins that nothing was happening that night, and so impromptu driving skills were honed on the flat and slippery grass.

After a quick look around the outside of the factory, it was clear it was yet another faulty alarm. Al confirmed the key holder was on the way to reset it and the lovers drove off towards the vast dark area of the marshes, illuminated only by the searching headlights of Panda One. Full of expectation, Norma drove to the side of the darkened changing rooms, a small eerie building shrouded in dense foliage; she was content this was far enough off the beaten track to prevent anyone finding them.

Inspector Wilkinson was just in the process of taking the alarm call to the engineering works, when he heard Panda One volunteer its services. *I can carry on having a five-minute fag break out of sight of the shift*, he thought. He sat in darkness, at the back of the Sunday league football changing rooms in a little cul-de-sac created by a redundant shed that had seen better days and a run of rotting wooden fence reducing itself back to the land. His attention was drawn to the headlights of a car, scanning across the neatly trimmed grass of pitch number one adjacent to him. He couldn't see the car as the lights faded to darkness passing on his blindside at the side of the changing rooms, but he figured it must be Norma and Fish doing a round trip as they continued their patrol. All was quiet as he continued his quest to acquire his own lung cancer, until the radio burst into life telling him that Al had been requested to meet the key holder on his arrival. Wilkinson's curiosity got the better of him; he stepped out into the still air of the night, thinking he would make them jump if he crept up on them, while perhaps they were having a crafty fag.

There is no way of putting it delicately. Norma sat astride Al on the front passenger seat and was riding him as he played with her ample breasts. Both were loving their physical closeness, him getting satisfaction from her enthusiastic pumping on his cock while she believed she was very definitely in love with the man she wanted to be with forever, once of course he had left his wife! The heat they generated inside met the cool air outside on the windows and succeeded in steaming them up. The lovers were in heaven as Norma shuddered to a climax, and the passenger door opened.

"What the fuck?" Wilkinson was lost for words; he wanted to say so much more but his unannounced presence left all those present completely dumb.

Norma scrambled back to her seat, apologising profusely, while Al fought with his zip to regain his dignity.

"Both of you see me before you go off duty at six," said Wilkinson as he left them.

It was difficult to know who was most in shock.

"Oh my god, oh my god," panicked Norma. "What are you going to say, Al?"

"What am I going to say? What's to say? We've been captured bang to rights," he said as he thought about the last time she had called out for her god in what were somewhat more private surroundings.

"Well, think of something, this is all your fault. I should never have gone out with you. You're married. Well, you'll have to leave her now."

Fish, feeling a bit pissed off – how all this could be laid at his door? – said, "Now hang on a minute, I don't remember you resisting, you wore the webbing tonight, didn't you? Not exactly routine for nights I think, or have I got it wrong? Don't think we can do anything but plead guilty."

They continued to bicker, in between protracted periods of silence, each dreading their exposure to the rest of the relief.

"I've got to meet up with Harry before I go off," said Al.

They crept back in the yard five minutes ahead of time. Harry was waiting with the dog handler; they chatted, having a fag before knocking-off time. Al joined them. There was a bit of laughter between them, which Norma overheard.

"How could you?" she said, challenging Al on what she had seen in the yard as they walked along the dimly lit corridor to face the man who held their futures in his hand.

"I didn't say fuck-all, sweet cheeks. We were joking about the geezer earlier tonight. I wouldn't do that to you."

They knocked on the drab blue paint-chipped door at the end of the passage where their fate would be learnt.

"Come in," said Wilkinson.

They walked smartly into the office and stood side by side in front of the seated Inspector. Al had a sudden rush of blood and thought he would take the initiative and the blame.

"Sir—" he said, but before he could explain that it was all a momentary lapse, and a complete one-off, Wilkinson said,

"Shut the fuck up. I don't want to hear any excuses. I know what I saw and I know this isn't the first time."

"But sir," said Norma.

Wilkinson said, "Listen, you dopes, I was uniform when you two were still in liquid form. I don't want to hear any bollocks from either of you. This is what is going to happen. You, Fish, are married, you are going to do a short report telling me that your wife is under a lot of stress and is missing her parents. You will ask for a move to 'L' division where she will be able to be nearer to her mum and dad. I will recommend the move on compassionate grounds, and you, madam, will ask for a posting to the domestic violence unit at the other end of the division, which has just started, so that you can widen your career, and not your fucking legs in two different postal districts. Now get out the pair of you, say your goodbyes and get on with your lives separately."

They turned and walked sheepishly out of the office to begin their respective new careers.

So this is how Fish, about a year later, having shown great promise on a number of crime initiatives, comes to be sitting in front of me. Now let's see what he's made of.

DI Trebor ran through all the usual background detail with Fish, outlining his expectations of him, confirming his wife wouldn't mind him doing some very late nights and early morning search warrants. He ran through a couple of hypothetical scenarios with him, and with a little bit of prompting from Paul Hazel he seemed to give a good account of himself.

"So you think you've got something to offer the Dip Squad? I expect nothing less than total commitment and loyalty to me and, as importantly, the squad. One final question. Do you have vision?"

Al was a little perplexed by the question, "Sorry sir?"

Trebor asked again, "Do you have vision?"

He could see his message wasn't getting across to Fish.

"Look I've just got to pop along to see the Chief Inspector. You two stay here." And he left the room.

Paul tried to explain, "You know how we work, we're good at what we do, the governor gets results from us and he keeps the bosses off our backs. Sometimes something will happen and you might be asked to confirm you saw something, or you might see something even though, you know…?"

As his voice tailed off, Al said, "Not a problem, I've seen all sorts before."

With that, Paul, happy that he had got his message across to the newest member of the team, saw DI Trebor re-enter the office.

"I trust the question has been answered, has it? Good. Welcome to the team, Al. Go with Paul, he'll sort out your desk and give you the low-down. Go and meet the rest of them. I don't expect you to be doing much today, play time starts tomorrow. But the good news is 5pm is 'beer o'clock' so see you there. Mine's a lager."

A little shell-shocked, Al left with Paul to settle in.

I know what you're wondering. What happened to Harry's prisoner? Well he appeared at the Magistrates' Court and pleaded guilty. Only Harry gave evidence. Strange thing was, he never made a complaint against police, something so routine, it becomes part of the defence strategy. But he didn't. Of course the Magistrate found the case proved against him, still dressed in his tartan outfit, despite his explanations. As Mandy Rice-Davis said, "Well he would say that wouldn't he!" Oh yes, and he lost his job. Too much of a risk to those kids, don't you agree? The moral of the story? Think very carefully about your dress code!

2

DANGEROUS LIAISONS

Mario Bergamot stood at his lectern; his instructing brief, a slightly built weasel with the look of a used car dealer by the name of Charlie Dickson, sat hidden behind him. Mario pulled his now slipping gown forward onto his broad shoulders, hiding his late-sixties corpulent frame. Years of practising at the bar and reminiscing his triumphs in the infamous wine bar near Middle Temple and the long lunches had taken their toll. He cast his eye around Court, falling purposefully on the jury. The venue for his latest performance was the historic Middlesex Crown Court, an imposing building built on the south-west corner of Westminster Square just before the outbreak of the First World War in the art nouveau gothic style on the site of the original belfry for Westminster Abbey. It had been the Guildhall for the county of Middlesex, decorated with medieval-looking gargoyles and other similar architecture. The two main courts, one and two, had magnificent stone blocks and oak-panelled walls, above which were oil paintings of various judicial dignitaries from a bygone age whose eyes and stern expressions seemed to follow you around the court room. There was some natural light at the top of the walls but it had to be supplemented with huge chandeliers, which would have been more at home in a castle setting.

"Now then, officer, I'm not going to beat around the bush, you're a liar. Your evidence is littered with untruths. To add to your efforts, you embroiled another officer in your conspiracy to pervert the course of justice. What do you say to that?"

DI Bob Trebor slowly but methodically took a sip from his glass of water, his right hand steady as he took in the assertion and dwelled on his choice of reply. He was no stranger to this kind of allegation. You could say it was par for the course. The defendant, a nasty little scrote called Gerry Monk, alleged corruption shortly after he had been charged at the nick. Basically it was a standard for a villain who had the kind of form he had to make a complaint against police. That way the defence could go on the attack from the start. If they succeeded in planting the idea that maybe the police hadn't been straight then they're halfway home. They'd say, "Isn't it the case, officer, that my client, following his arrest made an allegation of corruption against you?" The officer would have to admit it, even though it was a nonsense, and knowing that a public complaint such as this was regarded by those investigating as 'sub judice'. In other words it cannot be investigated until after the case. It's regarded by many in the force as an irritant, but it goes with the turf.

Monk sat mumbling in the dock. "This is another fit-up from those fuckers on the Dip Squad," he said as he shuffled, still seated, around on the bench.

Monk is and has always been a gobby shit, and always will be. He's a violent thief if challenged, and usually goes dipping with blacks because as he said to me, the 'old bill' usually nick them first because he says they're easier to convict. Monk will always exploit the situation, sacrificing if he has to, and coward that he is, any co-defendant, particularly if they are black. In this trial he's standing alone and so he needs to perform in court. Let's see.

Monk looked angrily across at the jury. They had been subjected to a constant commentary from him on the evidence given by the prosecution. Countless times the Judge, His Honour Judge Ramm, had to stop the trial, and require Mario to speak with his client to tell him to shut up, and that he would have his chance to speak later in the trial. Monk took no notice of this and continued with his outbursts, obviously working on the basis, in his mind, that throwing enough shit, some will stick. But the best theatre was yet to come.

DI Trebor waited until Monk took a breath, some of the jury giggling to themselves at his performance. It was nothing like what they'd seen on that new cop show in a Miami courtroom on the telly.

"Sir, that is not the case. What I have told the court is the truth, the whole truth and nothing but the truth. I understand why Monk would allege as he has, he's a professional thief. Just not, sad to say, a very good one."

This time Monk jumped to his feet and launched at the rail of the dock, "You're fucking sad! That's bleeding good coming from you, Trebor, you bent bastard. Listen, you tried to get me out of the cell for interview, didn't you? What for? If you're right and telling the truth, you had all the evidence already. It don't matter what I did, we could play Ludo or Snakes and Ladders, you would still fit me up. No fucking way was I coming out of that cell."

Judge Ramm boomed out across the court, "Sit down, Monk. Mr. Bergamot, this is the last time I shall say this. If you cannot control your client, I shall have him removed and we will hear the rest of the trial in his absence."

Monk knew not to push his luck any further. He felt happy the jury had got the message.

Bob took a measured pause before going over the evidence again.

"As I said earlier in evidence to this court, Monk was seen to move in behind the elderly female boarding the train. Hiding his right hand with the jacket over his left forearm, I saw him place his right hand into the top of her open shoulder bag, which she carried over her right shoulder. He then removed it empty. Detective Constable Champion grabbed Monk round the torso, pinning both his arms at his side. I moved in to try and speak to the female who, oblivious to the attempted theft, had gone further inside the carriage. Monk by now had started fighting with the officer trying to free himself, shouting, 'Get off me, fuck off.' I gave assistance to DC Champion who was struggling with the defendant. Regrettably, before I had a chance to secure the female and her details, the doors closed and the train departed with her on board."

The prosecution barrister, Rupert Hyams, stood. "Will you just go over again what happened next, officer?"

"Yes, Your Honour," he said, according the appropriate deferential recognition to the judge. "I went with DC Champion and the prisoner to an office at the entrance to the station to await transport to the nearest police station."

Hyams, knowing the answer said, "And this is where,

as you said in your evidence earlier, you conducted a search of the prisoner, prior to police transport arriving. Is that correct?" Bob confirmed his barrister's summary. "Just tell the members of the jury again, why you did this?"

"Monk has been known to carry a knife before, and a search would reduce any risk of him being able to use it."

Hyams responded, "Yes, officer, a list of his previous convictions is before the court, and I think among some twenty convictions, he has two for carrying an offensive weapon, and in both cases these were knives. Is that correct?"

"Yes, Your Honour," Bob said, directing his reply to the judge.

Monk started mumbling again. The judge glared at him. Bob Trebor went on to describe the search.

"I requested Monk to open his trousers to show he was not carrying anything. He said, "There you are you, queer, I'll drop me kecks as well." He fumbled to hold onto the top of his underpants. As he did so a wallet fell out on the floor."

With that, Monk leapt to his feet. "Oi, jury," he shouted, "another load of lies. Look." And with that he stood facing the jury and dropped his trousers.

"See, I don't wear skiddies!"

The courtroom erupted as they witnessed Monk's meat and two veg swinging in the breeze. The dock officer jumped on Monk trying to pull up his trousers at the same time. "Get off me, you poof. They're all fucking queer in here."

His Honour said, "Right that's it. Take him down, officer. Get him out of my court. I'm going to adjourn for a few minutes. Mr Bergamot, I suggest those instructing you go and speak with your client. I'm sorry, members of the jury, I think it prudent to have a break for ten minutes. Please go to your room now. Thank you." They filed out, completely bemused as to what had taken place. Monk, still shouting and swearing that the whole thing was a fit-up, was taken down below. The weasel slid out the back of court. The courtroom fell quiet.

"Court rise," bellowed the usher.

Judge Ramm rose to his feet, cast an eye round the courtroom, finally falling on defence counsel with a look of disdain. He looked up to the fine William Morris-inspired ceiling, admiring the neo-gothic architecture, sighed, picked up his trial notes and swept out of the door to the left, held open by the court usher.

The cell complex under the courts exuded that familiar smell of sweaty feet and stale body odour. In cell three, Monk sat on the bench muttering to himself. "Another fit-up," he repeated to himself. *But I've got Trebor on the run*, he thought to himself. Good move of his to mention he knew that Trebor was having it off with his mate's lawyer. Told him so, too, at an earlier remand; he even told him he wouldn't mention it at the forthcoming trial. Obviously got him going although he promised his discretion. Keep just saying the evidence is bent. Just get the jury to focus on that.

"All right, Gerry? Look, we just need to calm down a bit, just focus on the facts and you'll get a result," the weasel pleaded.

In the meantime, Trebor left the witness box, stepping slowly down the three steps to the well of the court. He looked across at his barrister, who appeared to be reviewing his papers, but deep in his lap was today's *Times* crossword. Trebor thought to himself, *Clue, to egg on, five letters; toast! Twat!* He carried on to the bench opposite the jury box and slumped down.

His mind drifted to the brief he'd met at Bow Street Court a couple of weeks earlier. *God she's fit*, he thought. A bet he had with DS Hunt that he would invite her for a coffee brought a wry smile to his tired face. He won, she accepted. Since that time they'd seen each other at least four times. She seemed keen on him. Last Thursday they met by Eros at Piccadilly. A couple of beers in the Kilt and Celt, then adjourned to a small police office overlooking the junction at the bottom end of Regent Street. It was a place that was unknown to the public, somewhere the police would take their arrested prisoners while they waited for transport to the local nick. It was secure; you needed a police key to get in, then once in there you could lock it from the inside. But you could see all of the junction through a large window with one-way glass. In other words, you could see out but the great unwashed couldn't see in. It was there they made love across the office table.

They laughed and joked with each other as they stumbled into the office. Bob closed and locked the door behind them. She turned, looked into his eyes and pushing her tongue into his open mouth, they kissed. Her right hand drifted straight down between his legs. Bob felt his manhood growing as she rubbed him gently on the outside of his trousers. He reciprocated, feeling from her knee to her thigh. He couldn't believe his discovery. Stockings! Fucking hell, she's up for it. *Why else is she kitted up?* he reasoned in his mind. *And she's married, mind you, so am I*, he thought. He gently laid her back across the Formica table. *That's handy*, he thought. *The tabletop is the right height, right at the top of my legs, and easy to lift her on to.*

She groaned as his hand worked its way round the edge of her French knickers, his finger pushing inside. He leant forward, the end of his tie dancing across the top of her fanny. The brief sank her tongue into his mouth again and again. She pulled him round the side of the table so he stood like a surgeon leaning over his patient. She lost no time in undoing his trousers and pulling his full penis out. In one natural move she began to suck on him, licking the shaft and his balls. He worked on her pussy, feeling her getting wet. He pulled her knickers down her legs as they draped over the end of the desk. They hung tantalisingly off her right shoe. In the light from the other side of the window he could see her neatly trimmed lady garden calling him to attend to her. Unable to resist any more he returned to the end, spread her legs wider, and pulling her towards him, he pushed up inside her. She let out another groan of ecstasy and a smile of approval toward him. As he looked to his left he watched a blonde combing her hair in the mirror glass, oblivious to the carnal gymnastics happening just in front of her. He smiled to himself as she brushed and pouted straight at him as he pumped vigorously and his lover moaned.

"DI Trebor, DI Trebor!" said counsel for the prosecution.

"Sorry what was that, sir?" said Bob as the barrister stood in front of him.

Hyams said, "What else is there to mention to the court before close? Anything?"

"No I don't think so, sir. That performance of his was enough. We've got his form in because of his allegations of corruption, so no I don't think so. The jury seem pretty switched on. I think they saw through the drama."

"Well I hope so, officer," said Hyams, "I think we can do without any more theatricals."

Just then a loud knock could be heard from the door through which the judge had left some minutes earlier.

The court usher entered followed by His Honour Judge Ramm. "Court rise," boomed the usher.

All stood, waiting for the judge to stand in front of his chair, where he bowed to those assembled in the well of the court. They each returned the compliment and everyone except counsel for the defence, Mr Bergamot, remained standing. The weasel scurried in and sat behind him.

"Defendant please, dock officer," said the clerk sat just in front of His Honour.

Monk reappeared in the dock. "Yes, Mr Bergamot," said the judge in a tired voice.

"Your Honour, my client is deeply apologetic for his outburst prior to us rising. His emotions had got the better of him and he now understands the seriousness of his behaviour. There will be no further acts of that nature."

Ramm said, "I sincerely hope so. Let's leave it at that then."

Bob thought what a load of rubbish that was. He remembered Monk doing the self-same thing in an earlier trial with him. *He just gets away with murder every bloody time*, he thought.

"Right, let's have the jury back in," said His Honour.

Another court officer opened the door at the rear of the jury benches and the twelve good men (and women) and true filed back in, sitting in their earlier seats. Bergamot sat down.

"Members of the jury, I'm sorry we had to break in the fashion we did and on behalf of the court, can I apologise for any offence caused? The defendant wishes to apologise to the court and I have an assurance there will be no repetition," said His Honour.

Several of the female members of the jury just stared across the courtroom, while a couple of the men looked sternly at Monk. Bob watched them and thought that maybe this time his little performance had worked.

DC Champion entered the 'bear pit' for his roasting at the hands of Mr Bergamot.

Hyams rose to his feet. "That's the evidence for the Crown, Your Honour."

Ramm said, "Mr Bergamot, will you be calling any evidence?"

Bergamot rose to his feet, "No, Your Honour."

"Right then, closing speeches," said the judge.

As was normal, prosecution first, then defence, then the judge's summing-up. Bob knew that he was in for about an hour or so of droning particularly by the defence who would claim what a victim of circumstance Monk was. How right he was.

Bergamot rose to his feet and trotted out a euphemism, which Bob was no stranger to, from earlier skirmishes with members of the bar. "Members of the jury, it is for me to address you on behalf of the defendant. His Honour will address you on matters of the law while it is my responsibility to deal with the evidence such as it is. It is for the prosecution to present their case, and they do so through calling witnesses whom you have heard evidence from. Imagine if you will, that you have to build a brick wall. You require a particular number of bricks and you lay those bricks using mortar to cement them together. So it is with this prosecution. Each piece of evidence is like one of those bricks, and the prosecution endeavours to cement them together with what they say are other pieces of evidence, to create a wall which cannot be breached. Well, it's my job to explore the weaknesses in that wall and knock holes in it, thereby exposing the weakness of the prosecution's case." Mario continued trawling through the case as he saw it, then turning to the lacklustre evidence given by DC Champion. "Now, members of the jury, we come to DI Trebor's partner in crime in this farrago, this tissue of, we would say, lies."

Judge Ramm gave Mario a steady glare over the top of his glasses as if to say, "Don't push it."

Mario went on, "Now you heard DC Champion's evidence. You will have noticed, as indeed I pointed out, that it was at odds with that of his fellow officer. In fact on a number of occasions he admitted he had made a mistake and had to correct himself. So if I had not knocked holes in that wall, he would have left you believing his version of events married with Trebor's. We now know it doesn't. So ask yourself this: is it mistakes through negligence, which would be random in their effect, or was it deliberate lying? He's like a waiter who always gives his customers the wrong change. If he's mistaken then you would expect the mistakes to be fairly even between the customer, or the defendant, and himself. But he is a dishonest waiter; all his mistakes work in his favour. He's been found out, members of the jury. This whole event is contrived simply to get my client into court again. Both officers have clearly never heard of the expression, 'Liar, liar, pants on fire'." Bergamot, happy he'd made the point, finished off, outlining how his client couldn't possibly be guilty, and sat down.

Speeches over, the judge summed up on the law on the two counts, on the indictments of theft and of handling stolen goods, and sent the jury out to deliberate whether they would add to Monk's list of form.

The judge rose again to the command of the usher, "Court rise," and swept out of the side door.

Monk was led back to the cells, and the weasel scurried off to see his client. The two barristers, who up until this point had exuded an air of ambivalence towards one another, now engaged in friendly banter about what they would be employed on next. For them, it was just a job. An academic exercise in who could best sell their story to the court. *Pure theatre*, Bob thought, as he went for a coffee in the police room.

As usual, this was down in the basement – no natural light and right next to the bogs! This was no different, as he remembered, to his experience at the overflow court for Middlesex Crown Court in St James Square. The court was a rather grand Georgian house over several floors in the corner of the square, adjacent to the Libyan Embassy. It had been loaned to the judiciary by Lady Astor and had been temporarily converted to accommodate Crown courtrooms for defendants who were on bail. How quaint, he thought, that the barristers and lawyers could use the main staircase, with its wonderfully lush deep-red carpet, but the coppers and detectives had to use the stone staircase, originally utilised by the servants when it was her main London residence. The police canteen was in the original basement kitchens. No luxury then for the common people! He remembered the converted courtroom on the first floor, in what he thought had been a ballroom at one time. You gave your evidence from a witness box on castors, which, if the court staff had forgotten to put the brakes on the wheels, could send you careering like some gloriously upmarket skateboard across the ballroom floor towards the windows overlooking the square.

The other thing that was weird about giving evidence there was that as you stood in the witness box, you looked at a long wall with elegant Georgian windows along its length. In between each of these was a large floor-to-ceiling mirror. As you swore by almighty God to tell the truth, you could see yourself in the mirror. *I reckon the defence set that up, to put us off our stride*, thought Bob. *Didn't work*. Bob paid for his coffee and sat in a battle-weary leather armchair, kindly donated or discarded, dependant on your view, from the barristers' robing room. Obviously, it wasn't up to the requisite standard for arses far more learned than those who now occupied it. He sat back with the case papers on his lap. He opened them and scanned through the antecedents for Monk. Putting his coffee on the floor to the left of his chair, he raised his hand to his forehead as if to shield his eyes from the bright lights of the room. In this pose, anyone casually passing would assume that Bob was diligently studying his brief. Reality was, he could close his eyes and have a snooze!

Last night on the "hit and miss" had taken its toll on DI Trebor. He was suffering – maybe five minutes of shut-eye would do the trick. His eyes closed and he drifted away.

3

SUSPICIOUS MINDS

One good turn deserves another. I don't want you to get the wrong impression, I've not suddenly become the 'Good Samaritan'. But sometimes you unwittingly do something which turns out to have a greater effect than you ever expected.

Dave Champion sat looking out of the front window of the taxi drivers' café in Eversholt Street. The delicious aroma of a full English breakfast wafted past his nostrils as the fully glazed door sucked the air out as it was opened by another black cab driver entering. Following in his slipstream was Paul Hazel. They agreed to meet there that Saturday as a precursor to hunting for dips plundering the Underground system of London. Paul went to the high counter and ordered two teas from the daughter of the owner, Del, who jealously watched over his girl, lest some silver-tongued lounge lizard should sweep his beautiful blonde-haired girl off her feet.

She called across to the elderly lady standing sentry at the chromed upright boiler, manning the large brown enamel teapot, "Two teas please, Josie."

And Josie nodded in acknowledgment. Until that point Paul had thought the blonde had an air of quiet sophistication about her, but her demand of Josie dispelled any thought of that, as she sounded off like some Dickensian street trader.

Dave looked up from his *Sun* newspaper as Paul delivered the two mugs of steaming tea to the Formica table. "What time did you tell the young offender to get here?" asked Dave quizzically.

Paul chuckled and said, "I told him four thirty, but you know what he's like, he'll have done it in, especially if he went back to hers last night. He'll service her before he gets here. How did he pull such a young bird? I mean she's fit but she's a bit young."

Dave sighed, "Dirty lucky bastard. But she is twenty, you know, just looks younger."

Paul and Dave sat on opposite benches chatting about the amount of overtime for payment they'd made so far this month. Ten minutes and two consumed mugs of tea later, Al breezed in, seemingly full of the joys of spring. No apology for lateness or any explanation for delay. "Teas all round?"

Paul responded, "Yeah all right, come on I'll give you a hand," and joined Al at the counter to retrieve the order.

"Two ham and one cheese please, Josie," said the blonde bombshell, repeating the order of the two cabbies in front of them. "Oh, and Josie, can I have some more tongue please?"

Paul looked at Al and with that they began to waggle their tongues at each other as if Maori rugby players waiting to take on the English at Twickenham. She didn't get the joke.

"That's nice," whispered Paul, "offer of oral sex, always appreciated."

"I don't like to talk about it," said Al quietly, seizing the one-liner as they returned to their seats.

I smell a rat, a particularly smelly rat, among my number. It was no coincidence to me that each time I organised a squad initiative to go out and nick the curse of the Underground network in London, the dips, mysteriously the ground would go quiet – no reports of thefts, or suspects. Most unnatural for a busy Saturday when the network was bursting with travellers and visitors to London. A detective, not one of mine, is tipping off the thieves that we're working. I've got an idea, but I need to flush him out.

He'd been given the green light by his old mate Frazer McKay, a seasoned detective sergeant who had made being indispensable an art form. Not only did he have an arterial route to the Area Commander, he had a web of contacts in all walks of life whom he could call on for a favour, from the left-wing press to security services, police, military, you name it.

The boss could see him now. Time was about 4pm on Friday as Bob wandered in to where the Area Commander's secretary had positioned herself to block any forward assault on his office door whilst still being able to see who was passing by in the corridor. She stood like a terracotta warrior until she saw that it was Bob endeavouring to negotiate the *Krypton Factor* of tables and chairs leading to his boss's office.

"Oh hello, DI Trebor, he knows you're coming."

"OK thanks, Mavis, how are you?"

"I'm fine thank you, Bob, go on in."

He tapped on the door and entered on invitation. Sitting at the far end of a long mahogany table, the Area Commander, resplendent in full uniform, rose to his full six foot two, smoking his trademark Half Corona cigar.

"Come in, Bob. Have a seat. Drink?"

Bob sat to the side of the table, and leaning on it said, "Please guv." He knew from earlier 'chats' with his leader that tea or coffee were not the intended beverages.

Eric Brown, or 'the boss' as he was known, poured two gentlemen's measures of a single malt into the Edinburgh crystal glasses he had retrieved from behind some strategically placed books and folders in the bookcase.

"Now then," he paused, "how are you settling in then? I was beginning to think I'd never see you, what with that long trial at the Bailey you had, then your Inspector's course."

Bob took a sip, "Yes guv it seemed like that. In answer, though, it's good. I'm enjoying the challenge of getting the Dip Squad to respond to my direction of strategy and operation. I've been in charge of them now for about three months, still work in progress," he answered like a politician.

Eric took a sip and said, "Mmmm. I see you've been organising specific operations over the weekends. How's your success with that?"

Bob thought, *He must know they'd been a failure in the main. But what was he driving at, or did he know already?* Detective Sergeant Brian Western, an officer with over twenty years' service, and now the newly created Scenes of Crime Officer had, in his earlier years, been part of an impromptu Dip Squad in the days when no specific team had been created to tackle the scourge of the Underground network. There were always rumours about Brian and those he worked with at that time. Some said that various officers were 'on the take' from some of the dips. It was known by those in the know as 'taxing' or 'giving a life' and came about when, say, a pickpocket was stopped and searched for stolen property. If none was found but the dip had a large amount of cash on him, say two or three hundred pounds, which was obviously the proceeds of crime from an earlier theft and which it was quite apparent could not easily be proved, then he would be given an option. He would be 'taxed' by the officer, by handing over the cash he had on him in return for a 'life', which would mean he'd be released with no further action by the police. If he didn't comply with this arrangement, he'd be arrested and charged with attempted theft from a person unknown or the earlier offence of being a suspected person, loitering with intent to steal, no longer on the statute books. This now defunct offence required evidence of two overt acts of stealing, whereas now, under the Criminal Attempts Act, only one is necessary. So those who railed against the old 'sus' law, some said, now found themselves more easily arrested and convicted! He'd still lose his cash, but now he'd be appearing in court, having been 'fitted up' for an offence.

I think I need to clarify my position… I hate thieves and particularly sneak thieves, the kind that prey on their unwitting victims, stealing purses or wallets. They often carry knives in case of resistance, turning the theft, if they need to, into an outright robbery. They cause such misery, taking the money, selling on the credit cards for fraudulent use and then throwing away those little personal items such as photographs of loved ones. If you know of someone who has had this happen to them, you'll know the hurt it causes. They are shits. But worse still are bent coppers. The kind who are on the take from the thieves having taxed them or given them a 'life'. This is the era into which

I've been promoted, and I don't like it, not one bit. My buzz is catching the shits and putting them away. Now if that means being 'visionary' to do so, then so be it. They get away with more than we catch them for, so need to be culled. Isn't that a kind of noble-cause policing?

Bob and the boss continued chatting about the operational effectiveness of the squad, and taking the boss into his confidence, Bob said how Brian Western would try to ingratiate himself with him. Over a drink at the end of the day he would try to find out what he was planning over weekends when specific squad operations were planned. At first, Bob saw no reason not to share that information with a fellow officer. But when no arrests were being made it was obvious someone was tipping off the dips and they wouldn't perform. So he changed tack, he would move the squad's rest days at the last minute, and bingo, arrests would happen. Now there's a surprise! The boss expressed no surprise at all. He had known Brian Western was crooked, he just wasn't able to prove it. But he did reassure Bob he was doing OK, and if Bob got the evidence, then he would be happy to pot Western. Bob went on to outline how he was changing the structure of the team and how recruitment was dependant on recommendations of those already on the squad. They chatted about Bob's Inspector's course, after which he asked to leave, unless there was anything else, as he was meeting up with his team for an evening's 'trawl' on the Underground system.

Hazel, Champion and Fish checked in with the Information Room, seeking updates of any reported dippings on the network. There had been three thefts at Piccadilly

Circus and another one on a train near Holborn. It was now about 6pm and the rush hour was in full swing. They made their way by tube to Kings Cross for a prearranged meet with Bob. As they descended the escalator at Green Park into the fluorescent world of the Underground to catch a northbound Piccadilly line train, the lights flickered against the white enamelled ceiling as if sending a morse code signal to those below that 'the boys' were coming. In the vestibule at the base of the escalators were two black men dressed in casual clothing entering the long tunnel to the platform. As they did so they were unnaturally close to a young white female just in front of them. The three Dip Squad officers spaced themselves out so as not to look connected to each other, as they followed the two targets past adverts for forthcoming films in London. Nothing was said, no signs were made, but they each knew who their targets were, and what to look for. All six made progress along the tunnel. The two suspects gave knowing gestures to each other with the taller one indicating the female just in front of them. As she entered the subdued lighting, doing its best to illuminate the grubby world of the platform, the targets moved in, one casually blocking her path as if lost, while the other shaped up behind her and tried to liberate her purse from the top of her shoulder bag.

The boys moved in, shouting their presence, appealing to the intended victim to wait, while they wrestled the two now violent targets to the ground as they fought to escape their arrest. As is so often the case, members of the public, not knowing the circumstances, expressed their disapproval of three white men attacking two black men. After the usually expected confusion, and allegations of racism, they were brought under control and handcuffed, at which point the plain clothes officers could better explain, not only to the victim, but also those remonstrating members of the public, who they were and the purpose of their arrests. They took the two arrested targets, still struggling to break free and appealing assistance in their release from the 'pigs', upstairs to a room in the booking hall where they could arrange transport to the local police station. She reluctantly went with them, waiting patiently outside the office. Fish emerged to say, "Thank you for following us up, darling. They were trying to nick your purse. Did you realise it?"

She looked visibly shaken, "I had no idea. I don't know how to thank you."

Al's mind was working overtime. "We'll need to get a statement from you; not now, I'll call you tomorrow."

She said, "That's OK, can you call me at my office? I live with my boyfriend and he's a bit of a jealous guy."

Fish felt he knew exactly what she was saying, and so confirmed he would do so, establishing that said boyfriend was away on a course for the next two weeks.

The uniform van arrived and the three officers together with their prey were taken to Vine Street police station, that being the nearest having space to accommodate two more 'customers'. Bob made his way there also, knowing that his boys would be tucked up with paperwork on the prisoners. He strolled from the tube at Piccadilly, musing at Eros and the 'meat rack', a run of metal railings where ageing homosexuals proposition young rent boys for sex, as he completed the two-minute walk to the nick. It was a modern building stuck in a cul-de-sac behind the grand frontages of Regent Street and Piccadilly. There was no station yard to speak of, just a small space for a three-point turn. By the time he got there, the captives had been taken into the charge room and were in the process of being searched and booked in.

Bob sauntered in; the custody sergeant recognised Bob from earlier encounters, and content that the Dip Squad boss was now present, he excused himself, explaining a need to use the toilet. Truth was, his mug of tea was getting cold in the reserve room.

The tall one, David Choo, tried to explain the little bit of ganja in a wrap was for his own use. Bob picked it up; it wasn't much, but it might be a lever. He pocketed it, as if it never existed. He said, "Now you really shouldn't have this, should you, David? You could get in trouble possessing it." It was as if he was rebuking a naughty schoolboy.

"No, Mr Trebor," said Choo.

In reality, Bob knew the cannabis was a pain in the arse. It would mean sending it to the laboratory for analysis, delay in charging Choo with it, and losing the impetus of a quick turnaround on the attempted theft charge. The boys saw this but didn't challenge the boss's decision. Choo's main concern was that he was in excruciating pain with toothache. He begged Bob for his help just as the sergeant re-entered and Bob, being the 'kind-hearted' detective that he was, arranged for a doctor with some expertise in dental problems to attend to Choo and give him some relief.

Well why wouldn't I? Now David's had his teeth sorted, he's mine. By the way, I haven't a clue how a Jamaican gets a name like Choo either. Can't see any oriental in him. Life's mystery, I guess. I'm not going to ask; it would sound like I really care, when I don't. They're both charged with attempted theft from that poor unfortunate girl, whose troubled mind Fish is going to ease, I suspect. David's little drug problem is now gone; I think we're on to a guilty plea from these two at Bow Street Magistrates' Court. To save you from suspense, yes, they appeared at court on the Monday, having been kept in custody over the weekend, and pleaded guilty. Their duty brief did a good job though. Despite them both having form for similar offences, the magistrate gave them six months' imprisonment suspended for two years. Six months later, and two in the afternoon, the twist.

4
COMPLACENCY

Dave Champion, the boss and an 'old sweat' on the team, Pete Farmer, sat around the battle-weary Formica canteen table deliberating where they would go next. It was late morning, and the rush hour was over.

"Your turn for the teas, guv?" said Dave.

"Don't push it, Dave. Don't you like what you're doing?" Dave realised his place and got the teas.

"So what's this new house like then, Pete?" said Bob.

"Oh. It's nice, boss, it's on a new-build estate, so everything's brand new. We even managed to get the carpets thrown in for fuck all. The wife and kids are well pleased with it. Pumps up the mortgage compared to the old place, but that's life, ain't it?"

Dave returned with teas in hand, "What's that then?"

"I was just telling the boss about the new gaff."

Dave retorted, "Yeah, yeah, we're bored with it now."

Pete, affronted by Dave's indifference, went for the jugular. "At least it's better than that fucking rabbit hutch that you live in!"

Bob fell about laughing as the two protagonists set about mutual insults, doubting each other's parentage and so on.

Teas consumed and scores settled, the three of them agreed it was time to check the Central line, as there had been two reports of a tall 'I/C 3', or Afro-Caribbean, (or black man or man of colour to the less initiated, or informed) had been seen acting suspiciously, pushing in behind various females as they boarded the trains. They descended the front staircase of Bow Street police station, with the neoclassical edifice of Covent Garden opera house opposite, and walked up to Long Acre, turning right into Great Queen Street.

"So, any ideas why there's no blue police lamp outside the nick we've just left?"

It seemed neither Pete nor Dave had a clue.

"It goes back to the time of Queen Victoria. She used to turn up in her horse-drawn carriage at the opera house and looking across at the front of the police station she saw a blue illuminated gas lamp with the word 'Police' written on it. She remarked that blue lamps looked a bit vulgar opposite such a centre for the arts. In no time at all, one of her flunkies, who knows, could even have been her close personal friend Mr Brown himself, had a word with the then Commissioner of Police, and they were removed and replaced with two white globes instead."

Pete and Dave were in awe of Bob's knowledge. It might have been wrong, but they weren't about to challenge it. They walked past the headquarters for Freemasonry, or Grand Lodge as it's known by those in the exclusive club, a building looking more like a very imposing bank than anything else. At the far end of Great Queen Street at the junction with Southampton Row they peered into the Blitz bar, where Spandau Ballet first performed, before finally arriving at Holborn tube.

"What do you think, Pete, trawl up and down the Central line?" said Bob.

Pete agreed, as they descended the longest escalator on the Underground network to the bowels below. Ignoring the signs for the Piccadilly line the three detectives continued down on to the westbound Central platform. Dave and Pete turned left for about ten yards while Bob went right. He was taken with the designs on the walls. What looked like a facade of the Acropolis ran along the length of the tube. Then the penny dropped. *Dickhead*, he thought to himself. *Of course, not the front of the old Euston station, the British Museum isn't far off. It's a symbol of that*, he surmised. He regained focus as the next train drew in.

Dave said, "Here Pete, you ever thought how dangerous this is? I mean here we are on a narrow bit of platform, looking for dips and robbers who usually fight us. Just a couple of feet away is a moat which we could easily fall into, and at the bottom is enough electricity to fry us to death."

Pete, ever thoughtful, said, "So what's your point?"

At which they both fell about laughing boarding a set of double doors, agreeing that their mums would tell them they were both brave 'little soldiers'. Bob stalled boarding until the last passengers boarded, then he entered a single door at the end of the carriage. The train swept out leaving the bright fluorescent lights of Holborn behind them. In no time the acceleration turned to braking as the train's sparse population of passengers lurched back and forth, grabbing whatever bit of carriage fitting would save their fall. Next were the

Eduardo Paolozzi mosaics adorning the walls of Tottenham Court Road station. *Somehow, the dim fluorescent light strips didn't do justice to what had obviously cost a fortune to create,* thought Bob, as he scanned the platform from within.

The train came to a juddering, thumping halt, the brakes squealing as it did, and then what seemed like an age passed before its doors opened, disgorging its cargo before enticing eager new passengers to enter. The two looked out towards Bob further down as he looked back along the platform's length. Almost in unison, the two parts of the team saw their quarry. At the back of a group of some twelve intending passengers, seemingly bemused foreign tourists chatting to each other, was a single black male 'shaping up' in preparation to steal behind a young girl who was carrying an open shoulder bag. Bob couldn't see what he was up to from his side, but the boys could.

Not that it matters, because whatever they see, so do I. That's what I mean about having vision.

They ran the short distance towards him, upon which he ran straight into the arms of Bob.

David Choo struggled to escape Bob's bear hug, "For fuck's sake, David, stop struggling. You're going nowhere except with me."

The other two were now with the somewhat robust dance partner. Pete, carrying his truncheon inside a Tesco bag, took a side swipe at Choo's right shin. Choo let out a yell of pain, as did Bob because the stick had connected with both of them.

"You prick," said Bob, wincing as the impact pain turned to throbbing.

Dave grabbed hold of Choo's left wrist, holding it in a vice-like grip, upon which David said, "All right, all right, I'm sweet, sorry Mr Trebor, I didn't realise it was you."

Bob released his wrestle hold, as Choo accepted he was nicked, and would be going upstairs to await police transport to the nearest station, which by curious coincidence was going to be straight back to Bow Street.

"Now David, we're going to go up the escalators to an office we can use where we will wait for the van to take us to the nick. Do you understand?"

David confirmed and asked if the handcuffs could be taken off, as he wouldn't struggle or try to escape, as if it was some kind of 'gentlemen's agreement'. Bob had known of this before with other dips. It was as if they were accepting of their fate but felt embarrassed at either being walked handcuffed in front of the public or even being held by two burly coppers as they re-emerged from the Underground. Bob agreed to this rather casual escort arrangement.

It's a risk, I know. But David is known to me, and now, of course, the other officers. He knows if he escapes, we'll catch him again, either at his flop, in which case his mum will also be pissed off when we turn it upside down, or somewhere else. And if we have to do that, he'll be gifted with so many 'extras', he'll know there will be even more porridge for him to serve.

As they rode the escalator to the top Bob said, "David, I don't want to have anything slowing us down, or causing me extra work when I get to the nick, so if you've got anything on you that you shouldn't have, let's deal with it and get rid to me in the office, before we get in the van. So have you got anything I need to have?"

David confirmed, "Yes, Mr Trebor, I have."

"OK," said Bob, assuming he was going to be dealing with another bit of ganja, aka cannabis, "I'll deal with it shortly."

With that, all four arrived at the office and closed the door, avoiding prying eyes.

Bob said, "Right, let's have it."

To his astonishment, which of course he dare not reveal, Choo pulled out an eight-inch sheath knife from the back of his waistband and held it as if to stab someone in the stomach. Bob, trying to appear unfazed in front of Choo or the two junior officers, took it from him without uttering a word. He jammed it into his own rear waistband, now hidden by Bob's blouson jacket. A knock on the office door announced the arrival of the uniform van to take them to Bow Street police station.

In the back of the van Bob said, "David, tell me, why have you got a name like Choo? It's oriental, you don't look oriental, in fact you're black. How did that happen?"

David smirking said, "You're right Mr Trebor. I changed it, cos when I went to my secondary school I found out that my birth name, 'Codrington', was an old slave name. I didn't like still being a slave. I saw it above a Chinese takeaway, so I changed it, and it's just stuck."

Upon which they arrived in the yard at the nick. In the charge room, Bob outlined how Choo had been seen shaping up behind a young girl, tried to steal from her bag, but because she was foreign and not speaking any English, she didn't want to get involved. No mention of the knife, no dispute from David. He was searched, put in the cell and the boys set about trying to break their record of processing the prisoner and getting him charged in under twenty-eight minutes. They did and left the nick twenty-six minutes later. They went off to the Maple Leaf pub to celebrate.

Let me help you here. I must confess, I asked David what he had on him thinking he'd give me some cannabis, which as you know I've done before. I would have dealt with it sensibly. The knife was a surprise, I'll concede. He could have pulled it at any time and stabbed us. He didn't, probably because he knew we knew him; what's his chances of getting away with it? Maybe, maybe not. But a deal's a deal. I disposed of the knife, he signed a property destruction declaration that he'd found it and he doesn't get another conviction for it. The result? He appeared, pleaded guilty, and went inside for nine months, so everyone's happy. We count ourselves lucky and resolve to be a bit more sensible about searching our prisoners.

5

CAUGHT AND CONVICTED

"DI Trebor!"

Bob could hear a demanding voice in his head. Where was that coming from? He drifted off again, the tired leather seat offering a comfortable retreat from reality. His mind went back to the early hours of two days before when as a result of a phone call from Brixton nick he went to St Thomas' Hospital and saw Michael Jackson, a black suspect he'd been after for the last three months. The fluorescent lights of the Accident and Emergency reception drew a tired Trebor towards the automatic sliding doors like the bright lights you're supposed to see as you pass from this world into the next. *The gates of St Peter's, maybe*, thought Bob as the doors slid back beckoning his presence within. He obliged, followed by his driver. Bob had been drinking, no sense in getting bagged! He sauntered over to the smart designer desk hiding a tired, battle-weary receptionist who'd obviously had a really shitty evening dealing with a conveyor belt of dross from south London, each doubtless demanding immediate medical assistance, finding any delay to their needs intolerable and prompting a tirade of abuse and belligerent behaviour.

He approached her, fiercely aware that ladies who sat there ruled with a rod of iron. They had to, it wasn't a job for the meek, or you'd go under. But by the same token, you didn't want to wind them up, as they were very capable of screwing around with you and making your job less than easy. Her peroxide perm remained firmly head down as she was obviously focusing on some papers in front of her, oblivious to Bob's presence at the counter.

"Hello, love."

She slowly lifted her head, her pen stopping writing as she said, "Yes, have you taken a ticket from the machine?"

At which point he was joined at the counter by DC Brian Kent.

Without drawing a breath she said, "There's a system here, one person at the counter at a time, and I bet you haven't got a ticket yet have you?" she quizzed Kent.

"Um, er, no."

Bob, tiring of the obvious confusion, resisted the devil inside him to wind her up for a bit longer and produced his warrant card, or brief, as it's more colloquially known.

"Sorry love, no, we're on an enquiry. You've not long received someone who I want to speak to. He should have a police officer with him preventing his escape."

Her attitude changed, "Whoops, sorry dear, you both together? I think he's up on the first floor. Hang on." She shuffled some papers in front of her. "Yes, he's on Westminster ward." Bob thanked her, and the three parted the best of friends. She went back to her paperwork.

The last time Bob had been inside this hospital, 'Tommy's' as it's known in the trade, was his induction into the job when he had to attend for the statutory X-ray, to prove he was alive he supposed, and to bend over, bollock naked, in front of a couple of quacks to prove he wasn't a practising homosexual or suffering from piles, at least that's what he thought at the time. On that occasion, though, the whole experience occurred in the old Victorian edifice next door to the comparatively new tower block in which he now found himself. They sauntered off in the direction of the lifts for the short ride to the first floor. *How strange*, Bob thought, *that staircases in modern buildings only seem to be for the purpose of providing fire escape routes*. Gone are the days of making a grand entrance via the staircase. Still, he was a bit knackered after a long day working, and then a rinse, so actually the lift was quite welcome.

Bing bong. "First floor," said the sultry voice over the intercom. "And menswear, lingerie, and wet fish counter," chimed Brian and they both chuckled. Following the signs to their quest, they were greeted by a uniformed PC sat to the right of Bob's subject of attention.

The officer looked up and politely acknowledged Bob's presence as he instructed the young officer to relax and not stand on ceremony. Jackson, finding it difficult to manoeuvre, turned his head towards Bob.

Neither had met each other before so Bob broke the silence. "Michael, I'm DI Trebor, and you know my boys have been chasing you for the past few weeks. You have been very shy, so much so you jumped out of a second-floor window in a house on the 'front line'," (a local reference to the houses on Railton Road) "just to get away from my colleagues from Brixton. Which is why you find yourself in here now suffering from cuts and bruises from the fall. How lucky you didn't break anything!"

DC Kent chuckled, as did the PC; no such responses from Jackson. He simply made that noise of disdain all the blacks seemed to do, he thought, of drawing breath through his teeth, finishing with the words "Blood clot."

Bob responded, "Ooh, not very nice. Way I understand it, Michael, you should be grateful to us. You accidentally fall out of a window, can't get up and run because you're injured, we call an ambulance, we get you to hospital, you get seen by a doctor who wants to keep you in overnight to make sure you get better, you have your own babysitter, you have guests, that's me, and still you're a miserable fuck! No grapes, I'm afraid. Hang on here a minute."

Bob left the ward, spoke with the gorgeous dark-haired sister at its entrance and explained that Michael was a violent escaper whom he'd rather not have to chase again.

He reappeared next to Jackson. "Michael, good news, I've spoken with the hospital staff and they agree with me. The view over the Thames isn't very good from this low down in the hospital, so I've insisted you have a better view."

Jackson turned away from Bob just as two ward orderlies entered the room and started wheeling him out to the lifts in the corridor.

"Go with him, chaps, and make sure he doesn't go walkabout. You're off to the top floor." Bob turned, saying, "Won't be a minute," as he went back to the sister.

He thanked the young sister, pledging he owed her a drink. She warmed to the idea and Bob, sensing the interest, left her his phone number so she could contact him if she felt hopelessly attracted to his charms. On arrival on the tenth floor, Bob introduced himself to the ward sister, who was obviously clued up on what was happening. She mentioned her husband was in the job, so she understood the importance of prisoner security.

"Right, Michael, your new home for the night. Now this officer will stay with you all night, so if you get lonely or think maybe you want some fresh air, do make sure you speak to him first. Now give me your wrist so I can take your pulse." With that he took Jackson's wrist, slapped on a handcuff and attached the other end to the metal bed frame.

Jackson, taken by surprise, said, "What you fuckin' doin'?"

Bob responded, "You tried to get away from me; it's not happening again. This will make sure you'll still be here in the morning. Sweet dreams, shithead."

Now to tell you the truth – 'Interesting,' I hear you say – I've been after Jackson for a few weeks. I want to speak to him about a very nasty GBH he committed on a plain clothes police officer in an effort to escape being nicked. So far all he and his family have been giving me is grief.

Bob and Brian left, making sure the hospital staff were happy and no problems.

"Take me home, Brian, will you? I'm too late for the last train. Then, if you want, take the car and bring it back in the morning. Not early."

Brian said, "Will do, guv, can I make it about eleven?"

Bob, happy with that proposal, slunk back into the passenger seat, and almost immediately fell asleep.

"Guv, guv, we're on," said DC Champion.

Bob stirred from his snooze, "Jury back then?"

They made their way back into court, nodding to the respective barristers. The clerk gave a nodding acknowledgment to the officers, confirming that there was no note from the jury querying the judge's directions. They had a result to the counts on the indictment. Monk, on being told the jury had verdicts, became uncharacteristically agitated as he paced towards the gaoler's door to the dock. The weasel tried calming him about the impending result, but his efforts to pacify were to no avail.

Monk was by now crawling up the wall, "Let's just get this over with; if those cunts have done me up, I'll go fucking berserk."

The gaoler's door opened and he was beckoned back into the dock. He eyed the jury up and down but couldn't get any kind of clue from them. Mr Justice Ramm nodded to the clerk to start the verdicts.

Having identified the jury foreman he said, "Members of the jury, on the first count of theft, do you find the defendant guilty or not guilty?"

There was a pregnant pause, like those game shows when they're trying to raise the suspense in the audience.

"Not guilty!"

Monk, standing for verdicts, hurled a string of expletives at Trebor and Champion, ending with, "Told you it was a fit-up."

Once again the judge warned Mario Bergamot against any further outburst from his client and he told Monk to calm down as an alternative to being removed from court again.

"And on the second count of handling stolen goods, do you find the defendant guilty or not guilty?"

Again a pause, then, "Guilty." The clerk confirmed it was the verdict of them all.

Monk slumped back on the bench, deflated. He knew full well what was going to happen: he'd be banged up, his 'form', or previous convictions, would see to that. Bob went into the witness box and outlined Gerry's antecedents. Mario addressed the judge on Monk's previous history, hoping to convince him that a 'bender', or suspended sentence, might be the appropriate way to dispose of the case.

Ramm was having none of it; the clerk told him to stand. "Monk, I have listened to the evidence in this case, and witnessed your performance together with your counsel's address. You are a career criminal who treats his arrest and incarceration as an occupational hazard, and if your efforts to intimidate and cajole this court fail, you treat your sentence in the same vein. You will go to prison for eighteen months; take him down. Just a minute; Monk, what did you say under your breath?"

Quick as flash he said, "Fuck all, judge."

Ramm, annoyed at his constant mutterings, asked, "What did he say?"

The clerk turned to His Honour and, believing he was helping, said, "He said, 'Fuck all, judge'," and sat down.

Ramm, mystified said, "How strange, I swear I saw his lips move; take him down."

Monk, once again, launched a tirade of abuse at Bob, claiming again that he'd been fitted up as he was led down below. Bob smirked at him and felt a huge sense of relief that, despite Champion's fuck-ups, they'd got him down. The court rose with Ramm, sweeping out for a well-earned cup of tea.

Bob, on the other hand, said, "Dave, you owe me a large portion of chilly lager. If you had kept to the script we would've potted him on the first count as well. You're fined. Ring the chaps, tell them it's a duty commitment, be at the Maple Leaf at five thirty. No excuses." Dave, realising his need to make amends, made the necessary calls back to the office. The boys, on hearing this, to a man, raided their nearest hole in the wall to replenish funds and knowing that as Dave was having to confess his shortcomings it might well turn into a 'wet' night.

My corroborating officer and witness messed up his evidence. Not badly, as it happens. We've been really active, nicking any number of dips and basically what happened was that Dave mixed up his evidence about where he was when the theft occurred, which Underground platform we were on and in what direction the train was travelling. At least he got the date right! It happens, it's unfortunate, particularly with this gobby shit, but it happens. My sanction is to enforce a form of discipline which will ensure he doesn't forget his gaff, never to repeat it again. So much better than some crappy internal enquiry, don't you think? We surely don't want some wanker from Complaints and Discipline crawling all over this. In my experience very few of their number comprehend the pressure to produce results that we're under. We're not bent, not on the take, unlike some that went before us, that's why my recruiting system works. But if they 'see' an offence, I expect them to take out the bad guys. Someone brighter than me once said, "Why let the truth spoil a good story?" I don't think you want me to comment, do you?

The Maple Leaf is a Canadian-themed pub in Maiden Lane just on the south side of Covent Garden. It has loads of ice hockey memorabilia adorning its walls, and for the benefit of the boys, loads of lovely ladies. But best of all, it's the only pub serving Molsen lager on draught – rocket fuel in pints, sheer heaven! So just before six, all the usual suspects were there, and as Dave entered with the 'guvnor' a big cheer went up as they hijacked the offender, frogmarching him to the bar and dipping his wallet, relieving his funds to pay for the round. A few of the punters were bemused at the boys' behaviour. Not all, as there were other groups scattered around the pub acting in an equally boisterous manner. The group continued to replenish their pints, laughing and joking as the evening progressed into a full-scale lager frenzy. One of their number, Paul Hazel, was getting well oiled, no more so than the others but his eyes were drawn through his beer goggles to a group of some ten to twelve young ladies, sat near the back of the pub, who were obviously celebrating something with one of their number. Al Fish suggested the pair of them go over and chat them up. They established the girls were celebrating Sophie's imminent wedding and they were doing their best to get her pissed as it was her last chance to have 'fun'. Al, being the silver-tongued lounge lizard that he was, immediately struck up a chat about the impending marriage, and pointed out that her betrothed would be out on the town seeking to sow his wild oats, therefore sauce for the gander is sauce for the goose. Sophie, in her inebriated state, seemed to be warming to Alan's advances. Bob looking across just thought, *Here we go again. Wish he would just keep it in his trousers, but the one-eyed pink python was dictating to the 'Fish' on what and how he would secure his quarry.*

"That's a lovely flower in that vase," said Paul seeking to gain some advantage in the chatting-up stakes over Alan.

Sophie swung round from Al's advances and said, "Yeah, it's lovely ain't it, these girls got it for me. It's an orchid you know."

Paul thinking, *I know it is you dopey bird*, said, "Is it? Beautiful. It's in its own little vase and in a lovely presentation box."

Sophie smiled approvingly and said, "Do you want to have a look at it?"

Paul picked it up, removed the vase from its box, revealing the bloom, and in one fell swoop he ate the flower, swallowing it whole. The girls' table erupted as Paul struggled to digest the last of the flower. Sophie was fuming, shouting a series of expletives, unimaginable from such a demure person thirty seconds before. Al tried to calm the full-scale verbal assault which ensued but it was quite obvious he wasn't going to get his end away and the girls meant business. With that, the rest of the lads, having heard the ruckus, moved towards them to give some support, not actually knowing what it was that had prompted the tirade.

"You fucking ate my flower, you bastard, I'm going to call the old bill."

Paul just grinned, as Al said, "We are the old bill."

Upon which Bob beckoned the lads away and told them to get the fuck out of there. They all decamped from the pub in a bomb burst as they hit the street, each of them knowing they were to meet for a 'spin', otherwise known as execution of a search warrant, the following day.

Dave Champion checked his watch and reckoned he could get his last train home. He jumped on the tube to Liverpool Street making his train to Chelmsford just as the guard was blowing his whistle for the off. He was down for the raid the following morning so he tried to grab some sleep as he fell into a snooze and the train rocked him off to sleep.

6

KNOCK KNOCK –
WHO'S THERE?

Kinver House is a block of flats on the Woodbury Down estate on Seven Sisters Road in north London. The road runs south from south Tottenham towards Manor House at Finsbury Park and along its length the estate has several blocks of flats, regimented like rows of soldiers standing to attention at Trooping of the Colour at right angles to the road. The flat of interest to Bob was number four on the ground floor just to the right of the central staircase, a known address of Michael Jackson. The two CID cars crept onto the estate as Capital Radio announced the time being seven in the morning. How was it the DJ sounded so full of beans at this time of the morning? Could only be that he'd got to bed early, unlike the troops, who were each suffering, although they daren't show it, from varying degrees of hangover while the Weather Girls were booming out "It's raining men, hallelujah," from the radio.

I'm here outside with my troops and a plain clothes officer who's armed. Why? Well information came to me that Michael had upgraded from knife to gun in his armoury of protection and for the purposes of evading capture. I'm not surprised; I want him for that very nasty assault. He knows I'm after him and of course he wants to avoid me like the plague. With any luck, my informant, whom I met the other night, pointed to this flat door where he had come in order to buy ganja from Michael. So here we are. I'm a bit pissed off that Champion has failed to make my briefing this morning, I'll deal with him later. By a stroke of luck another detective from the Divisional CID office who's known as 'Little John', a great fridge of a man, was on early turn, so I've commandeered him for our little excursion.

The boys decamped from their cars with Bob and Little John leading the charge. The officer with his gun was right behind them in a state of readiness.

"Go on, John, put in," said Bob, upon which he barged at the door just above the lock.

It went in, the door falling like a drawbridge from its frame crashing to the worn brown shag-pile carpet within. The firearms officer, his beige trench coat billowing back, rushed in, gun drawn in his right hand, closely followed by Bob and the rest of the team leaving Little John standing like a night club bouncer at the gaping hole where a door used to be. All was quiet in the flat as they ferreted through the rooms, until they came to a closed door at the rear of the flat. Two of the bedrooms were empty, and this was the last to be tested. Carefully, Bob turned the old brass knob anticlockwise, releasing the latch. With his fingers on his right hand he silently gave a visual countdown. Three, two, one, as the door flew open the gun went in first and found two people – a bloke and his bird – in a sleepy loving embrace underneath a Brentford Nylons quilt. The officer shouted,

"Police," and pointed the gun at the heads of the lovers. She immediately started screaming hysterically, pausing only to draw breath and then continue. Her man immediately crapped himself in the bed and with embarrassment he tried to calm her whilst at the same time endeavouring to control her screams, which were split between her shock at having a gun six inches from her nose and her abhorrence that he had shat himself. As Bob looked in, it was immediately apparent to him there had been a fuck-up. Both occupants were white, not the black Michael Jackson they were looking for.

The rest of the team left the flat moaning about piss-poor planning leading to piss-poor results. *Smart arses*, thought Bob. He beckoned Little John into the premises, as he was a Detective Sergeant, so he got lumbered with the profuse apologies to the lovers, and a promise to get a chippy (carpenter) in to re-hang the front door. Then and only then, her screaming subsided. John gave her reassuring promises about the unfortunate circumstances of their meeting while lover boy cleaned up and made good the damage he'd caused to her bed. Bob in the meantime reflected on why on earth in this day and age anyone would want those three Carlton-ware ducks flying across the wall of their hallway. Surmising that it takes all sorts he regrouped with the team next to the cars to decide their next move. Remembering what Champions' 'snout' had said, he looked again at the flats and decided one more attack should be launched at the flat next door.

It looked like a shit hole; the letterbox plate was missing, revealing a huge gaping hole in the middle of the door, just like those you see at a fairground when you throw wooden balls into the mouth of some surreal-looking clown's head to win a cuddly toy. Also someone had painted a large number four in a very tasteful purple emulsion across the whole of the lower half of the door, but in the early light it was barely discernible against the council dark blue gloss. Looking to the right of it were numbers one, two and three. Obvious really, they'd hit number five instead of number four! Bob sent one of his number over to the suspect address to test the 'robustness' of the front door. Reporting back, the conclusion was that with just a heavy lean, the door would go in. As Bob once more briefed the chaps for this onslaught, Champion arrived.

"Sorry guv, I did it in this morning," said Dave.

This was the squad's phrase for oversleeping and it covered any variety of reasons for lateness without raising too many questions about what might have actually occurred.

Bob, with as much dignity as he could muster, said, "Yes you fucking did, you twat. We've now got a busted door to a wrong flat, a woman who's only just stopped screaming, a boyfriend with an incontinence problem, a firearms officer who's just itching to shoot someone, and at this rate it might be you, and a DI with crew who are severely pissed off, because you couldn't get up this morning. Am I getting my message over to you?"

Dave, looking like a dog who'd just been scolded by his master, just said, "Yes guv."

Paul tried to find out what had happened to Dave, while Bob spoke with the firearms officer. Dave explained that he woke up in a blind panic and that he'd overshot his station last night. He had leapt to his feet and stumbled off the train at Chelmsford just as it was pulling out. A lucky break, he thought, as the red light of the rear carriage disappeared round the bend at the far end of the platform. Dave, thinking he'd take a short cut through the park to his house, wandered past the fishing lake, where he encountered the tennis courts. In his still drunk and somewhat confused state from the station episode, he decided to take a short cut through rather than walk round the outside. So in he went, clang went the gate behind him, not registering whereabouts to his rear the noise had emanated. He walked diagonally across six courts, he thinks, until he reached the fencing the far side where he would just slip through another gate and home. Coming face to face with the fence he looked for the exit gate. Nothing. He looked up and saw the fencing was not only high but also very wobbly. Deciding against scaling its perilous heights, he gripped the fencing as he made his way along it replacing each hand as he stepped along its length, pacing as if some trapped lion patrolling the perimeter of its confines. Round and round he went, checking the whole of the fencing, and still pissed, he overshot the gate he had entered at least two or three times. Frustrated at his stupidity, with an hour wasted, he saw a park bench next to the court which looked attractive. Without further ado, he laid out and fell asleep almost immediately, happy in the knowledge that at least it was a dry night, and that nobody would know, despite him being a detective, that he couldn't detect his way out of being held prisoner by the tennis courts. Early morning saw Dave shivering into life, the overnight dew on his thin clothes just failing to reduce him into hypothermia. He quickly made good his escape, ran home, gave some cock-and-bull story to his missus about prisoner-processing making him late, showered, changed, and with a peck on the cheek and a promise of his undying love for her, ran back to catch the fast train back into London. Hence he had done it in!

They lined up again, Bob with the firearms officer leading the charge. With a nod the command to enter the real number four was given. In they charged, this front door putting up very little resistance to a detective's boot. *No carpets*, Bob thought, just a cheap strip of lino, the walls displaying signs of people rubbing along their wood-chipped length, and a solitary lightbulb, hoping to shed light on what was now happening. As they again rattled through the rooms, one closed door beckoned. On bursting it open they found just a mattress on the floor with a black male in his early thirties, Bob estimated, hiding underneath a single discoloured cream blanket. The firearms officer, having pointed his gun at the once sleeping beauty, saw there was no further cause for his services and re-holstered his gun, leaving the team to get 'acquainted' with their new bedfellow.

Bob said, "OK, I give in, I know you're not Michael, so who the fuck are you?"

Coming round from this early morning start to his day he said, "I'm David, his older brother. And who the fuck are you? Before you start, I haven't seen Michael for a couple of months."

Bob went on to enlighten David about his desire to speak with Michael, somewhat urgently, by reassuring him that whatever happened after the flat had been searched, he would be nicked, if only on suspicion of obstruction of the police.

The team went through the process of searching the flat, which none of them thought would take long, as there appeared very little in it. The bathroom didn't look as if it had been used for a good while. There were telltale signs: no toilet paper, just some torn newspapers on the floor next to the pan, the bath was dry as a bone with what looked like a yellow urine stain running its length, and the sink had a large piece missing on one side as if someone in a fury had taken to it with a hammer, having been told to go and have a wash. In any event, the plugs were missing from both scenes of ablution. *Nothing unusual about that*, thought Paul. But it was in the kitchen where the team were educated in the need for cleanliness. Each step taken into the culinary cavern found their shoes stuck to a glutinous mess pervading the whole of the floor surface. Paul and Dave found with each stride they had to pull the sole free from the floor before taking the next step. Bob, seeing their plight, remained at the doorway of what was once a smart kitchen fully appointed by the local council. What a war zone it had now become! A quick search of the drawers found they were occupied only by a couple of dirty knives and forks but had the added attraction of a colony of cockroaches scampering for cover whenever a drawer revealed their shy presence.

But it was the cupboard under the dented stainless-steel sink where the boys found a little 'pot of gold' in the form of a dark green plastic bucket, the first nod to any form of cleaning. Underneath a grey towel ripped in half was the largest hoard of credit cards and bank cards either of them had ever seen. There was a look of delight on Dave's face as he retrieved it and showed it to Bob in the hope he was redeeming himself for his early morning indiscretion.

Paul looked at the now dressed Jackson and said, "You're nicked for the stolen cards. Let's go." David Jackson, still coming round to the real world, said nothing. After a cursory glance around the flat, Bob led the squad back to the cars for the trip to Bow Street police station.

Well, that turned out OK in the end, a few fuck-ups along the way, not least Champion 'doing it in', a screaming woman who seems now to be more upset with her lover crapping in the love nest, a body – not 'the' body – but a body nicked for a load of obviously stolen credit cards, and intelligence from his brother that Michael had been at the address a couple of weeks earlier. By the time I've finished this, the script will have a strong aroma of roses and all will be well with the powers that be. Why Bow Street nick I hear you ask? Well, they know us there. The crime squad based there are forever wanting to work with us, and I can convince the sergeant in the charge room that, because the cards have been stolen from a variety of locations all over the capital, some of which are bound to be from thefts on Bow Street's ground, it's likely that some form of conspiracy to steal or handle stolen goods within the jurisdiction of the Central Criminal Court is going to be the charge for this little lot.

Al Fish led the way into the charge room of the Victorian edifice from the yard, as light rain fell on the group; the irony of the Weather Girls on the radio wasn't lost on him. Jackson's Afro glistened as the light mist settled like a sprinkling of icing sugar across his head. He had been routinely handcuffed for the journey but was released from his manacles as he stood at the door to the charge room. Al led them through the door, seeing as he released his grip of the dull, unpolished brass door handle the familiar face of a rotund uniform sergeant sat behind his desk, eagerly awaiting the arrival of the Dip Squad. He had been forewarned of their imminent arrival by two other members of the team who had made their way straight to the nick, as it appeared there might be a lot of enquiries to be made on the haul of cards, in the hope of quickening the pace of resolution. And so it was that Al, Paul and Dave were now greeted by John Conroy, a thickset Irish lad, short and stocky, aged about thirty, with hands that looked like slabs of meat, capable of delivering a decisive punch. His partner in crime was a skinny Indian guy, same sort of age, answering to the name of Basil Chakrabarti, dressed in a pale blue shell suit with purple and white flashes. Bob joined them, thus completing the ensemble, having left Little John and Dirty Harry (with the gun) at the scene to tidy up any other cock-ups from their early morning visit.

The sergeant continued to sit at his desk munching on a strawberry Mivvi as he mused what kind of tale of woe the miscreant before him had been involved in. He was surprised the arrest was not the normal attempted theft from persons known or unknown – hand went in, came out empty scenario – but instead a theft or dishonest handling of some forty plus credit and debit cards, believed to be the proceeds of a number of thefts or 'dippings'. *Lovely*, he thought, as Al related the facts of how, searching for his brother, they had arrested him at his home address having found the bucketful. Needless to say, no mention was made of the earlier indiscretion at gunpoint. Seemed unfair to cloud the issue.

Al said, "Sarge, those are the facts, the boys will start on the cards; can we bang him up in the Peter till we've got somewhere? Then hopefully we'll be able to do a short contemporaneous interview before you decide?"

The sergeant nodded approvingly saying that cell three was available for Jackson to make himself familiar. With that, Jackson sucked through his teeth, making a sound similar to that of a budgerigar, signifying that he was distinctly unimpressed at being nicked for the cards, as he was led away by Al.

The boys set about enquiring about the cards. Sometimes the banks were helpful, but often they'd play the 'more than my job's worth to give you the details and address of the account holder'.

"What is it with these fucking banks?" said Paul to John. "Anybody would think we're the villains. We've recovered their customers' property and they go into denial."

Bob, sensing Paul's frustration, told them to focus on any crime reports over the last three months as a start point. Then they'd be able to pick up the slack on the other cards later.

Now here's the rub. I'm after David's brother Michael for the very nasty assault on a police officer. At present I've got David with a bucketful of nicked cards, although no direct evidence of his involvement, but I reckon with a bit of 'investigation' I can make that stick. I need him 'over a barrel' to pressure him into telling me where his brother is. I suppose I could visit the third brother, Winston, and question him. Shouldn't be difficult to find, he's coming to the end of his incarceration at Her Majesty's pleasure, so I should really 'extend the hand of friendship' to him as well. Otherwise I can see some snaky defence brief for David claiming that the cards were either Michael's or Winston's, and fuck all to do with his client. What's a 'Peter'? I hear you ask. Its origin I'm told is from the world of safe blowing: the heavy steel door of a cell looks like that of a walk-in safe. Now the safe blower, using a fairly basic explosive containing saltpetre, was known as a 'petreman', hence the police cell became known by some as a 'Peter'.

Paul and Al were happy with the boys' efforts finding the victims of the thefts. Better still, bearing in mind that Jackson protested he hadn't seen his brother for a couple of months, six of the cards were from thefts about a week ago, and two of them from theft or dipping two days ago. John and Basil had done well in uncovering the crime reports; it seemed they were 'dippings' on the London Underground. Bob decided that Al and Basil would do a short interview with David, if only to get his denial on paper to knowledge of the cards. The same sergeant was still covering custody when they asked for their boy to be let out and placed in the interview room next to the doctor's examination room just off the charge room. A contemporaneous note interview is one of the slowest forms of interview known to man. It means that the officer, Al, having cautioned that he needn't say anything, etcetera, to the interviewee, Jackson, then asks questions about his involvement in a crime. The second officer, in this case Basil, then has to write out in longhand the question. They then wait to see if Jackson wants to make any reply. This system was brought in because it was alleged that police would 'verbal' the villain, otherwise known in the fraternity as 'fitting him up', and seemingly have a fantastic sense of recall as to what had been said, verbatim, since the time of arrest. A nonsense, of course, as any career detective will tell you. And so the contemporaneous note interview was born. What it meant, though, was that the interviewee had loads of time in which to formulate a response, the element of surprise completely gone, reducing the art of interview to formal banter. Many were at a loss to see where the fun was in that.

Bob briefed the two officers, telling them to just stick to the cards they knew the whole story about. So in essence the two cards nicked in the previous week. They were under strict instructions from Bob to come out of the interview immediately after they'd finished. With that they kicked off the interrogation of Jackson.

Having done the caution, Al said, "Now David, I want to ask you about all the cards found at your address this morning."

He quickly answered, "They're nothing to do with me."

Al went through the evidence again and finished with, "These two cards were only nicked last week! You said you haven't seen your brother Michael for a couple of months. Your other brother Winston is banged up in prison; nobody else according to you uses the flat, so these two and all the others are either stolen by you, or you are handling stolen goods." Jackson, realising he'd have to give something, said, "All right, those two, but none of the others. I didn't steal them though."

Al then asked him how some of the cards no longer had

signatures on them. "Is it because you've used brake fluid on them to clean them off?"

No reply.

Al pressed on, getting no reply, but realised he wasn't going to get much further and so terminated the interview. He stepped out and apprised Bob who was standing just outside with some blank sheets of paper. Al teamed up with the rest of the boys to say they had a load more enquiries to do on the cards, while Bob entered the room where Basil was endeavouring to convince David to sign each page of the contemporaneous notes of interview. But David, obviously having seen many TV detective dramas, knew his rights, and with an attitude of 'You're not taking me alive copper', refused to sign, wouldn't touch them, and didn't even want to look at Basil.

Bob, completely unfazed by his outright refusal, and seizing the opportunity to completely and utterly have him over, said, "David, now I understand what you say about the cards, but of course they might have been used in frauds to buy things."

"Not by me, I don't know nothing about that."

Bob said, "That's fair enough. But I need to prove that you're innocent, so will you give me a sample of your handwriting, your signature, at the bottom of each of these pages? It needs to be at the bottom so we can stick an exhibit label on them."

David obliged, believing this would divest him from any involvement in 'kiting', or fraudulent use. *As Phineas T. Barnum said, "One born every minute"*, thought Bob as he thanked him for his help in excluding him from suspicion.

Jackson was put back in his cell by Basil and Bob.

"Thieving black bastard," said Basil to Bob as they emerged back into the charge room.

"How can you say that, Basil? You're Asian and actually darker skinned than he is."

Basil retorted, "I know, boss, but he's a lazy arse black fucker, who's never done a day's work in his life. And I can't be racist, because when push comes to shove, I'm black as well."

Bob thought, *I suppose you have a point.* The team reconvened in the canteen on the first floor. John Conroy was sent for the teas, while the boys looked through the cards and paperwork to see where they were in relation to what, at this stage, they could charge Jackson with. Bob stood at the Georgian window musing at the street scene outside. Opposite was the Royal Opera House, where 'posh' people, as Bob thought, paid shit loads of money, to listen to someone warbling. *Philistine*, Bob thought to himself, and walked back to the long Formica table the boys occupied, to establish what the state of play was.

"So to summarise, we have losers for most of the cards, and they've been contacted and say they were dipped on the Underground network. We've got two that Jackson has put his hands up to, then we have a number of the cards that have had signatures cleaned off, with the usual brake fluid. Did we recover anything in the paperwork recovered from the flat that has any practice forged signatures of any of the losers?"

Paul chipped in saying, "I've got this, guv, found under the mattress he was lying on."

In a clear polythene evidence bag was a yellowing copy of the *Jamaican Weekly Gleaner*, a weekly newspaper for the

West Indian community. This one, Bob observed, was four months old, and had some writing down the margins of the front page.

"Guv, if you look closely," said Paul, "you can see they're all signatures of people. And when you look at the cards, it's those people's names. Nice?"

Bob smirked, "Paul, that's very good police work. Would I be right in thinking we weren't able to find the pen used at the flop?"

"Absolutely, guv. I might not do or say much, but when I do, it matters."

Bob laughed and said, "Very profound, Paul. Nice touch."

You're probably wondering what happened next, well I'll tell you. I charged Jackson with the theft or alternatively handling stolen goods of all the credit cards. He was not impressed because he thought he was going to get away with two cards, hence the admission in the interview. I'm not going to include that yet in the evidence, and I've done nothing at present in relation to the signatures on the newspaper or the 'handwriting samples'. That'll be a nice surprise for him later, when I serve it as additional evidence. In the meantime, he's been committed to stand trial at Middlesex Crown Court, on the statements of Basil and Paul, which deal only with the finding of the cards and his arrest and will be kept in custody until his trial. And if you're wondering about me mentioning the pen, I needed to establish that however the signatures came to be on that newspaper, the pen was no longer in existence. Imagine the difficulty of explaining that the signature pen's ink was the same as that in the officer's notebook? You get my point, I'm sure.

7

BEST EVIDENCE

"Oh. It's such a perfect day, I'm glad I spent it with you," sang Lou Reed, the words filling Bob's head as the transistor radio boomed out the lyrics in his office.

He felt good; thoughts of the woman he was seeing, and her willingness to see him that evening, filled him with an eager anticipation. Bob was married with a couple of kids, but his wife was, to say the least, frigid. She saw him as an inconvenience to have around at home but viewed his existence as a meal ticket for her. The 'brief', on the other hand, was going through a shitty, acrimonious divorce so in essence, the bet on a cup of coffee actually brought these two lost souls together. The squad were in their office, catching up on their paperwork from previous encounters with a number of dips, which meant they were now facing prosecutions either at Magistrates' or Crown Courts throughout London. It was a Thursday; the time, eleven in the morning. All was right in the world. Bob, who this week was standing in for the Detective Chief Inspector while he was on leave, was just finishing off his overnight paperwork, which had landed on his desk as a result of his additional responsibilities. The window cleaner, a young skinny lad in his early twenties who had been sitting on the window ledge with his legs dangling into the office, and by the way he talked was obviously from an Eastern European country, dropped back into the office. In broken English he confirmed he'd cleaned Bob's windows and asked if he could go in the main office where the squad were and clean theirs. Bob approved.

The window cleaner entered the squad room to an indifferent audience within. It was a large office with tables running down the centre, so the team members faced each other down its length. Then at one end was another desk for the Detective Sergeant to sit at. The walls had a sort of plastic-coated wallpaper in a boring beige, and the boys did their best to hide it with court lists, wanted posters, and other police publications. And underneath some of the adornments, carefully concealed, would be a full frontal of some 'fallen Madonna with the big boobies', the boys not wanting to offend of course. The Eastern European opened the first sash Georgian window, leaving his bucket of water beside him on the floor as he squeezed out the residue before leaning out on to the window ledge. He carefully edged himself out, sitting as before on the edge, while his legs provided the counterbalance as they dangled inside the office. As he had done in Bob's office, the lad simply balanced on the ledge. The squad listened to John Conroy as he told them of an old lady he'd seen at Clerkenwell Magistrates' Court the other day who was up for shoplifting from a little supermarket in Kings Cross, while he was getting a remand.

He said, "Purcell was the magistrate, he took the plea of guilty from her. Cos she had form for 'hoisting', and so before he weighed her off he said, 'I see you have your husband with you in the public gallery. Now remind me, what was it you stole?' She said, 'A tin of peaches, your worship.' 'And how many in the tin?' She said, 'Six, sir.' 'Right,' said Purcell, 'I'm going to give you six days' imprisonment suspended for six months.' Just then, the old boy at the back leapt to his feet and said, 'Please excuse me your holiness.' 'Yes what?' said Purcell. He said, 'Actually she stole a tin of peas as well.' 'Get out!' And with that the old girl was taken down."

This immediately prompted a tirade of abuse at John together with any number of bits of office paraphernalia being thrown at him, including heavily soiled ashtrays, pens, paper clips, in fact pretty much anything that wasn't nailed down. Calm then resumed and the boys got on with their paperwork, leaving a somewhat bemused window cleaner, still working, trying to fathom out what he had just witnessed. John pushed the fag ash from his desk on to the carpet-tiled floor and with a couple of sweeps of his foot, worked the deposits into the pile. The rest of the detritus, he simply scooped into the waste-paper bin. Making use of one of the ashtrays which had arrived via 'airmail', he leant back, pulled a pack of twenty Marlboro from his jacket pocket and, imagining he was James Dean, slowly but purposefully lit one of its number. The acrid pale grey smoke he exhaled mixed with the blue smoke emitting from the cigarette, hovered above where he was sitting until the light breeze flowing lightly into the room, courtesy of the window cleaner, caused it to dissipate across the entire squad room. Bob, looking for some case papers, entered the room.

On seeing John having a 'Marlboro moment', he said, "John put the fag out will you, I don't like it."

John did no more than take a small drag and then dropped it into a discarded half-full cup of tea.

"Better," said Bob; he found the papers he was looking for and left the room.

As he left, John reached into his pocket and retrieved another cigarette, which he promptly lit and resumed his position.

Basil said, "John what are you doing, the guvnor just told you to put it out."

"And I did," said John. "I did as I was told, but he said nothing about this one," in a defiant tone.

Bob opened his office door to the dulcet tones of the Thomson Twins singing, "We are detective, we are select…" As he sang along he heard a gunshot ring out, coming from the squad office. John, being the office joker, had a small starting pistol which he would fire at quiet moments. This time it scared the shit out of the window cleaner, causing him to topple backwards out of the third-floor window, meaning certain death had it not been for the quick thinking of Dave and Paul who grabbed his ankles before he disappeared off the ledge. They steadied him back to regain his balance.

Bob re-entered saying, "What the fuck was that?"

John confessed, claiming it went off by accident, as Bob rebuked him for petrifying the window cleaner.

"And put that fucking cigarette out, I won't tell you again."

He left, slamming the door as the boys patted down the failed jumper, apologising profusely for John's antics.

As Bob got back to his office, his telephone let out the shrill sound of one of the new phones, demanding his answer. *Damn modern phones*, he thought.

I've just been told of a very nasty assault on one of my officers, which sounds like a bad GBH (or grievous bodily harm for the uninitiated). He's a uniformed officer who was out on plain clothes enquiries when he came across a 'dip' performing right in front of him. When he challenged the thief, he was slashed right across the face and because of his injury he was unable to apprehend him. The woman who was blissfully unaware of the thief's attentions, as is so often the case, just carried on her way, ignorant of what had just happened. So I'm off now with one of my officers, and the scenes of crime officer, known as the SOCO, to University College Hospital where poor bastard is being treated.

"Blimey, guv, the brakes need sorting on this Astra, I'm really having to pump hard to get any traction," said Al.

"Just get there in one piece, no need to drive like a nutter, or we'll be checking in as well!" said Bob.

The newly appointed SOCO rolled from side to side on the back seat as the bends or corners appeared, having a pretty good idea what would be required of him, photographs and maybe some blood samples before transfusions, as Al negotiated the roads. They pulled up at Accident & Emergency, dumping the car in one of the police bays. Bob led the charge into the hospital telling the SOCO to bring his camera, stopping momentarily to introduce himself to the receptionist who in turn pointed the way to his injured officer.

The three officers turned into a brightly lit curtained area with, Bob assumed, any number of patients, all in their minds requiring urgent medical attention. A gaggle of staff were busy at the central nursing station. Several doctors, stethoscopes draped around their necks, were diligently filling forms and writing what looked like prescriptions. Nurses sat chatting about diets they must go on – *Not before time*, Bob thought – or the date they were either meeting or dumping later. At bay four behind the pale blue curtain they turned right to see the young officer spoken of. A doctor, attending to his wound, looked up, acknowledged them and beckoned Bob outside while Al and the SOCO engaged in small talk with the traumatised officer. It was apparent the medical staff had stemmed the flow of blood from the wound which, for the time being, had just a light gauze covering the extremis. The doctor briefed Bob that, although he'd lost a fair amount of blood, he didn't think he required an immediate transfusion. However, many of the nerve endings in the cheek and down towards his neck had been severed, and considerable work would need to be done in an effort to prevent permanent paralysis. Bob, a seasoned campaigner, knew this was no five-minute job. This was at least a GBH if not attempted murder, depending on how the evidence shook out. Not wanting to delay the officer's further medical attention he thanked the doctor, who promptly advised that another doctor would be along shortly to apply the stitches. Bob saw his chance; he rejoined the officers and having spoken with the young victim he directed that the SOCO take several pictures of the open wound before it was stitched and dressed.

Now why would I do that? Strategy my friend, strategy. You see, all being well, we're going to catch the shit who did this. My intention is to get that open wound photo into the bundle to go to the jury. That way they don't just see a sanitised version of the wound, which although will look pretty nasty, won't have the necessary shock value. That's what I'm after, I'm selling a story to those twelve good men and true. I want them to imagine they'd been slashed across the face, I want them to feel his pain, to imagine what kind of lasting injury they might have for the rest of their lives. This is theatre, and they need to know the awfulness of it all. This is not just headline-grabbing, brave 'bobby' steps in, this is a case of that poor bastard, all he was doing was trying to stop a sneaky pickpocket, and now he's scarred for life. That's the message I need to get over.

While Al applied himself to investigating the circumstances of the crime, the SOCO patiently waited until the officer was stitched before taking further photographs, including once the dressing was applied. Bob left instructions with Al to get as full a statement and description as he could and to get the officer home safely in police transport to the bosom of his family, saying that a fuller statement could be obtained once the poor bastard had had the chance to recover. In the meantime, the SOCO had the 'pleasure' of driving Bob back to the scene of the crime for more photographs, and perhaps blood spatters or marks if the scene hadn't been sanitised by the lacklustre cleaning staff at the station. He briefed the bosses over the radio as much as he was able, reassuring them of a fuller picture on his return to the nick. In the meantime, he called for an office meeting of the squad an hour later, to direct the operation. It was obvious to Bob that his team would have to start 'rattling a few cages' and hassling the dip fraternity – his briefing reflected this – while he would organise the public appeals, posters, etcetera, and appearances on *Police 5* with Shaw Taylor.

Happy that everything that could be done at this early stage had been, he disappeared at 6pm to meet his date.

SECOND NATURE

He awoke to her attending to his old chap, still dressed in the basque and stockings from the previous night's liaison. He was comfortable in the knowledge that she cared for him, her objective to give him pleasure come what may, unlike his soon-to-be-estranged wife, whose only interest was how much money he was bringing home. It was 6am and DC Kent was coming to pick him up in a 'job' car from her house in south London. They were on their way to Lewes prison to see the third brother, Winston Jackson, who had been put away for a string of knife-point robberies on the Underground system. Kent was a trusted confidant of Bob's and would be deliberately evasive if anyone was to ask about Bob's whereabouts. The previous night, the lovers had a nice meal at Rules restaurant in Maiden Lane, reputed to be the oldest restaurant in London. She, as usual, had the oysters to start with, Bob fantasising as she swallowed each one whole. He stuck with the soup, before they both indulged in steaks, washed down with the house red. But disaster struck when they adjourned to the Punch and Judy pub at the far end of Covent Garden for a late drink.

My god that feels good, her attention to detail is divine, and I love her all the more for it. I'm renowned for self-discipline, so while I 'endure' this I'll let you in on the secret of last night. We were a bit pissed by the time we reached the pub, but ask yourself, what's the worst thing that could happen to the head of the central London Pickpocket Squad? Exactly, the woman he's with having her handbag stolen! I went fucking ballistic; some sneak thief nicked it from under our noses. Bastard! I did my best – the boys turned out for me and tried to find the shit without success. The shame, the embarrassment, to say nothing of the piss-taking I will now have to endure. At least we got her cards cancelled, and I made her laugh when we got to her place. I now realise why they call it doggy fashion; there I was attending to her every need on the edge of the bed when I suddenly felt the presence of something behind me. Her cocker spaniel was busily licking my arse and balls as I pumped away! Lucky it's a bitch. Serious worries otherwise. Still, a new one on me I suppose. Guess that's how it gets the name cocker, as a promise to the future. Must dash, my driver's just arrived. Lewes, here we come.

As he slumped into the passenger seat, still wearing the same shirt from the day before, and a suit straining to keep its shape after twenty-four hours, he was greeted by the car radio blaring out "Last night a DJ saved my life," which in his mind he converted to "BJ". The journey down to the south coast was fairly uneventful and allowed Bob to close his eyes for a much needed snooze after the night's 'gymnastics', oblivious to DC Kent getting lost in south London before retrieving the situation, and guiding the CID car through the heart of the South Downs and the jewel in the crown of Sussex that is Lewes. Unfortunately, the same cannot be said for the prison, a Victorian edifice built in the 1850s, originally occupying a site on the outskirts of the town, but more recent expansions meant that it stood at one end of the town on the Brighton Road. The large car park to the front of the main gate beckoned them onward into a space reserved for 'Authorised Vehicles'.

Bob came round to the prophetic Talking Heads song 'We're on the Road to Nowhere' as he picked up his black leather portfolio case, his papers within, which found its way onto the back seat, courtesy of Brian Kent. They strolled in the autumn chill diagonally across to the visitors' door. Bob introduced himself to the warder within. They were both allowed access, escaping the wind relentlessly blowing leaves that were racing, seemingly without purpose or indeed a winner, across the rough tarmac car park, leaving the application form that sought an interview with an inmate with the same warder. His fat frame led them, long chain slapping against his right thigh, through a couple of gates at either end of a small yard, to a building welcoming prospective visitors. The persistent and regular unlocking then re-locking reminded the detectives why they could never be 'screws'. The tedium of routine and essentially being a prisoner all the time one is at work reinforced their abhorrence of such a crap job.

They entered a large hall housing about two dozen tables, regimented in three lines and bolted to the floor. Three chairs were also arranged at each table, two opposite one, and again screwed to the floor. This ensured everyone visiting could been seen with the minimum of prisoner supervision and would avoid the understandable temptation of a sexually repressed prisoner engaging in hanky-panky with a loved one across the table, or the reorganisation of someone's face with the legs of the chairs kindly provided by HMP. The lines of fluorescent lights hanging on long chains from the angle iron girders above revealed the pale green emulsion on the walls had seen better days, with large areas divorcing the old stone walls underneath. Some of the paint bubbles could hang on no longer with pieces the size of tabloid newspapers falling to the ground. A few wives and girlfriends were already seated, waiting for their respective 'absent partners'. Kent and Bob sat to the far left of the females in the hope that they might not be overheard by them as they chatted to Winston. This wasn't going to be a formal interview, otherwise they could have requested a separate room, but Bob knew he wouldn't get much change out of the inmate, and in truth he didn't need it.

A few minutes passed, the next of kin, shall we call them, getting louder in their chatter. "Shall I get the cards out yet, boss?" Brian enquired.

Bob, still feeling drained after last night's carnal gymnastics, said, "No, leave them in the bag. It'll be a nice surprise for him. I don't really need much; if he'll sign a short statement saying he knows nothing about them, that'll be fine. It'll mean his brother David or Michael will be on their own on this one. Just need him to say he shares the flat with David and nobody else, and of course that he hasn't seen Michael, which he'll be happy to do, as he's been banged up in here for a while."

With that, the door at the far end was released and about a dozen 'lags' sauntered in. Each looked as if they were wearing some sort of public-school uniform, grey jumpers with a blue stripe round the collar, blue and white striped shirt and – the dead giveaway of their residence – the ill-fitting grey trousers looking as if they'd had an argument with their boat-like shoes. After recognising their respective partners, they sat down as if attending an interview for a job.

Winston, craning his neck over those in front to see who was so interested in seeing him, wandered in and, seeing there were no other prospective visitors, sat down opposite the pair of officers. Silence reigned supreme as Winston, guessing who the two were, stared at them waiting for their overtures. Bob introduced themselves, which produced no response from Winston. Brian laid out the cards retrieved from the flat across the table.

Bob said, "Now Winston, as I just said, you're under caution. We recovered these from your flat where you live with David. They are stolen 'dippings' which happened on the Underground in London, did you steal any of them?"

Winston's response was immediate. "I don't know nothing about them, innit. Never seen them before."

Bob said, "Are you sure? Only you and David live at that flat, they were hidden. So it must be someone who knew where to hide them. You were living there with him until you got banged up?"

Winston continued to deny any knowledge and accepted the invitation of doing a short statement to that effect. *Good news*, thought Bob, *David now well and truly tucked up by his own brother!* And he didn't really give a toss whether he knew where Michael is, he'll come.

Kent took the statement, only a one-pager, which Winston signed without quarrel, and they left without further ado. Winston, sucking air through his teeth, and feeling nothing but hatred for the two officers, rose to his feet and walked, feigning that limp that they'd seen so many do, back to the warder at the far end. Once he had been locked back through the gates, Bob and Brian nodded to the warder to be released from the visitors' hall. As they wandered across the yard to the car, the wind let them know it hadn't given up. More leaves cascaded like confetti to the ground, before joining the meaningless race around the car park.

"Get that heater on, Brian, it's bloody freezing. Let's get back to sanity."

As they headed north towards the 'Smoke', Bob outlined how he was going to use today's little adventure to his best advantage.

Some might say today has been a waste of time. I don't. I could've created a situation whereby Winston could've been implicated either in some of the thefts or dishonest handling of them, before his current incarceration at Her Majesty's pleasure. But that would've meant more verbals, more vague allegations of 'fit-up' and really a lot of aggro. Then follows a not-guilty fight with the chance that because he's already banged up, he would only get a concurrent sentence to that he's serving. So there's no sense in attracting a load of corruption allegations just for the sake of it, and besides, I wanted brother Michael and not to get caught up in a side show. I'd much rather use Winston to convict his brother David of the cards, thus causing family disharmony. You know what they say, divide and rule. Well, that's what I'm going to do. And I knew he couldn't help me on that shit of a brother, Michael, I'm already on it. Now it's back to the office for a chat with Fish and Hazel.

Paul and Al, having had a briefing with Trebor, were sitting around a desk with Basil at the far end of the office, avoiding unnecessary contact with the infrequent tide of officers flowing in and out of the squad room. The boys had all the papers together with the bag of cards on the table and were running through the evidence which had committed David Jackson to stand trial at Crown Court. Now was the time to evaluate that evidence before discussing what else was needed to 'assist the court' to return a conviction.

"Have you got the original 'contemp' notes there, Basil?" said Paul.

"Yeah," said Basil, "they're still in the plastic folder, here. He just talked a load of crap, basically, just admitted two cards, and then refused to sign the notes."

The boys confirmed with each other that David needed help to reconcile himself with the truth, as they saw it. "How many pages?"

"Just the four," said Basil.

Al said, "Right, Basil, we've got the blank sheets the governor conned David into signing. He gave them to me, and I've kept them locked away, so no one else has touched them, nor have they been indented, so there's no impressions of handwriting on them. And the pen used by David is in there as well. So far the only fingerprints on them will have been the governor's, mine, acting as officer in the case, and soon to be yours, Baz. Before you touch them, leave them in the plastic folder, get four more sheets of paper, same size, so we can do a run-through of the questions and answers, trying them for timing and fit."

They then set about constructing the interview as they

saw it, which would explain how David had come by all the cards, how he'd practised signatures on the newspaper that Paul had recovered, and how he used brake fluid to carefully remove the signatures from the strip on the reverse of the cards. Obviously, the signatures on the newspaper only related to cards which had been 'cleaned', which showed he was practising with a view to fraudulent use of the cards. By the time they had finished, David Jackson had at first resisted the line of questioning, but by the fourth page he had made a full and frank admission of his criminal possession of the stolen cards and his efforts to clean and then use the cards on various 'shopping' sprees. What he wouldn't say, and this was because the boys at the time of original interview wouldn't know the detail, was how he had acquired the cards or what frauds had at that time been committed. He also refused to say who had stolen them, or implicate anyone else, but would sign the interview notes. The last part in this little scenario was to get the contemporaneous notes countersigned by the interviewing officer and the note's author, still using the same pen used for David's signatures, and the notes themselves. Bob told Paul that unless they heard from solicitors defending Jackson, the notice of additional evidence shouldn't be served until the morning of the trial so they'd have to take further instructions from their client. That way, the learned judge would ask them why they weren't ready, because it was obvious the evidence was outstanding in the weeks before the trial! And just to add to the 'unfortunate' delay, Paul had to submit the newspaper with the signatures on it to establish whether there was any scientific way of establishing when they were written, and whether by the same author. They already knew the answer: not a chance. But this was needed so that scientific services could be blamed for the lateness in serving any evidence on the defence.

9

A SHOT IN THE DARK

I'm going out with the boys today looking for thieves who look to have a Mediterranean appearance. We've been hit by what seems like a swarm of locusts on the Underground network who are attacking members of the public going about their lawful business and relieving them of their purses and wallets. Common sense would suggest that we are being besieged by South American thieves, probably Chileans or Columbians, the finest dips there are. The trouble with common sense is that it's so common, don't you think?

John Conroy arranged the meet out on the ground, the café next to Russell Square tube station. At about 9am he was joined by Dave Champion, Al Fish and the guvnor. There had been several thefts from the person reports from visiting tourists passing through the nearby station heading on their way into central London. Russell Square station is situated just round the corner from the Hotel Russell and many other large hotels in the Bloomsbury area. It's the station in that part of the world that tourists usually use to get around London on their sightseeing trips and is served by the Piccadilly line running north and south. Looking at the tube map, the station beforehand is Kings Cross, a large terminus which decants many hundreds of travellers onto southbound trains towards the metropolis, and the rush hour in the morning often means the carriages are packed to the gunnels as the train sweeps into Russell Square. This is a prime hunting ground for the would-be pickpocket.

The crew polished off their teas and bacon rolls and having settled their own 'national debts' they turned right on to the street and then right again into the station. They descended in the lift to the station platforms which lay at the far end of a dimly lit corridor in need of refurbishment to the peeling pale green gloss paint, the sort of colour that is on offer at a pound a tin in a discount store. John, knowing the intimate geography of the station, walked halfway along the corridor to where the half-tiled walls gave way to painted steel panels forming the obvious structure of a bridge over the southbound line. The upright support bands were regularised with rivet heads every six inches. One was missing on the left-hand side, and John leant down to waist height to look through the hole. There was much speculation as who had removed the rivet affording the vista, whether it was the Dip Squad or pickpockets. The rest of the team looked on as John had a bird's eye view of the single entranceway onto the platform. He could see the intending passengers standing three or four deep, many of whom were excited tourists eagerly awaiting their first experience of the London Underground.

Bob leaned against the cold steel of the bridge next to John. He could feel the chill of the structure as it diffused through his Harrington jacket. As he waited for the 'off' from his observer, his mind drifted back to a year before, when part of his squad were nicked and banged up on the strength of a moody allegation of corruption against his boys. This was the very station where a homosexual dip called Andrew McMurray made an allegation against the then dip squad, which Bob was in charge of. He alleged that they had 'taxed' him, taking any money he had, and given him a 'life', or let him go, rather than fitting him up for an attempted theft from persons unknown. This kind of corruption was rife in the years prior to Bob being promoted into the position of being in charge of the squad, hence the challenges which Detective Sergeant Western had presented earlier, and this had been the topic of the 'fireside chats' with Bob's commander.

In essence what had happened was that McMurray was a prolific thief who preyed on unsuspecting tourists. He had been arrested many times by various squads in earlier years and had been given a 'life' on some occasions in return for whatever money he had on him at the time. Having been taxed, he would then have been freed and not fitted up. This time, my squad had arrested him and charged him with a couple of thefts. What we didn't know was the close connection he still had to a former dip squad sergeant who had in the past not only corruptly taken monies from the thieves, but in this case had a casual homosexual relationship with McMurray. Needless to say, the dip was not impressed that he had been charged by my team, who were not averse to editorial licence when it came to evidence, shall we say, but were certainly not bent in the truest sense of the word. McMurray feared, given his previous convictions, that he would be going inside for a number of years. He pressured the sergeant for a solution, and between them they came up with a cock-and-bull story of how my officers had stolen from him when they arrested him. But to make it look credible, the sergeant, a man by the name of Greg Dennison, contrived to arrest him for an attempted theft, and having called for urgent assistance with the arrest, would then be 'assaulted' by McMurray. He would then be taken off to hospital, leaving McMurray clear to make his spurious allegations to those officers turning up to assist. And all this happened while I was on annual leave, on holiday with my family! I came home to find an anonymous note through my front door telling me that my squad had each been arrested and suspended from duty, and someone looking out for me said they'd be in touch. What I can tell you is that I smelt a rat straight away. The investigators were investigated, but it may not surprise you to know, not suspended, with three of them, including the sergeant, being put up for prosecution for perverting the course of justice. And guess what, the Director of Public Prosecutions decided it was not in the public interest to prosecute them. My officers were returned to work with no further action being taken! The whole thing stank, as you can imagine. But be assured I didn't get mad, but I did get even.

John turned to Dave and said, "Fuck me, it's 'Gambian Billy' there. He's on his own but he's not wearing the usual African clothes, he's got a black leather jacket on his shoulder, jeans and a dark red shirt."

The four of them waited as another lift disgorged passengers into the corridor and chattering tourists passed them, turning left to descend the stairs to the platform. The distant rumbling of the southbound train gave the team their signal to start their descent to the southbound platform. The fifteen or so steps wouldn't take them long to negotiate, the first two taking the lead with Bob and Dave bringing up the rear. Al and John turned left onto the platform as the train came to a halt and the crowded platform surged forward to board. Billy had moved about five yards to the right, 'shaping up' behind a bemused woman boarding at a single door at the end of the carriage. She held her shoulder bag over her left shoulder thinking she had adequately secured her belongings close to her. She didn't reckon on Billy, who by now had moved in so close to her that his jacket partially concealed the top of her bag.

With one swift movement his left hand extended from underneath his jacket and plunged into the top of her open bag, as his efforts were masked by the jostling of the surrounding group trying to board the train. As his hand located her purse he pulled upwards just as another nudge from behind resulted in him losing his grip so that it fell back into the bag. The woman, believing she had just been jostled in the crowd's efforts to board the train, pushed through onto the train.

John grabbed his target in a bear hug and pulled him back saying, "You're fucking nicked, Billy."

Fish leapt on at the next set of open doors in a vain hope of speaking with Billy's intended victim, while John struggled with the thief as he shook him from side to side like a wild animal trying to break free.

"Get off me, blood clot, I'm going to fucking kill you," said Billy.

He broke free of John's grip. With that he swung round just as Dave and Bob arrived to see a flash of silver swing round towards John. As it did so, John saw it coming and instinctively raised his hand to defend himself. The three-inch blade swept across the back of his hand resulting in a light scratch from his thumb to his little finger, and a yelp from John, confirming that the knife had connected.

The boys jumped on him and Bob rescued the blade in what looked like a violent 'pass the parcel' encounter. Billy became all the more determined to break free, first losing his jacket used to conceal the intended theft and then ducking under the other two in a move which any rugby player would have been proud of. His break for freedom saw him leaping and running like a gazelle down the length of the platform, not realising there was no escape. The doors of the train closed with Fish still on board trying to convince the 'victim' that she was a very fortunate woman indeed. As the train pulled away, disappearing into the black hole, Billy, realising his only option for escape lay in him following down the pipe, slowed with a view to jumping down onto the tracks. As he did so, John, in hot pursuit and winning the race with Bob and Dave, pulled the starting pistol from his jeans pocket.

He shouted, "Stop, armed police."

He raised the gun in the air and with a loud crack let off two rounds. Billy, believing those chasing him had a serious attitude problem, dropped to the ground, put his hands on his head, and begged not to be shot. Dave, not knowing of the gun, shat himself, wondering how he was ever going to have a job after this, while Bob quietly cursed John under his breath, doubting his parentage, and working overtime in his mind on how the hell this could be written up.

Armed plain clothes coppers on the Underground? Now that's a first, if of course it were true. I'll let you in on a little secret, and I bet you go looking for it next time you're travelling on the tube. The trains have what I think is something to do with the electrics, like a circuit breaker or something similar, underneath them, which seems to kick in as the train is pulling away. It makes quite a loud bang either once or twice as it does so. Fortunately, there were no members of the travelling public nearby as they had all just left on the southbound train, so the only ones were the next lot arriving down the stairs as we had just done and who were oblivious to the fucking Hawaii Five-O *drama seconds earlier. If anything registered it could be innocently explained as just that. We handcuffed Billy and took him off to Holborn police station. I still had the blade and anticipated that Al would join us sooner or later. As for Dave, well, only the laundry man will know how worried he was. He'll get over it.*

The uniformed van driver pulled up outside Russell Square tube and had a quick fag while the boys loaded their latest statistic into the back of the transit. John and Dave sat either side of him refusing to engage in conversation with Billy, who was seeking to confirm he'd been nicked by armed police, while Bob rode upfront, casually dismissing any talk of shots being fired as the words of an attention-seeking nutter! The journey to the nick remained uneventful save Billy's persistent assertions that he'd been shot at. The van driver reversed the back of the Transit right up to the charge room door and released his cargo into the 'caring' hands of the uniformed sergeant who sat facing their entry. Bob did the talking, relating who the prisoner was, his nefarious activity at Russell Square tube, and his efforts to resist arrest in trying to 'stripe' John with the blade, showing it as he did so, and conveying in a reassuring air that Al would be arriving very shortly with the victim, or at the very least, her details. The sergeant, unimpressed by Billy's behaviour, expressed his satisfaction at the scenario, despite Billy still protesting he'd been shot at. The performance of the three officers in expressing their complete disbelief at such a bizarre story was worthy of an Oscar, and Billy was neatly despatched to the cells.

By pure chance, Bob, when he was on a sergeant's course, had met the balding, corpulent officer who had just ignored Billy's claims of firearms being waved about. They renewed their acquaintances once more, as each brought the other up to speed with where they were now in their 'illustrious' careers. The sergeant had been busted from CID for drink driving a couple of years before, when he was found slumped on the drive of his house, engine still running, in the police station's general-purpose car! This was basically a plain car used by either uniform, crime squads or CID and on this occasion very usefully employed to convey a pissed DS home, without authorisation, of course! Hence, his rise up the slippery pole had come to an abrupt halt. They both agreed, though, there seemed to be a wind of change blowing through the service, since breathalyser offences were now regarded as crimes. This meant, of course, if you were convicted of this, you became a candidate for dismissal from the job.

Not a situation anyone wants to find themselves in, particularly as most of the top brass were totally uniform orientated, with a considerable dislike bordering on a loathing of CID officers. The irony of course was that they didn't mind quoting how well their respective stations were doing when it came to arrests, charges and convictions, perpetuated in the main by CID! Two-faced shits. But that's the job I'm afraid. So coming to Billy, it was obvious he wasn't going to shut up about this firearm. The sergeant and I came to the conclusion the only way to take the wind out of his sails at the eventual Crown Court hearing was to dispense some summary justice from our side. And so it came to pass that Billy was deemed under the Mental Health Act for seventy-two hours. This basically meant he was sent to a secure psychiatric unit for assessment as to whether he was fit to be charged. Needless to say, he protested, but there was nothing he could do, so off he went. This gave us time to get together to straighten out our case for the attempted theft. And the victim? Al tried to convince her to come with him to the nick, but she wasn't convinced she'd been the victim of anything. She did however agree to give us a statement at a later date. Turns out she gave a false name and address! So another day drew to a close. I gave John a bollocking for the stunt, told Al he was a wanker for not securing the victim, and calmed Dave's nerves, which had taken a bit of a battering.

10
GAME, SET AND MATCH!

Paul Hazel and DS Jim Hunt knocked excitedly on the door of Bob's office. The office had just been told Michael Jackson was fit to be released from hospital and requested a time for collection. He was still attached to the bed by the bracelets with a police 'nanny' by his side, but he was now considered a bed blocker, and in need of transfer to the caring custody of the Dip Squad. The boys arranged his collection and met Bob at Bow Street nick where he was 'booked in'. Because he was coming back into police custody the first thing was to get a police doctor, otherwise known as the Divisional Surgeon, to give Jackson a quick once-over to confirm he was fit to be interviewed and detained. As is so often the case, the doctor is an enthusiastic supporter of the blue serge, and only too willing to concur with the train of thinking of the police. After all, he's on a retainer; in other words, for a regular fee, he is willing to turn up any time of day or night at any police station and perform a medical examination; for a price of course! DC Kent, as with the visit to Winston, brought the property bag of stolen credit cards, and knowing what Bob wanted to do, neatly laid out the cards across the desk in the interview room.

Jim spoke with the custody sergeant and by prior arrangement Michael met Bob in the interview room parking Jackson's arse on the chair opposite them. He looked around at four tired grey-painted brick walls, a lone fluorescent light suspended from the drab white ceiling. A single radiator had obviously been working overtime during the winter months creating yellowing stains like exhaust fumes up the wall where the open door into the room provided the only natural light.

Jackson can best be described as a wiry little shit, looking in need of a good meal, other than Colonel Sanders of course, loads of surly attitude, and wearing the latest fashion we have in custody clothing, the all-in-one white boiler suit. His clothes were removed from him at the time of his arrest and bagged, just in case any of the items were the same as those at the time of the GBH. Needless to say, it's miles too big for him, but I'm afraid we only do one-size-fits-all. He looks as if he's wearing a giant baby's sleep suit, all dignity and self-respect removed from him. Anything to throw him off his stride is worth a try with this nasty, violent little shit. What he doesn't know is that I have a witness to him slashing the face of the officer, who says she could recognise the 'assailant'.

As he sat belligerently leaning back feigning a casual indifference to his custody, his eyes were drawn to the thirty plus cards spread out across the table. Bob saw the look of concealed surprise in Jackson's face while DS Hunt shuffled the sheaf of papers in front of him as if to suggest they had a lot to talk to Jackson about.

Bob reminded him that he was still under caution and said, "OK, Michael, have a guess what we want to talk to you about?"

Jackson, leaning back on his chair with his arms folded

and distancing himself from the table of cards, sneered in a seemingly confident tone saying, "Them, innit."

Bob leant forward and started slowly and methodically picking them up, one by one. He said, "No, fuck all to do with it. You striped one of my officers right across the face when he stopped you from thieving. Now, I'm going to give a once-in-a-lifetime opportunity to put your hands up to me right now, or I'm going to fuck you over completely, you horrible little cunt. I'll just write you up in an interview that you did it, a complete plea and that you refused to sign my interview notes, charge you with attempted murder because you tried to stab him in the neck, and you'll stay in custody until your trial. Choice is yours."

Jackson got up and hurled abuse at Bob, leaving him in no doubt he was in no mood to negotiate. Jim leapt up and with one punch to his chest, planted Jackson straight back down, with a "Shut the fuck up, and sit down."

Winded, he assumed the position trying not to look as if he had been bothered by Jim's directive.

"Now, Michael, I tried, but the fact is you're a dumb twat who doesn't listen to the nice policeman when he's trying to do you a favour!"

Bob outlined the scenario of that day when the plain clothes officer had intercepted him as he tried to steal from the passenger in the corridor between the two platforms, and instead of being apprehended, Jackson chose to produce a knife, and to assist his escape, he viciously sliced the officer across the face, causing a severe life-changing wound to the officer. His response? No reply to everything that Bob said, and every question he levelled at him.

As Jim tidied away the cards into the property bag Bob said, "As I said to you, you fucking shit, the custody record will show that we've been in here long enough for a short interview. Now I'm going to fuck you over in our notes of that, just so you know what's coming. Oh. Yes. One last thing, I've got a witness to your assault on that day, so what's going to happen is that you're going on an identification parade to get you picked out and then I'm going to charge you, fuckwit. I've already got your brother for the cards so maybe I'll think about a conspiracy to handle stolen goods and defraud. What do you think, Michael? So you'll stay with me for another night so I can arrange the ID parade.

Jackson was dumped back in the Peter while I spoke on the phone to a good mate of mine, a uniform Inspector who is like a bald-headed version of Del Boy, and he readily agreed to set up the parade for the following day at Brixton nick where they have a specially designed Identification Suite. I've known Steve, or Slippery Steve as he's known, since we did a covert job over to Holland, and as we had an overnight there before returning to the UK we got pissed in Amsterdam and went and saw the Jaws *film with Dutch subtitles. In our inebriated state we thought with a title like that it was going to be a blue film. Dickheads! He got the title 'Slippery' from having been caught on an internal discipline job coming out of a massage parlour having benefitted from a free 'muscle rub' from a grateful madam paying her tax to the local plod. He wouldn't have got caught but the DC he went with signed in the visitors' book in his own name! Whereas Steve wrote 'Michael Mouse'.*

"Can you phone Jackson's sister for me, Paul, and get her to drop off some of his own clothes at Bow Street tomorrow morning before he's taken down to Brixton for the ID parade. And impress on her how important it is that the investigation is being carried out fairly for dear Michael. You know what I mean."

Paul with a wry smile on his face said, "Of course, guv, leave it to me, parade set for one o'clock, is that right boss?"

Bob leant back in his captain's chair and nodded in agreement. Paul could see he was deep in study of a load of crime reports that needed signing off, so he left. Bob looked up as the click of the office door indicated he was alone once more. He mused about Paul and his passion – apart from eating orchids of course – that of train spotting. He had a vision of an overweight dumpy man dressed in cheap jeans, sandals and the statutory anorak waiting excitedly at the end of Kings Cross platform until a particular locomotive came into view and the smug satisfaction of ticking it off in his little book. *What a wanker*, Bob thought to himself as he shook his head vigorously trying to rid his mind of Paul's peccadillo.

He was just indulging in another daydream, in preference to signing off the deluge of crime reports, when a loud trill announced someone wanting to speak with him on the phone.

"Oh, hello Steve."

Bob ran through the strategy for the following day, and meeting with his approval, Steve outlined that, because of Jackson's singular appearance, it might be better if, instead of a formal parade, he proposed doing a 'street identification' on the escalators at Brixton tube station. He was content he had enough officers to contain the scene and ensure no escape for Jackson. Bob told him that he'd received a phone call from a brief, some slick-sounding bloke with an Italian surname, who was attending the nick tomorrow and would want ten minutes with his client before the parade started. Happy that all the t's and i's were crossed and dotted, Bob replaced the phone knowing that he would take no part in the parade, although he would be present while his trusted Del Boy did the business for him. While he thought of it, he took the opportunity to phone the female witness who had come forward following Shaw Taylor's *Police 5* appeal at the scene of the crime. A brief chat with her and a reassurance of her safety, he arranged to meet her at Brixton nick thirty minutes before the start of the parade, advising her that parades were notoriously slow and very often delayed but that her help was deeply appreciated. She had already done her statement, witnessing the GBH, with Al Fish, and as per the nature of the beast, he had begun 'charming the knickers' off the prime witness! But he knew not to push it too far before she had done the business at Brixton.

Bob left liaison with the recovering injured officer, PC John Innes, to Jim Hunt asking him to meet with him before taking him to the nick for the parade. He was acutely aware this was going to be a tough ask for the officer, young in service, with limited experience, and possibly reliving the whole incident and receiving the dreadful injury across his face, which he would see in the mirror for the rest of his life. He needed handling with kid gloves, lots of quiet encouragement, to help him play his part in screwing down this nasty, evil little shit. Bob knew he could rely on his team to do whatever was absolutely necessary to 'pot'

Jackson. Content that he had lined everything up for the following day, Bob's next call was to his 'love interest'. They had now fallen into a routine for contacting each other. She could phone him on his extension but there was always the risk that the police operator could listen in. He had a new gadget called a pager but again, you had to call an operator to activate it, and it only had a red flashing light on it which indicated the recipient must contact the CID office. The brief, on the other hand, had the next generation pager which could actually display a short message. If Bob knew the connection through the switchboard was safe, he'd just send the message 'phone x9', his extension, otherwise they used codes for various locations in central London.

He came off the phone wryly smiling to himself; he knew carnal gymnastics were on for later. She had booked tickets for the evening performance of a comedy drawn from television called *'Allo, 'Allo!*, a favourite of his ever since he saw the supposed English undercover *gendarme* say, "Good moaning, I was just pissing by the door!"

With a renewed skip in his step, he peered round the doorway of the squad office, overhearing the boys arranging lager frenzy for an hour's time, and declining their invite to join them. He dared them to fail to make the meet at Brixton the following day; to a man they reassured him they wouldn't let the side down. Those that couldn't get to the comfort of a bed, whether their own or someone else's, would be sleeping on the armchairs in the fifth-floor canteen. Bob slipped out of the nick making his way down to Oxford Circus courtesy of the Bakerloo line where, on arrival, he was obliged to negotiate the rush-hour one-way passenger system, which fed him straight into Argyle Street and The Palladium.

Realising he was a bit early for curtain-up, he went into the pub opposite, a very old mahogany-bedecked establishment popular with tourists, for a quick 'livener'. Using the public phone just inside the main door to the saloon, he phoned home to give his missus the good news that he wouldn't be back tonight as he was still out on enquiries and then had the commitment to the ID parade the following day. Needless to say, she wasn't bothered, the kids were on sleepovers with their schoolmates, and she was meeting up with a couple of her equestrian pals, for cheese and wine. *How appropriate*, Bob thought, *she's forever whining, she'll enjoy it!*

So tomorrow's the big day for Michael. My pal Steve will do a good job with the parade, he's done them before at Brixton tube station, so he knows exactly how many officers he'll need to prevent any escape of the suspect. I, on the other hand, will be enjoying a night at the theatre with a most stunning-looking woman, who is intelligent, such good company and someone who I've grown very fond of. This will end with us going back to her place and falling into a night of unbridled passion. But then you know that, don't you?

Bob sauntered into the office at first light, having been dropped off by, he believed, a very contented lady who he was getting more and more fond of. Office unlocked, coffee on, radio on.

"Can't start the fire, can't start the fire without a spark…" Bob joined in, "Even though we're just dancing in the dark."

Springsteen brought him into life. He leant back in his chair, remembering that night a couple of weeks ago when she came to his office, ostensibly representing a dip who had been further charged at court with conspiracy to steal. On went the lock and they were at it like rabbits, bending her over, lifting her black and white striped dress to reveal that gorgeous peachy bottom being restrained by grey suspender straps leading to black lace-top stockings. He felt himself getting a bit of a beat on and to divert his fornicating thoughts he mused at his cracked Arsenal mirror, thinking about sending one of the boys to the supporters' shop to get a replacement.

"Da-do-do-do, da-da-da-da, that's all…" rang out from his radio as the door burst open allowing the corpulent frame of one Chief Superintendent McVicar, officer in charge of the nick, to barge in. He went straight to the radio, and in one fell swoop, switched it off.

He angrily said, "Trebor, what the fuck are your blokes playing at? Bob, they've got to stop this, or I'll stick them on!"

Bob said, "Guvnor, I don't know what you're on about. What's up?" He knew that when McVicar was in this mood, he could go a bit psycho.

"Your squad came back to the nick pissed and had a fight with the fire extinguishers. They're all fucking empty now and the carpets on the floor above are wringing wet. This has got to stop. If there was a fire we'd be in shit creek!"

Bob, looking to mediate the situation and perhaps take some of the sting out of it, apologised on behalf of his team, quietly cursing them to himself under his breath.

"Sorry guv, I'll speak with them, I trust you'll leave it with me. All I'll say, and it doesn't excuse it, but if you have a look at the two boards over there listing our current bodies, you can see how busy they've been, they're all working well, under a lot of pressure. Perhaps it's best explained as a bit of high jinks. But I get that it's not right, guv. I'll speak with them once they're all together in the office. They'll be there shortly, we've got the ID parade for John Innes today."

McVicar mellowed, enquiring how John was, and hoped for the best at Brixton, the fire extinguishers taking a lower priority in his conversation.

With that he withdrew from Bob's office saying, "Sort it, Bob; by the way have you got a debrief in the office this Friday?"

Bob confirmed, saying of course, he was invited. Might be good, he thought, to heal the rift over last night's stunts. The debrief was a euphemism for a bit of wine tasting with nibbles, behind locked doors to avoid discovery by wankers looking to 'grass', when the squad could relax, talk about various cases or problems they had. Truth was, though, that very often squabbles between members of the team might result in punches being thrown. However, miraculously, come the early evening, a retirement to the local drinker would result in honours even and all friends again.

"Gentlemen," said Bob as he entered the squad office, "I have just had the pleasure of entertaining the Chief Superintendent in my office, giving me the benefit of his opinion as to what happened in the dead of night in this very police station. To my surprise he told me that you have been having a sort of duel involving the launching of a number of the fire extinguishers. I want to know who was responsible for this flagrant abuse of my instruction after the last time this occurred, in my office in five minutes. This comes only a week after I had a soaking wet WPC in my office complaining that one of your number had emptied a plastic bin full of water from a fifth-floor window. I won't tolerate this fucking about gentlemen. Five minutes!"

He swept back out, and immediately went to the toilets in the basement.

Dave and Basil, knowing they were the main culprits, decided to fall on their swords and take their punishment. DS Hunt said nothing but followed them both to Bob's office. Basil elected to knock but there was no reply from within. Hunt checked the room was empty and, telling them to wait outside like a couple of naughty schoolboys, he went off to find Bob. After checking the canteen on the fifth floor he went down to the basement toilets and ensuring no one else was on 'the throne' or within earshot, he called over the occupied trap.

"Guv, the culprits are outside your door."

Bob, sighing, said, "Oh for fuck's sake, what's the world coming to when my officers start pleading guilty to this load of bollocks? Get rid of them will you, and they had better keep quiet about this or I will get seriously pissed off. I'm staying here for another five minutes." DS Hunt assured Bob of this, returning to see the miscreants looking like a couple of scolded puppies still outside. He told them to get back in the office and get on with their paperwork and say nothing to anyone.

Just so you know, I returned to my office to find that no one had come to confess. I was now able to say to McVicar that sad to say, despite my investigations, no suspects had been revealed.

However, everyone knew I was somewhat pissed off with the behaviour, but it now meant that maybe a couple of other officers, maybe even uniformed officers, had been responsible. Either way, nothing was certain! Deep joy. I'm off to set things up for the parade at Brixton.

Bob called a quick office meeting with the squad just to ensure everything was covered for the parade at Brixton. He told them that Steve and his uniformed officers were already at Brixton nick awaiting their arrival, and that two of his squad were en route with the prisoner Jackson and on arrival would book him in to the cells, handing him over to the uniformed officers involved in the parade. Jim Hunt met up by prior arrangement with John Innes in a café just round the corner from Baker Street nick. Over a cup of tea, Jim went through what was going to happen that day and John's role, as this was not something which John, being young in service, had experience of. Jim at this stage didn't want to say what kind of ID parade this would be, whether formal or what's known as a street identification, which would take place at Brixton tube station. Al Fish, in the meantime, had renewed his charm offensive with the female witness, a soon-to-be-married Janet Flynn, having picked her up from her home and taken her to Brixton in the squad's CID car. Al, being the silver-tongued lounge lizard that he was, put his Ultravox tape on. "This means nothing to me, oh-h-h Vienna." Having met with her approval, he left the tape playing while he engaged her in seemingly casual banter, all the while eliciting her background.

Al was well versed in briefing witnesses on their obligations in an ID parade, although his intention with Janet was to 'debrief' her at some later stage. In the meantime his patter revolved around his being separated from his wife, and although not the case, wanting to see his children as often as possible, finding it difficult because of work but seeking to get a sympathetic ear from Janet. She warmed to Al, being such a nice man, trying to do his best by his children, while they steadily progressed towards the nick. She found him to be very approachable and quite an attractive guy although of course she was getting married to her beer-swilling, rugby-playing fanatic who in her mind had been taking her for granted in the past few months. Her thoughts weren't conveyed to Fish. They pulled into the yard at Brixton, parking up adjacent to the Identification Suite.

Al, familiar with the layout of the nick, opened the front passenger door of the car saying, "This way, love, we'll go into the witness waiting room and I'll get you a cup of tea."

They sauntered across the yard under a cloudless blue sky, past the outer cage leading to the charge room, and by good fortune, as they arrived at the combination lock door to the suite just as a PC was coming out. He recognised Al and held the door for him as they exchanged pleasantries before going in. Closing the door to the witness room, he met up with Jim who'd arrived at the nick with the young Innes parking him in the canteen on the first floor.

"I hope you don't mind. But I got you a sandwich and some biscuits to go with your tea. I wish I could've offered you something stronger but we can't do that till later," said Al with a cheeky grin as he slipped the refreshments across the table to Janet.

"That sounds a good idea, what time?", she daringly said.

Al, quick as a flash, outlined the itinerary and confirmed he would be driving her home. *In more ways the one*, he thought to himself.

Just to bring you up to speed, I've spoken with Slippery Steve and he's sent his uniform guys out to see if he can rustle up enough 'stooges' otherwise known as fine members of the public willing to do their civic duty to stand on the parade with Jackson. Usually the ID suite here at Brixton organises that for you beforehand, but unfortunately the dickhead in charge of the unit, who's only just recently taken over on promotion to the exalted rank of uniform Inspector, forgot to jack that up. As you can imagine, I expressed to him my sadness and disappointment at his fuck-up. Coincidentally, I've known the resident Detective Chief Inspector here for some years. A giant of a man, he used to box super heavyweight, was a previous Lafone Boxing Cup winner and a dead ringer for George Foreman, and someone I mentored in his earlier career. It gives me no pleasure to 'fix' a fellow officer, but having outlined my, shall we say, concern, I've been assured that for the foreseeable future, or until I indicate to my friend otherwise, the new boy is in for some 'corporate oppression', just to reinforce the importance of not pissing off his 'customers' i.e. me! You'll be wondering if Michael is to appear on the parade in his lovely white 'romper' suit. Well, the answer is no. His sister, who I'd never met or even known of before, turned up earlier with a change of civilian clothing for him. What I find curious is that she's a really nice person, who holds a senior and responsible position on the staff at Selfridges, articulate and no attitude, unlike all three of her brothers. Still, no time to wonder, I've got to meet Michael's 'brief' downstairs at the front counter. He's someone whom I've done battle with in the past, a silver-tongued lothario, so he thinks; Sicilian man by the name of Luca Zengretti, sharp-suited, swept back black flowing locks, and in his mind, irresistible to the opposite sex. He's known by my boys as 'shotgun', because he's a smooth bore. I've kept him waiting long enough now, just to let him know who's boss!

"Ah. Detective Inspector Trebor! Robert Trebor, that well-known palindrome."

Bob quizzically asked, "What the fuck are you on about Luca?"

The brief said, "Your name, Bob, it's the same either way round, Trebor or Robert, it's a palindrome."

"And your name's a fucking anagram for wanker, now let's get back to business. By the way, Luca, how many savvy lawyers does it take to screw in a light bulb?"

"Not a clue, Bob," said an impatient Sicilian.

"Thought not! Your client is in the cells at the moment changing into the gear his sister brought in earlier. I guess you'll want to have a word with him. There's a bit of delay as we're still trying to get enough to stand with him on the parade. Trouble is, trying to find that many skinny little shits like him isn't easy, but we're giving it a go," said Bob as he cursed his parents for giving him such a dumb-arsed name.

It was bad enough that many of his contemporaries called him 'Minty'!

The Sicilian said, "OK, Bob, and I'm guessing if we don't then we'll be doing a street ID?" Bob confirmed as he walked him down the cell passage towards Jackson's temporary accommodation, outlining that the street identification procedure would be Brixton tube station with Jackson coming up the escalators as the witnesses waited at the top to see if they could pick him out.

About twenty minutes later, Luca emerged from the cell, courtesy of the gaoler PC, his head full of Michael's remonstrations as to the delays in getting all this sorted. It's fair to say that Bob wouldn't be on Michael's Christmas card list – he was annoyed with the choice of clothing his sister had delivered, clearly believing he belonged on the catwalk in better threads! And one final thing, he wanted a woollen hat to wear, so that his early attempts at growing dreadlocks could be hidden from view. That last bit of wisdom was imparted to Bob, who, sensing Michael was already trying to pull a stunt, sent one of the boys out with a fiver to Electric Avenue to buy the cheapest he could find. In the meantime, he met up with Steve who confirmed their joint suspicions that, in Brixton there is an underlying mistrust of anything to do with the police, – even when trying to bribe them a tenner each, just to stand there! The irony is, they believed if they were mistakenly picked out by a witness, they'd end up getting charged and banged up. Their 'irrational' fear of a fit-up ensured their lack of interest in anything which meant they had to enter the nick. *That really would be taking a detective's efforts to secure a result a bit too far*, Bob thought.

And so it came to pass, no volunteers meant Steve organised the 'street' ID to take place. Fortunately, the tube station was a 'stone's throw' from the police station, and so he was quickly able to speak with the staff there who still had to run a train service. Steve had organised them there before and was comfortable that the prisoner would remain secure throughout. All it took was a sergeant and one PC positioned a short way from the foot of the escalator, with the prisoner. At the top would be another three officers to ensure no escape into the street. Steve, in charge of the parade, would call over the radio for one witness at a time to be escorted to him from the nick. On their arrival, he would do the formal bit, advising them that they may or may not see someone they recognised emerging from the top of the escalator. He would then position the witness in a good viewing position and would move away to communicate by radio on a dedicated channel, ensuring sterility of the parade with everyone else out of earshot with the offices down below. They in turn would release the prisoner or suspect to join the escalator for the ride to the top at his own discretion in his own time. The process would get repeated for all witnesses, in this particular case, two.

"Luca, I think we're about ready, do you want to go with your client to the tube station, and then when he descends, wait with the uniform Inspector at the top, to observe?"

Luca nodded approval and chatted with Michael as the two uniformed officers booked him out of the cell and walked him in handcuffs to the tube station. Bob spoke with his two witness escorts prior to walking down to the tube station. He was fiercely aware, as indeed was Luca, that he could take no active role in the proceedings other than to watch as Steve worked his magic, hopefully getting the desired result. As the heat of the day increased, Bob was relieved he'd thought to put on a brown linen suit, which he kept in reserve at work.

Jackson was now at the base of the up escalators with his two babysitters. He remained in handcuffs much to the passing interest of the predominantly black travelling public, who registered their disdain at one of their 'brothers' attached like a hand-in-hand lover to a police officer. Any rescue attempt of dear Michael at this stage was futile unless they wanted to drag a great lump of a copper with them as well. And it was obvious his sergeant, who was constantly on the radio waiting for Steve's signal, would be able to scupper any release by screaming for urgent assistance. So an uneasy peace prevailed over the circulating area at the base of the escalators, with many making the telltale sound of resentment through their teeth while others supplemented with the expression 'Blood clot!' Steve summoned the first witness on his personal radio – the injured officer, John Innes – to the tube station together with his chaperone DS Jim Hunt, to enter the booking hall where he'd be met. The Sicilian listened in as Steve went through the standard instructions for the parade, while a studious Luca made notes in his blue brief's book, endeavouring to fill as many pages as he could, in the hope that he would con Steve into believing he'd somehow transgressed from the rules, and of course to show to the passing travellers that he was indeed earning his legal aid fee at taxpayers' expense! Steve turned away, and using channel two on his personal radio, told the babysitters that Michael could ascend in his own time.

After about thirty seconds, Michael emerged at the top of the escalator, apparently in deep conversation with two other black men wearing dusty clothing as if they had just come off a building site. To add to Michael's avoidance at identification, he was carrying one of the men's holdalls in one hand and a yellow spirit level in the other.

His stunt, as cute as it was, served only to show what a sneaky little shit he was, because John had no hesitation in stepping forward indicating to Steve, "That's him. The man who slashed me across the face."

With that, Jackson threw the holdall and spirit level to the ground, shouting, "Blood clot!"

A wry smile emerged on Bob's face as uniformed officers robustly seized the assailant by the arms, ensuring no escape. The builders retrieved their kit and sauntered out into the bright sunshine of the High Road. Luca raised his eyebrows as if to say, *That's me stumped*, as he resumed making copious notes. A brief word to his client Jackson saw him descend the escalators in handcuffs once more. Steve thanked PC Innes for his attendance and he was escorted back to the nick by DS Hunt, ensuring there was no cross-pollination with the second witness, Janet Flynn, who was being 'put at ease' in a separate room by Al Fish.

With everyone back in place, Janet was summoned by Steve for the same procedure to be repeated, while Bob and the Sicilian mused as to Jackson's next trick to avoid detection. Al, sensing he was making progress towards a 'satisfactory' conclusion, walked her to the tube station, continuing to make small talk about the weather, the nice Laura Ashley dress she was wearing, and giving her an insight as to what might occur on the parade in an effort to take away any fears or misconceptions she had. He held her hand, gently squeezing it, furthering his intimacy with her as they arrived. Turning into the booking hall, she was blissfully unaware of the bright sunlight making her dress transparent when seen from the dimly lit station. Bob was pleased to see her, although of course at this stage he was fiercely aware that he couldn't tell her so.

The Sicilian's only response was, "Nice," under his breath as he made a careful note of her description and Steve's address to her.

Here we go again, thought Bob, the lights irritatingly bright at the head of the escalators. *I wonder what the little shit's going to do next*, thought Bob as Steve radioed down to release Jackson once more. His release saw him immediately speak to a very pale-skinned black girl about twenty years old who was pushing a baby's buggy and baby within. He saw that she was wearing a 49ers baseball cap and after a short chat he was now wearing it, as he threw the woollen hat to the ground. They boarded the up escalator as if they were a family group, Jackson lifting the buggy to his hips as he continued his conversation with the girl. One of the uniformed officers at the bottom retrieved the woollen hat, unsure what he should do with it. The couple blocked anyone else coming up behind as they reached the summit. He carefully placed the buggy on the floor, the baby not stirring from its 'impromptu abduction', and they continued chatting as they walked towards the exit. *Crafty bastard*, Bob thought, as he gazed across at Janet.

She moved forward one step, then as if briefly hesitating, two more steps, saying "That's the man there, with the pushchair."

On hearing the positive identification, Steve signalled to the waiting officers to recapture a subdued Jackson whose only response was a smirk towards his brief. Steve quickly thanked her for her help as Al shepherded her back to Brixton nick.

So what happens now, Bob? I hear you ask. Well, Jackson has to go back first of all to Brixton because that's where he was booked into custody when the boys picked him up earlier. I don't intend interviewing him anymore, because I suspect the Sicilian will have told him to say fuck all and a 'no comment' interview is frankly a waste of everybody's time. So, happy that he's banged up again and his brief is now waiting patiently at the front counter, I shall speak very briefly to both the witnesses, thanking them for their positive identification in what were extenuating circumstances, and send them on their way. John's dreadful injury looks less red and angry since the last time I saw it, but reality is that he will have one hell of a 'Mars bar' for the rest of his life. Janet looked terrified, like a rabbit caught in the headlights of a car, but I have every confidence Fish will 'ease her tension'.

It had been a long day when Bob met up with the boys at Bow Street nick having ferried the belligerent Jackson back there. He told Luca that he wasn't bothered about interviewing the little scrote but invited him to be present when he would be charged with an attempted murder and GBH with intent alternative, plus an attempted theft and a conspiracy to handle stolen goods, the bank cards. He was careful not to mention what had happened in the first 'interview' when Jackson had made a full and frank confession to all his criminal activity; seemed a better idea to give dear 'shotgun' a nice surprise when he would be committed for trial! Some twenty minutes later, Jackson was indeed charged and told he would be going nowhere other than to his first appearance next door in the court at Bow Street and the strongest objections to bail would be made to ensure he stayed banged up until his trial at Crown Court.

SKIN THE CAT

"You'll never guess who I've just bumped into," said an excited Steve, sounding more like Del Boy than Del Boy!

"I give in," said a bleary-eyed Bob as Steve planted himself in the one easy chair in his office.

"Well, yesterday went all right, didn't it?" said Steve.

Bob, beginning to lose his patience, said, "Who the fuck have you just bumped into?"

"Oh. Yeah. So there I was, I'd just been into the ID suite at Victoria, and I was walking across the concourse of Victoria Station to get the tube to come and see your good self. I must admit I looked bloody lovely in my smartly pressed uniform with my cap worn at a jaunty angle when coming towards me, in a group of about five or six people, was Clint Eastwood. Yep that's right, Clint fucking Eastwood. I couldn't believe my eyes. Well he walked up to me, obviously saw the uniform, liked the 'cut of my jib' and spoke to me. Apparently him and his group wanted to get a train to Gatwick airport and he asked me which platform. I know, I know. It was too much for me to resist, I just went all serious in my face and I said, 'I know what you're thinking, is it five or is it six?' Now to tell you the truth in all this excitement, I kinda lost track myself. Then I said, 'But you've got to ask yourself one question, do I feel lucky? Well, do ya, punk?' He just gave me such a look, I thought he was going to draw me one off, then he said, 'Five.' I said, 'Na, six.' He looked at me with that aggressive squint he did in Dirty Harry, but returned to his group, I suppose part of his film crew. After a few seconds they all fell about laughing as they walked to where I'd told them. He waved goodbye and said, 'Good one.' How about that, that's how you command the respect of the members of public! Bet your day's been shit by comparison!"

Bob leant back in his chair and related the story of Al Fish's latest, shall we say, challenge. He was taking the nervously shaken female witness from yesterday's identification back home when he had the brilliant idea of taking her for an early evening drink, just to calm her. One thing led to another and having found a quiet spot under some railway arches so they could swap spit, the drinks having had the desired effect of loosening her tongue and inhibitions, she got down to it. One small problem, it wasn't far from her home! Her soon-to-be husband, out walking their Heinz 57 dog, came across his betrothed with her head firmly in Al's lap. By some sheer fluke he had just missed her playing the pink piccolo, and so the scene was innocently explained as her being overcome with emotion and the kinky officer simply extending the 'hand of friendship'! Somehow, this implausible tongue-in-cheek story grew arms and legs when Janet burst into tears as 'hubby' yanked the door open. Fish, quick as a flash, thanked him for turning up; he'd tried to console her but obviously the experience had affected her more than anyone ever imagined. The only reason Bob learnt of this dalliance was when his phone rang first thing, a concerned husband-to-be worried about the likelihood of a forthcoming trial and seeking reassurance that Bob would do everything in his power to protect her. Of course, Bob was happy to do so, cursing Fish under his breath and his preference for birds with big tits, something with which Janet had been handsomely appointed. Steve's contribution was to laugh like a drain, leaving Bob's office with the assurance his statement would be with him in the next couple of days. Bob's response was to tell him to go forth and multiply, as he was getting ready to go to court on a not-guilty fight, having been warned to attend 'not before 2pm'. This kind of court warning usually comes about where the court finds that one of its current trials will fall short and finish earlier than anticipated, and so they go to the early warning list and pick off the next trial to be scheduled. The early warning list is where the court advises any number of police stations or offices that particular trials are going to be listed over a nominated two-week period. It basically gives you a reasonably fair warning of when trials are listed for, in case there is any sickness or leave of any of the witnesses to be considered.

Well, here I am at the all new Southwark Crown Court for Gambian Billy's trial, which apparently should last for between two and three days, dependant I guess on what 'alligators' are released by the defence. Allow me to walk you up the grand but sadly very modern staircase to the first floor where the police room is. As we ascend the beige-walled vestibule, probably painted in a colour designed to calm people's nerves or tempers, you see a huge painting some three metres square on a canvas high on the wall to the right, boasting three, yes only three, blobs of colour, grey, purple and green. It has no obvious meaning, no apparent style and word is that it cost over thirty grand of public money! The artist, if I can call him that, must have thought, Suckers, *as he laughed all the way to the bank. This new courthouse has about fifteen courts, much bigger than the old Guildhall on Westminster Square, the site of the original Middlesex Quarter Sessions and of course its overflow court rooms in St James Square, so we should call this progress. I can't help thinking it's more like a modern conveyor belt of justice with very little of the historic gravitas that the old Middlesex Court had, but we are where we are. In the brief time that my chaps have been using this new facility, not only have we managed to bed in well with the officers on the court staff but also the ladies in the list office, the place where all court warnings emanate from. I'm now just waiting for my star gunslinger, 'Butch Cassidy' Conroy and his sidekick Sundance, or Dave Champion, to honour me with their presence, then we're ready to kick off.*

An elderly barrister, who had done thirty years in the police force, now qualified to wear a wig and gown, by the name of Hector Classe, entered the police room in search of a senior officer in the case of du Port, Billy's chosen surname. He met up with Bob who by this time was indulging in his second cup of tea whilst chatting with the court sergeant, who had just invited him to one of the regular cheese and wine parties taking place on the following Friday after close of play, or for the uninitiated, after all the courts had risen for the weekend.

"Have we got all our witnesses here, officer?" enquired Hector.

Bob, aiming to create the right impression that he had his finger on the pulse, said, "Yes sir, the other two officers, Conroy and Champion, will be here in time for kick-off. Unfortunately, we weren't able to trace the female victim, but as you know this is so often the case. People, for whatever reason, just don't want to know."

Hector nodded in agreement as he scanned Billy's extensive list of previous convictions, a list that went into two and a half pages. Hector confirmed this was a trial of a professional, or perhaps not so professional, pickpocket, having no legitimate means of support, who was not averse to resorting to robbery or carrying weapons if the need arose. Bob, sporting a Prince of Wales check suit, loud pink tie, and matching pink socks, worn for a squad bet of a tenner, readily agreed, citing two previous convictions on page two for possession of an offensive weapon and another three for a variety of assaults in his compendium of crime.

With that, Butch and Sundance appeared, carrying the leather jacket and the penknife, now both exhibits in the trial. Hector, content all his ducks were in a row, left the officers to continue their tea tasting, while he swept off, gown in full voluminous flight, to find Mr Orlando Van Hagen, barrister for the defence. On learning the name of the defence brief, Bob afforded himself a wry smile, knowing from previous trials in which he had defended that his defence would be robust and his closing speech to the jury would follow a fairly obvious line. Bob couldn't wait for the cross-examination, so he could steal the thunder from Van Hagen, mentioning nothing to the others. A dear old judge by the name of His Honour Judge Crook – *How pertinent*, Bob mused – would be sitting in Court 13 for this little extravaganza. John and Dave waited outside while Bob, together with the two opposing barristers, entered the courtroom while the jury were sworn in. Some twenty bemused members of the public, both male and female, filed in, unaware of what was to be required of them; clearly this was their first experience of something they had only ever seen in some drama on the television. This was, of course, now the real world.

The clerk of the court rose to his feet for his Warhol fifteen minutes of fame. Judge Crook sat back and watched proceedings as the clerk, chest inflated, grandly called the potential jurors to the stand, impressing on them the full weight of their impending duty. After the usual swearing on oath that they would faithfully try the defendant and give a true verdict according to the evidence, twelve 'good men and true', comprising of eight women and four men, assumed their positions in the jury gallery. Some in suits, some smart-casual and three of them looking as if they'd just surfaced from Glastonbury or a peace camp. Nobody could say it wasn't a cross section of society; the days when a jury member had to be of a mature age and a householder or homeowner and even further back, a man, had long gone. Du Port stared at his peers from the dock, the glazed panels preventing any physical contact with anyone in the courtroom. He sat, weighing them up, like a captive fish in a huge aquarium, his eyes running back and forth along the two lines of jury members, looking for someone he could focus his attention on, but they were consumed with the address from the judge, giving them a few pointers on court etiquette.

And so battle commenced. Bob, being the officer in the case, went into bat first. His evidence in chief procedurally ran through how on the date in question he together with Butch and Sundance entered the southbound Piccadilly line platform at Russell Square, where he saw the defendant, du Port, leather jacket over his right shoulder, manoeuvre in behind a female intending to board the stationary train via a carriage door just diagonally right of the egress onto the platform. He rummaged around with his hand firmly in her shoulder bag, clearly with the intention of stealing something from within, then removed it without successful plunder. At this point the 'cavalry' stepped in to arrest Billy, whilst at the same time Fish was rescuing the damsel in distress. However, Billy had other ideas. Intent on making good his escape, he produced an open penknife with something like a four-inch blade and slashed out at those trying to arrest him. He succeeded in striping Conroy across the back of the hand, which in all honesty was the lightest of scratches, a point not conceded by Bob, but obviously delivered with the intention of serious harm. To reinforce the account, both the leather jacket and the knife were then shown to the court, though not given over to the jury. Their opportunity to examine the aids to offence would come at a later stage. Having been given exhibits one and two, they were placed on a large bare table just in front of the clerk.

Hector, not wishing to stop Bob's flow, asked him what happened next. He told the court that du Port ran off down the platform as the train was pulling out. Amongst the noise of the departing train a couple of loud cracks were heard, which to the uninitiated could sound like gunfire but were in actual fact something to do with the electric motors on the train. Du Port, not realising this, dropped to the platform floor, begging not be shot. Hector Classe chose not to interrupt Bob's colourful account of the incident, utilising the 'less is more' policy. He assumed Orlando would do his best to destabilise the prosecution, not knowing at this stage if he intended a full-on assault, calling all the officers liars, thereby allowing the prosecution to introduce evidence of Billy's bad character – in other words, his previous convictions. The alternative to this robust attack was simply to suggest the officers were mistaken, avoiding the horrendous criminal history being revealed to the jury. Bob continued his evidence, outlining how when du Port had been told he'd been arrested for attempted theft, he frantically asked who had tried to shoot him. So traumatised was he by this imagined incident, a wet patch appeared on the front of his strides and a strong aroma of someone having had a bumper crap filled the air. Bob, in a quietly concerned tone, explained that Billy was essentially talking gibberish during the journey in the van, on his way to the nick. Once there, ever aware of the need to ensure the welfare of the prisoner, du Port, he consulted with the charge room sergeant who would assess him once he'd been charged. Needless to say, Bob didn't allude to their cunning plan to deem him for seventy-two hours for some spurious mental enquiry – besides, a theft is a theft, even if committed by a nutter thinking he's going to be assassinated!

Orlando, a short arse, rose to his feet, a full five foot six inches draped in an oversized gown, looking as if his mum had dressed him, visually emphasising that Ede &

Ravenscroft of Chancery Lane, robe makers since 1689, did not cater for children on youth opportunity schemes.

"Officer, I see you referring to your pocketbook throughout giving your evidence. As you have made it public, would you now with the leave of the court pass it across to me?"

Judge Crook, sensing a fishing expedition by the defence, made no comment other than to nod in approval as Bob, seeking guidance, passed his well-worn pocketbook over to the court usher, who in turn ferried it across to the 'angler' in the front row. A pregnant pause then ensued as the frustrated Orlando, unable to immediately find the relevant entry in the book, masqueraded as if he was forensically examining its content.

"Ah. I see your notes start on page twenty of this book and go on to twenty-eight, is that correct?" Bob confirmed, believing that to be the case.

"Officer, I can see you say you made your notes at Bow Street police station. There is a problem though. I can't read them, I can't make head nor tail of what you have written. It could be about anything or anyone. Why is that? What are you hiding?"

Bob took a sip of water from the glass provided by the usher, paused to increase the theatre of the occasion and said, "Absolutely nothing, sir, the notes are not meant for you. They're my notes, to aid my recollection of events. I then made my witness statement based on the content of my notes, which of course you have."

Three of the jury smirked with an expression of, 'That's stuffed you, mate' on their faces.

Orlando, refusing to accept he'd been made to look a dick, took a deep breath, and sacrificing Billy's otherwise 'impeccable reputation' said, "Detective Inspector Trebor, I'm not going to beat about the bush. I will say it as I see it: my instructions are that you and your cohorts are lying. This whole story, from start to finish, is a tissue of lies, a farrago of fact and fiction. None of what you've just said to the court happened in the manner in which you say. The only piece of evidence on which we concur is that you and your team bumped into my client at Russell Square tube station. The rest of it is an account worthy of *Grimm's Fairy Tales*. My client has been a victim of you and those working for you, a regular culling of those less fortunate, with whom you have a particular vendetta! And this nonsense of noises coming from underneath the train, another pack of lies. My client believes either you or one of your number fired two shots at him. Whether the gun was real or imitation, we know not, but so terrified was he that it was the former, he immediately surrendered. You turned him into a petrified wreck, requiring him to be detained for seventy-two hours. How did you manage that?"

Bob sipped again. With a look of 'Here we go again' he said, "Sir, I appreciate you have been instructed by your client. But I'm afraid he has led you astray. What I have given in evidence of your client's attempt at theft on that day is as it happened. I have not misled the court; to do so would, as you know, mean I had perjured myself. You impugn my reputation, which I find offensive."

Judge Crook interjected before matters descended into a slanging match. He reminded Orlando of this fact and indicated that as his client had alluded to his own good character and made allegations against this prosecution witness, he would be expected to reveal to the court at a later stage anything known by the authorities about his client.

Van Hagen, sensing he needed to get the judge off his case, changed tack in his line of questioning. Something that had worked for him before when cross-examining police was to ask them to summarise the significant points of evidence they felt were important in proving their case. His purpose was to draw a contrast between what they had given in evidence already as against that which they saw as important. This would sometimes have the effect of presenting two different accounts, which he could exploit with the officer or better still, play one or both accounts off against those officers following when it came to cross-examination. Having seemingly innocently asked Trebor to do his best with this, Bob saw his opportunity and struck.

"Well, you see, sir, an offence of this nature breaks down into a number of component parts, many of which are common to the commission of this kind of offence, by anybody at any location and at any time." Orlando smiled to himself, believing he had a gullible officer who was about to be overconfident in his analysis of this attempted theft, and let him go on.

Bob continued, "If you imagine that the various contributing parts of this offence are like bricks, which cement together to form a wall of evidence which is presented to the court, then of course as the counsel for the defence you have to test that wall, and discover the weak parts, if any, punching a hole through to reveal the poor construction of the evidence. I think that's probably the most useful analogy I can give."

Van Hagen's face visibly drained as he recognised where he had seen Bob before. They'd had a trial some six months earlier where he had used the 'brick wall' scenario, often practised by many a defence barrister, in his closing speech to the jury. Bob had just scuppered him using it again, knowing he came from the same chambers as Mario Bergamot!

Judge Crook nodded as Van Hagen slumped back down on his bench reluctantly announcing that he had no further questions for the officer. Hector rose and asked for the jury to be sent out whilst a point of law surrounding du Port's background was discussed. Crook, knowing immediately what he was alluding to, explained to the jury their need to retire whilst matters which need not trouble them at present be discussed. The usher escorted them out to their room and Hector raised the issue of the defendant alleging bad character by the police, which he submitted meant that Billy's long list of previous convictions could be known to the jury. The judge invited a response from Orlando although he'd already made his mind up. Van Hagen's only observation was that only those previous convictions of a like nature, not the two for indecency or the three for drugs possession, should be put to the jury.

Crook said, "I might have agreed with you had your client not, on each and every occasion, pleaded not guilty and subsequently been found guilty, so no, he's a proven liar and all offences should be listed."

Bob, relieved that he wouldn't have to edit the list of

pre-cons, nodded, not that it was required, towards the judge as if agreeing with his decision.

Bob, feeling he'd taken up residency in the witness box, waiting to be released so that 'Sundance' could be called, was now the focus of the judge's full attention.

"Officer," he said, "I trust the matter of the list of previous convictions will not cause any delay or difficulty for you? I just want to have a look at the exhibited knife."

The court usher, eager to please his master, retrieved it from the clear plastic property bag nestling next to Billy's leather jacket, which had been similarly bagged. Having broken the security seal he passed the closed knife to the clerk who in turn passed it up to His Honour. The judge, unable to resist the urge, opened the blade from its protective cover. In a *Tom and Jerry* moment, when the eyes come out on stalks, he looked at the knife more closely, and in particular, a small dark brown discoloured area towards the point of the blade. *Bingo*, thought Bob, he's clocked it.

"Detective Inspector, have you examined this knife in any detail?"

Bob, feigning a quizzical look, confirmed he hadn't, as if to say, "Should I have?"

Crook, believing he was Sherlock Holmes, said, "It looks to me as if there is a staining on the knife which could be blood. What do you say about that? I think we had better have it forensically examined, have it done overnight for court tomorrow. I want to know whose blood it is."

Bob maintained his bemused composure as he assured the judge every effort would be made to have it analysed to establish its origin and he undertook to Crook that he would return tomorrow with an answer. Inside he giggled to himself that the judge was now playing amateur detective, and being a Dickens aficionado, the line from *Great Expectations* sprang immediately to mind: "What larks, Pip."

Bob left the courtroom, knife in property bag; as he passed Conroy and Champion outside he said, "Back tomorrow, boys," whereupon they went back to the police room to get their jackets.

Whilst there Bob told them he was off to the forensic laboratory at Lambeth for the knife to be analysed. He reassured them there was nothing to worry about and that all was going according to plan, Conroy knowing what all that was about, although of course if anyone was to ask, they hadn't spoken about the case.

So why is the judge so interested in the knife? I'll tell you. A few weeks ago I looked at the statements in the case history folder on du Port and I just felt there was something missing. The leather coat, no problem, du Port had used it to hide his attempted theft, but the knife was a different issue. We said he used it, open, to help him escape the clutches of John. But the 'injury' to John was just a scratch, it didn't even need 'official' medical attention. No excuse, though, we all know what he was trying to do, he just didn't succeed. So I called John into my office, asked to look at the back of his hand. Nothing! I picked up a pin from the dish on my desk and in one sweeping motion pricked the top of John's thumb just below the cuticle. He yelped as he did on the day, asking why I'd attacked him. I made reassuring noises such as, "Don't be such a tart, and do you want du Port to go down for this or what?" I squeezed the thumb and a small bubble of blood appeared like a raindrop on a newly polished car. I told him to shut up and learn as I slowly drew the knife through, just enough to show traces of his claret. Carefully closing the knife, I put it back in the property bag, to await Billy's trial. My thought was that at some stage the two exhibits would go to the jury. When they did, they could play detective believing they'd cracked the case, teaching old bill how to suck eggs. Never in my wonderfully wildest dreams did I imagine the judge would lead the charge in amateur sleuthing! I must admit I was a bit concerned the laboratory might be able to age the bloodstain as it had been 'applied' a few months after Billy's arrest, but I knew they could only group it to John's donation.

Day two saw Bob and his two caballeros marching confidentially up the stairs at Southwark Crown Court towards the police room on the first floor. Once inside, Dave was nominated to buy the teas from the tea club in the corner while Bob renewed his acquaintance with his pal, the court sergeant, Terry Bells, or 'Jingle' to his mates. Knowing they didn't have much time, Bob got them together to outline in a fairly discreet part of the room the results of forensic examination directed by that ace sleuth, Judge Crook. Their faces visibly brightened as Bob reassured them all that very little could be said about the blood. The door to the police room flew open and Hector, noting the hinges could do with oiling as it let out a long lingering groan on shutting, enquired what the result of the test was. Satisfied he'd got an answer, he dragged open the door again and left.

All three made their way to the courtroom and Bob entered for his final performance in the witness box while the other two slumped on the long bench outside, awaiting their inevitable 'roasting' from the defence brief. The court was called to order by the usher as Crook made his entrance from the door at the far end of the bench. Settling down, he acknowledged both counsels and turned towards Bob who was by now standing in the witness box with the knife in its clear property bag balancing precariously on the front rail. Hector rose, reminding Bob he was still under oath, and enquired what was the result of His Honour's forensic enquiry. The judge looked attentively at him while he outlined that, sadly, the laboratory had failed! Well, not quite. It was able to confirm that it was human blood but there was insufficient to be able to group it, to identify whose it might be. Crook looked a little deflated as he directed that the jury should know that, but nothing more and nodded to the usher to recall them. Having settled down, they were given exactly that by the judge who then turned to Bob thanking him for his efforts and releasing him from the witness box. Butch and Sundance went on to swear by almighty God etc., but the only point of note was Orlando's continual allegations of a fit-up, which of course was robustly denied by both of them, and as a postscript he extracted from John that the injury to his hand didn't cause him to be signed off sick. His point, as he performed to the jury, was that obviously it wasn't very serious. They were both released from the trial by the judge leaving Bob, as the officer in the case, sitting behind the brief as the defence case commenced.

Orlando van Hagen rose to his ill-fitting form again pronouncing that his client du Port was not going to give evidence and sunk back down with an air of judicial superiority, as if to quote Wilde with "I have nothing to declare but my brilliance." *Pompous arse*, thought Bob. Fish, who had snuck in the courtroom in case of any challenges about the non-appearance of the female, left once more with Bob's blessing, content he could 'cover' the remainder of the trial. Hector's closing speech was a very brief affair, highlighting to an attentive jury that they were looking at a career criminal who made no secret of his past, relying on courtroom slander of the officers to defend his case. But his reluctance to 'take the stand', to quote those American soaps, may be his undoing, which the judge would address them on. He assured them they would have every opportunity to examine the two exhibits when they retired for their deliberations and as the defence had introduced it, du Port's weighty tome of antecedent history would also be theirs.

Van Hagen gave his closing speech but I'd fucked him using his usual brick wall analogy. In all honesty, it was something of nothing, he just commented on the credibility of us fine, upstanding chaps. The suggestion that we would fit up an innocent man having first shot at him? The very idea! The judge summed up and sent the jury out with the goodies to help them reach a decision. After five minutes they were back in with a note saying they'd found two little white tablets deep in one of the pockets of the jacket, were they anything to do with the case? Crook glared at me and told them not to attach any importance to their discovery. Dave, you twat, you didn't search it properly. I'll deal with you later, making me look a dick in front of His Honour! Ten minutes later they re-emerged with a result. Guilty, of course. Quite right too, agreed Crook. Van Hagen tried to plead that it wasn't the most serious offence in the criminal calendar, at which His Honour took issue. Sensing the judge was a bit more pro-police than he had realised, Van Hagen tried to soften his mitigation. He succeeded in winding up the judge with every tack he tried, so much so that, at the end, when he weighed off du Port, he commended Butch, Sundance and me for our professionalism and diligence. It's fair to say that was the first time I'd received a commendation by default. Still, it made up for those times when I hadn't got recognition. Billy, doubting my parentage, was sentenced to two years' porridge and taken down. I saw van Hagen afterwards. He told me I was a shit for stealing his analogy, but the offer of a beer from me meant we buried the hatchet with a couple of chilly lagers. Proves there's more than one way to… We parted the best of enemies or friends; he's OK, just misguided, but he had a job to do.

12

THE WARM-UP ACT

"Guv, I think we have a problem. Paul is missing, well, not missing. Just don't know where he is," said Dave Champion as Bob leant back in his chair trying to galvanise himself ready for David Jackson's trial that day at Southwark Crown Court.

He had originally been committed to stand trial at the historic Middlesex Crown, but with the early grand opening of the new court overlooking the Thames and HMS Belfast, he was to stand trial there. Last night had been a bit of a session at the Maple Leaf pub in Maiden Lane, following the arrest and charging of an old dip going by the name of Pettigrew. No, nothing to do with Tom, this one was, like his name suggests, a petty criminal who was just a pain in the arse. Upon his arrest, his usual stunt was to claim to have Aids or HIV and then spit at the officers engaged in his arrest in an effort to get released from any further involvement with the police. Bob had toyed with the idea of getting him detained under the Mental Health Act as it had met with such success with those trying to play the system, du Port being one of the most recent. However, Aids and HIV were very new medical conditions only recently coming to the notice of the media, and the fact so much was still unknown understandably affected how people generally feared infection from those allegedly having the condition. In Pettigrew's case, he hadn't actually connected with the skin of those nicking him, so on that basis a large portion of 'fuck you' was employed. Why should a shit head thief get away with it?

"Come on then, what's the problem, where is Paul?" asked a knackered Trebor who, post last night's lager frenzy, had been obliged to sleep across four chairs lined front to back in his office, as a very poor alternative to his legal lover.

She'd obviously given him a body swerve in preference to a night of drunken snoring. *He couldn't blame her, who would want that?* he thought as Dave continued the sorry tale of the previous night's escapades, while the guvnor's radio released the dulcet tones of Spandau Ballet ironically singing, "I don't need this pressure on." *Same shit, different day*, thought Bob. He recounted post-Petty how Dave, Paul, Al and the guvnor had agreed that a round of beers in the Sugar Loaf pub in Great Queen Street would be the perfect venue for a 'debrief' on the evening's events before catching their last trains home. Having got the taste, the session advanced with a pilgrimage to that favoured watering hole of theirs, the Maple Leaf, where the Molsen draught went down like the finest honey for the 'bees.' In no time they had found they were victims of the last-orders bell and turned out into the street. After the guvnor left, mistakenly thinking he would be rescued by his femme fatale, the boys had other ideas. Stringfellows nightclub, a short stagger down Long Acre towards Leicester Square tube, beckoned their attendance. They were greeted by two burly doormen who seemed to be as wide as they were tall and were quite obviously a couple of well-paid thugs masquerading as jolly commissionaires greeting the night's punters. Undaunted, the chaps feigned familiarity with them and sidled up, surreptitiously revealing their warrant cards and with the briefest of banter, they were in, free of charge. Nightclubs such as this, whilst accepting the old bill were poncing a free entry to their establishment, figured it was better to have them in the tent pissing out than outside the tent, etc. In case of some kind of skirmish within, the security could call on them to assist in cases of 'violent difficulty'. And so it was that Dave, Paul and Al danced the night away trying to move in on a couple of *Sun* page three girls, obviously invited by the host to dress the place up a bit.

"He looks like shit, guv," said the sergeant in the charge room at Bow Street nick, as he spoke to Bob over the phone relating last night's 'entertainment'.

Seemingly, the boys fell out of Stringfellows at about two in the morning having been treated to several glasses of Moët courtesy of the management, straight into a Mexican stand-off with a group of young stallions trying to gain entry to the place. Seeing the doormen were outnumbered, the chaps decided to even up the score. This resulted in a street fight which the night duty area car and plain clothes car, or 'Q boat' as it was sometimes referred to, found it difficult to resist attending. On arrival, a 'bomb burst' of participants saw the rivals scattering to all points. Paul, being the persistent little shit Bob knew him to be, remained as last man standing, only to find that the young uniformed probationer constable, riding as observer in the area car, needing a quick arrest to improve his quota in his probationary period, handcuffed him and dumped him unceremoniously on the back seat. Paul, now realising he had a little local difficulty, immediately calmed and said nothing. By some good fortune, two of the officers who were attached to the local crime squad in the Q car recognised Paul, having worked with him before.

When both cars arrived at the nick they offered to help the naïve young officer by searching his prisoner for him, and in doing so they dipped Paul's warrant card and wallet away, holding on to them to ensure they weren't recorded on the charge sheet. As Paul swayed in the non-existent breeze in front of the custody sergeant's desk, the crime squad boys reassured the sergeant and the probationer that they knew Paul, neglecting to reveal his true identity. So it was that 'John Mullins' of no fixed abode was placed in number one cell, the drunks' home, to sleep it off till the morning. The stench of poorly cleaned vomit and urine ensured there was always that recognisable aroma as you entered the no-star accommodation, and Paul, still heavily influenced by the rich drinks menu, was in no fit state to notice or indeed complain. So he settled himself under the foul-smelling blanket for a night of recovery.

You may be wondering how it is that Hazel doesn't get the full wrath of my displeasure he may have clearly anticipated. Simple. The early turn sergeant, who I believe I mentioned earlier, who had had an unfortunate meeting with a breathalyser, rang me first thing to say that on handover at six this morning he checked on the prisoners being handed over by the night duty skipper. Imagine his surprise, as they say, when looking through the wicket gate in the door of the cell, he spied one Paul Hazel, masquerading in his sleep as J Mullins. Rather than show out to anyone at the nick he bided his time then rang me. Having learnt the scenario leading to his incarceration, between us we agreed with Charles Dickens in David Copperfield: *least said soonest mended. The crime squad boys had sealed the warrant card and wallet in a brown envelope, signed it across the seal and shoved it in the sergeant's pigeonhole together with a suitably coded note for him. And so, when Paul woke, he was given a full English breakfast, infinitely better than the other residents, followed by a bollocking, a caution for being drunk and incapable in the pseudonym and therefore no further action, and the assurance that he would return to the nick here, where he would have a shit, shower and shave and get dressed in his emergency suit kept at work, making himself ready for the trial. I left the troops unaware of my course of action as I couldn't have them thinking they could, on a whim, degenerate into this sort of behaviour.*

Bob thought, *Another day another dollar*, as he ascended the stairs to the police room on the first floor at Southwark Crown Court. He'd risked the journey to court without a mac but reflected on his error when he saw fine rain falling over HMS Belfast moored under the windows of the court building, facing the river, with the spring tide sweeping past its bows. A huge black barrister resembling Frank Bruno, the heavyweight boxer, hovered outside the closed police room door, wondering if his entrance might evoke the wrong kind of response from within.

In his vast flowing robes, he turned to see Bob walking purposefully towards him, and recognising his familiar pale face with 'ruddy highlights' he said, "Ah. Detective Inspector Trebor, it is Inspector, isn't it? Or have you been promoted since we last met at this house of correction?"

Bob, still a little bleary-eyed, saw the barrister now coming into recognisable focus and said, "No sir, still Inspector, I don't play golf and I'm not a mason."

Upon which the man mountain of a barrister exploded into uncontrolled laughter at Bob's revelation, causing other court attendees going about their business to turn in their direction as if to say, "What the hell was that?" Bob took the initiative guiding his Bruno into a side counsels' room as the brief's laughter subsided. On closing the door, the two sat at the familiar beige broad civil service table seen in many a government building, the chairs frayed at the edges revealing the cheap sponge within.

Bob slapped his briefcase on the table saying, as it came to rest, "So sir, good to see you again. The other officers will be down in a moment, I'm the forward raiding party I guess you'd say. Have you seen the defence? What's the game plan?"

Bruno, or his real name Gideon Ireland, leant back in his chair, the tubular steel frame creaking beneath the weight of the giant of a man. He said, "Well I've spoken to counsel for the defence, Mr Rufus Soles, do you know him? He's from One Gray's Inn."

Bob nodded, acknowledging that he knew him all too well as someone who had made his hatred of the police an art form and would cause no end of aggravation for him if it meant his client could walk from the overwhelming evidence against him.

Ireland went on, "He's pleading not guilty, probably no surprise to you, claiming that you've fitted his client up with contemporaneous notes which he says were filled in after the event, admitting his involvement in dishonestly handling the bank cards, and also that the trial signatures found on that weighty tome I'm familiar with, the *Jamaican Weekly Gleaner*, are simply a stunt to make his client look as if he's more involved in the use of the stolen cards. He's claiming foul in that you didn't serve the additional statements regarding this evidence until yesterday and that he hadn't had time to take full instructions from his client about this."

Bob shrugged his shoulders saying, "More like he's not had time to concoct an alibi I should say, sir."

Ireland sighed, "Well there it is, officer, it's going to be a little dirty I fear. I wouldn't be surprised if defence ask to have the trial stood out while they have forensic tests conducted on the contemporaneous notes."

Bob thought to himself, *Well good luck with that one!* All the necessary homework had been done on that, so Mr Soles could do what he liked. *We're fireproof,* he thought. The two of them left the room to be confronted by one of the court officers telling them that their judge had a couple of bail applications in before them so the trial wouldn't be kicking off until after eleven o'clock. *Just as well,* Bob thought, *gives time for the rest of the cavalry to arrive.* And so they did, meeting up with the guvnor indulging in his first cup of coffee of the morning. The day had turned into a bit of a Dip Squad reunion with Dave, Basil, Al, John and a rather ashen-faced Paul in attendance.

Bob confirmed the boys had brought all the exhibits with them, with nothing missing, pocketbooks matched with times of entries, and the contemporaneous notes were pristine, no overwriting indentations, and times coincided with the defendant's full and frank admission contained within them.

"I hear we've got Mr Soles looking to give us a hard time, boss. Mr Rufus Soles, R Soles, fuck me, all we need is for one of our victims to be Betty Swollocks and we've cracked it," said Dave, upon which the rest of them nervously laughed, knowing the reputation of defence counsel.

They made their way up to the top floor to Judge Ranjit Singh's Court, where they met up with Gideon Ireland, reclining as if he were some Greek god waiting for his grapes, along one of the long benches outside the double doors of the Court Thirteen. They hovered while Bob sorted out a batting order for the police witnesses, there being no members of the public to give evidence, as all the victims had no idea who had stolen their credit cards or indeed that David Jackson had kindly accepted them from whichever thieves had relieved them from their owners' possession! It was agreed that Bob would go in the box after the rest of the chaps had given evidence so that he could do the mop-up of where the officers had deferred answers, for he could give any policy decision answers required. With that they each retired to the police room leaving Paul to be called first after the jury had been sworn in. Seemed only right, thought Bob, given the aggravation he'd had to sort out from the night before.

"Right, who's up for a game of Trivial Pursuit then?

Basil, get the board out, Al you get the coffees, Dave you help me set it up," said Bob.

Other officers who were booking in for their respective trials looked on bemused at the seemingly casual manner in which the group appeared to take their court appearance, as if seasoned campaigners. Not unreasonable, really, as on many occasions the Dip Squad might have three sometimes four trials running in the court building at any one time. Most of the trials were ordinarily two to four days in duration and so a fairly high turnover ensued. It made them very popular with the list office, and Bob had wasted no time in garnering their favour by 'taking tea' with the head of the operation. She had a direct link to the resident judge or top judge at the court. As was usual with newly opened courts, the Lord Chancellor's office would monitor and scrutinise the throughput of cases. If there was a shortfall in turnover the resident judge would be up for a bollocking from the gods. To avoid this, on one occasion, a message came down to 'she who must be obeyed', as in *Rumpole of the Bailey*, a favourite TV programme of the time, that the judge was looking for quick, short cases. On the promise of two cases of champagne from His Honour to be shared between the list office and the Dip Squad, Bob duly obliged in greasing the faltering wheels of justice. Everyone was happy, the judge showed he was cracking the whip, the list office galvanised their high regard for Bob and his boys, and the squad got pissed gratis! Deep joy.

Paul in the meantime had just been called in to give his evidence following the jury being sworn in. Gideon swept through Paul's evidence, while he continued to sober himself up to be ready for the anticipated onslaught of Rufus Soles.

Having enquired if the white-faced officer felt well enough to give evidence, he asked him a few questions about who found the cards, where they were found, who was there at the time, and how he came to find the newspaper with the signatures on it, mindful that he wanted to come over to the jury as a considerate barrister not wishing to cause any distress to the quite obviously unwell officer. Judge Singh then adjourned the hearing apologising to the jury that they had to retire whilst he dealt with an earlier trial which was coming to an end and reminding Paul of the usual nonsense about not speaking to any of the witnesses in the case as his evidence was part-heard. Soles dropped back down on the bench, resigned to the judge's whim at the moment when he was just about to slaughter Paul in cross-examination. Now it would have to wait until after lunch, back at two!

Hazel shambled his way back to the police room and met up with me, now the victor in the first game of Trivial Pursuit! I told the rest of the crew to go off to the little hole-in-the-wall café in the arches up by London Bridge. I've been reassured, if reassured be the word, that there will be no repeat of Paul's fuck-up last night. It's just not acceptable. Putting himself on offer like that puts us all on offer, and we have a hard-earned reputation to maintain. So, lecture over, we're out for a bit of lunch in the Grapes pub; they do the best roast beef doorstep sandwiches and Paul, for his sins, is paying. I've clocked a runner for the defence brief peeking round the corner at the end of the first-floor corridor – no damn idea of surveillance, but let's give him the runaround over lunch, see if he can keep up.

Bob and Paul, having given the others the chance to leave the building first, stepped out from the privacy of the police room. As they descended the stairs past the expensive waste of taxpayers' money, or huge abstract oil painting, floating menacingly above them, they continued in quiet conversation, quite obviously chatting to each other, for the benefit of the brief's runner who followed their every move. Paul opened the door on the far left, holding it open for Bob to pass through. Seeing the misty rain had stopped, they continued towards the four steps leading to the pavement and service road running across the front of the court building. Striking out across the road, taking the short cut to the pub, they had only got a couple of yards from the kerb when a loud screech of tyres to their right saw a lime green Ford Capri lose its grip as it spun into the service road to their right. The driver, struggling to regain control, drove straight at the surprised detectives who leapt back onto the kerb as it swept past, coating the pair of them in the earlier rainfall from the gutter.

"You fucking dick!" shouted Paul as the driver completely lost it and the car went into a broadside halt some twenty yards on from them.

The driver fell out of the door, regaining his balance as he stood up in his very loud turquoise blue shell suit, revealing his identity as none other than Winston Jackson.

Bob shouted to him, "You're a shit driver, Winston," as the pair of them laughed at him, serving only to infuriate him further. He ran to the boot hatch of the car and struggled to open it, without success, while the detectives continued ridiculing him as they walked off in the opposite direction. Winston slammed his fist on the boot, then jumping back into the driver's seat and with a screech of tyres and blue smoke disappeared at the far end of the service road. Unperturbed, Bob and Paul went off to the pub where the doorstep roast beef sandwiches beckoned.

"What can I get you, love?" said the peroxide-blonde landlady to Paul as he set a ten-pound note free from his pocket.

He leant on to the bar adopting what he thought was a familiar air as he requested a couple of Cokes and two of the establishment's finest doorsteps. He fell back as she told him that more than the one note he proffered would be required. A second note produced saved Paul's embarrassment, and they sauntered away from the bar to a perch adjacent to the leadlight window near the door. Bob asked Paul how last night's escapades came about. He explained how he'd stepped in to help the bouncers when a rather enthusiastic young probationer arrived seeing the opportunity for a quick arrest. He spent the night in a stinking cell but at least it had been put to bed. Bob had to smile at Paul's sorrowful tale, noticing at the same time the brief's runner had poked his head around the corner to see what was going on. Bob counselled Paul on 'plan B', which Paul understood, and the two of them left with the runner in what he thought was discreet pursuit.

On the way back Bob said, "You know that brief I'm seeing, did you know she's split from her old man and she's going for a divorce? He's a copper on the staff at Horseferry Road Mags, and by pure chance I bumped into him the other day on a remand I was covering. Someone must have bubbled me to him because he obviously knew I have been seeing her. Do you know what he said? 'How's the sex with my missus, is her fanny loose enough for you?' In front of the others. I thought, *Fucking cheek*, so I said in front of his audience, 'Only the first two inches, after that, it's as if she's never been fucked before.' Twat!"

The two of them laughed, agreeing that he was a twat and now they would go about spreading the rumour that he only had a little cock and that was the reason she was divorcing him, as they re-entered Southwark palace of variety, making their way back to the police room on the first floor.

The boys had started another round of Trivial Pursuit, Paul aware that he should make his way back to continue his evidence. Bob, devil inside him, went with Paul to see if defence counsel took the bait. Until this point he hadn't bothered to sit in on the trial, albeit as officer in the case he could, but the opportunity to make defence look like dicks was just too much of a temptation. Jackson was led into the dock chaperoned by two dock officers, and saw Bob turn towards him as he surveyed the court.

"So young to die," he said, directing his words to Bob.

"What did you fucking say, shit for brains?" said Bob as he stood to face him in the dock.

"So young to die, you pussy clot," asserted Jackson.

Gideon proposed that perhaps Bob might assist their strategy if he were to retire from the court before the judge and jury came back in, and not wishing to inflame the atmosphere but happy that he'd stood his ground against the shit in the dock, he left, leaving Paul to spring plan B.

Paul rose to his feet, together with the rest of the court's occupants as the knock on the door by the bench saw it open to Judge Singh's entrance. The clerk of the court, having spoken to the Judge in hushed tones, summoned the usher to retrieve the jury from their lunch break. Everyone settled, Paul stepped into the witness box to await R Soles' cross-examination, which commenced with, "If it please Your Honour, now, officer, remember you are still under oath. In that oath you declared you would tell the truth, the whole truth and nothing but the truth. Now, before lunch, His Honour told you not to speak to anyone about this trial. You were seen going to the Grapes public house with Detective Inspector Trebor, a fellow officer in this case, yet to give evidence, where you had lunch and you were in conversation with him over lunch and indeed on your return to this court."

Some members of the jury leant forward sensing something important was just about to be revealed.

"Do you admit doing so, officer?"

Paul simply said, "That is correct, sir."

Soles went straight for the jugular. "You were in discussion with Trebor about this trial, weren't you?"

Paul again, "No sir."

Soles, "Oh really, officer. You were told by His Honour not to speak with anyone about this trial. So what was your very deep conversation about?"

Paul asked for a glass of water, playing the delay in answering for all he was worth.

"We were speculating about why it was that the defendant's brother tried to run us over outside this court as we left for lunch. And we had a bet with each other. I bet DI Trebor that you would allege we had spoken about this case with each other and he didn't think you would be so foolish to try. There was a tenner on it, so I'm ten pounds richer now, sir. Thank you."

The jury masked their mirth at Soles being so publicly shafted.

Soles, smarting from the ridicule, looked to the judge for some support by way of a bollocking for the officer's smart-arsed reply, but saw that none appeared to be forthcoming, Paul seemingly just on the right side of contempt of court. He pressed on with cross-examining, confirming that Paul had been present when the cards were recovered and that he alone found the newspaper with the 'practice signatures' thereon.

"How do you explain the only signatures are where the card has no signature?" asked Rufus.

Paul responded saying, "I can only speak from previous experience, sir. When a fraudster wants to use a stolen credit card, rather than try to copy a signature, some have found, dependant on the quality of the biro pen used and any wear on the signature strip, they can use car brake fluid to carefully wipe the ink away. This then allows them to personalise it with their own signature."

Soles said, "But that's not the case here is it, officer? The cards may well have been cleaned, but my instructions are that he absolutely had nothing to do with that process. What I do say is that you've 'over egged' the pudding by falsely writing those signatures to implicate him."

"No sir," boomed Paul in an effort to show his indignation at such a scurrilous allegation. Soles, realised he was getting nowhere with his line of questioning, simply sat down with a flourish of "No further questions."

Gideon simply clarified that Paul's explanation came from earlier experiences of investigating similar crimes, and that he found the *Jamaican Weekly Gleaner* complete with practice signatures at the flat. Paul was happy to confirm, and with that he left the witness box. His journey to exit the court went past Jackson glaring at him from the dock.

As he reached the double doors, unseen to the jury, he surreptitiously mouthed "Fucking wanker" to him, resulting in the defendant leaping to his feet shouting "Blood clot!" and having to be restrained by the dock officer, all in the full glare of the jury members who had turned towards him, surprised to see the commotion.

Next was Basil Chakrabati who, having given his evidence-in-chief, was then treated to Soles' ritualistic abuse, claiming he had fitted up poor innocent David using the sheets of paper which had been handwriting samples demanded by DI Trebor. Naturally, he denied such outrageous allegations as did the others called, each saying that Bob was the officer in the case. Having given his evidence-in-chief it was Trebor's turn to be roasted by Soles.

"So, Mr Trebor, you are the officer in charge of the previous officers we've heard from. To hear them give their evidence we would be forgiven for thinking they are all telling the truth. But that's not the case, is it officer?"

At which point Singh intervened to enquire whether Soles was actually going to ask any questions of the officer.

He confirmed and said, "Officer, as a person of senior rank you used your position to force the officers to commit perjury on your behalf and you did likewise with the bogus handwriting samples, didn't you?"

Bob, exhibiting his best poker face said, "No, Your Honour, the circumstances of the defendant's arrest, the seizure of the credit cards and practice signatures are as have been outlined in evidence. He was interviewed contemporaneously, not by me, in which he admitted his part and no more."

Soles, trying to wrong-foot Trebor, said, "That's simply not true, is it? You gave him sheets of blank paper to sign at the bottom of each page, telling him the space above was for the exhibit label to be attached."

"No, only an idiot would do that, sir," said Bob again.

"I'm wondering, officer, what we would find if we were to subject the pages to an 'Esda' test," alluding to a machine that can reveal any indentations from other writing on the pages, which might suggest the interview notes were written out of sequence with the signatures at the bottom.

Bob confidently said, "Sir, it would be pointless as the events occurred in the manner stated. But if the court directed, I assume that could be arranged, although I suspect some delay in getting the test completed during the duration of the trial may be difficult."

Judge Singh glared at Soles who realised he was up against it, the judge not being with him on this quest. He asked a few more questions alleging smoke and mirrors by the squad, and realising his time was up, sat down deflated.

The jury came back after about thirty minutes with a finding of guilt. The judge weighed him off with eighteen months' imprisonment. That'll teach him to fuck with us. Two days later I took a call from some DCI on Rotherhithe Robbery Squad. He said, 'Do you have a DI Trebor in charge of the Dip

Squad?' and I confirmed he was talking to him. He asked me if someone had tried to run me over outside Southwark Crown the other day. I asked why. He told me his team had nicked Winston, David's brother, for a series of armed robberies. Music to my ears, I said. He went on to tell me what happened, how he'd tried to bowl us over and then screeched to a halt. I confirmed we took the piss out of him when he fell out of the car and was obviously frustrated that he couldn't get in the boot of the Capri for whatever reason before roaring off. He then delivered a chilling scenario. Apparently, Winston was trying to get in the boot to get a sawn-off shotgun he had on board. He was going to shoot the pair of us! The penny dropped, hence David's 'So young to die' from the dock. I told the DCI if he wanted to load that on the charge sheet, I'd be happy to knock out a statement in that regard. With that, he assured me Winston, with what they had on him, wouldn't be seeing daylight for some considerable time, and rang off. Paul just laughed at the near miss we'd had. Good boy!

13

PETTY CRIMINAL

"I used to be, oh fucking hell, no," said Arthur Peter Pettigrew, useless, know-nothing, lousy pickpocket of this Parish.

This was in answer to a question levelled at Arthur by Al Fish who, in the early evening post rush hour on the Northern line at Leicester Square tube station, said, "Aren't you Arthur Peter Pettigrew, that well-known pickpocket?"

It was just before Halloween, and revellers were out in force trick or treating across central London. The squad had gone out from the office late afternoon to trawl around the usual dipping hotspots. Bob and a couple of the others were at Piccadilly Circus tube while Dave Champion and Al had moved on to theatreland's main tube station at Leicester Square. Both the lads, the devil inside them, thought it necessary to get into the party spirit by donning false wigs and bright red noses. To supplement this cunning disguise, Al had gone one better and was wearing a pair of glasses with no lenses in them. On any other day they would've looked like a couple of nutters. But this was Halloween and basically anything goes. Dave, resplendent in a blonde curly wig, nudged Al in the direction of Pettigrew who was sat on a bench about halfway along the Northern Line platform.

The two of them sauntered along as if oblivious to the crowded platform. There had been some delay to the trains, which unsurprisingly caused a build-up of waiting passengers. As they approached the apparently relaxed Pettigrew, they saw him vacate his seat moving straight forward towards the edge of the platform. Nearing him they could see him casually bump into an elderly female shopper loaded down with three or four weighty shopping bags originating from various boutiques in the nearby Covent Garden area. He was paying very close attention to her small shoulder bag on her left shoulder. Something spooked her. She turned and glared directly at Pettigrew who adopted a casual confused look as if he was studying the tube map on the far wall adjacent to where the train would pull in. Sensing he'd been rumbled he slowly stepped backwards giving the impression he'd gleaned what necessary information he needed from the map and with the arriving train attracting those seated on Pettigrew's bench to vacate, Arthur was able to sit centrally, allowing space for others to sit either side of him. The woman, seemingly learning the penalty of her casualness, reorganised herself and her bags holding them closer to her, as the train came to a halt from left to right in front of her. Pettigrew did his best to ignore her obvious awareness of him as the crowded platform emptied, jostling on to the train.

As it pulled out, the doors straining to close round the passengers now packed like upright sardines in the carriages, the platform was bare save a few recently entered passengers and some frustrated at not being able to get on. Al and Dave wandered the last five or six yards to where Pettigrew was seated and sat down either side of him, as if ignorant of his presence between them. The flickering light of the train indicator board told those who could be bothered to read it, even less to take any notice of its reliability, that another train would be along in five minutes.

Dave, facing forward, not acknowledging Pettigrew's presence, started very quietly singing to himself, "Happy birthday to you, happy birthday to you," then stopped.

He started again, "Happy birthday to you, happy birthday to you." He stopped again.

On the second occasion, it registered with Pettigrew that Dave was singing. He surmised the weirdly dressed bloke next to him must be a bit of a nutter.

"Happy birthday to you," he went on, "happy birthday to you," and then louder, "happy birthday dear Arthur…"

Pettigrew turned quickly to see how it was that this nutter knew his name, as Dave grabbed hold of his right forearm and Al grabbed his left, pinning him to the bench. His mistake was not to recognise the two officers, who one year to the day earlier had nicked the lowlife for attempted theft from a woman at Hyde Park Corner tube station! Hence the question at the beginning of this sorry tale.

Dave said, "Well have I got a surprise for you," in true Eamonn Andrews style, "you still are and you're fucking nicked."

Pettigrew's disbelieving response was to tell the pair that he had AIDS and they ran the risk of being infected if they kept on with the arrest. His threat to spit at Dave in an effort to scare him resulted in him receiving a robust response and a bleeding top and bottom lip.

"Try it again and you'll get very fucking dizzy! You tried this bollocks last year, it ain't going to work for a second time. I suggest you just shut the fuck up, and take your medicine," said Dave.

"You hit me, that's assault, you wait," Pettigrew whinged.

Dave, 'mystified' as to how Arthur had a bloodied mouth, enquired of Al if he knew how it had happened, of which, of course, he had no knowledge. But for certain the script would reflect that, just before they had arrested him, they saw Pettigrew try to dip a middle-aged man, the description of whom, to save any confusion, and to ensure it was well memorised by the time they came to trial, would be that of the Chief Superintendent of their division. The 'victim' would feel Pettigrew trying to steal a wallet from his back pocket, whereupon he turned and challenged him thereby resulting in the bloodied mouth, before he strode off telling him to go forth and multiply! Police appeals to locate and identify the victim will undoubtedly reveal no trace.

As the diminishing crowd boarded the next train, Al and Dave saw their opportunity to escort Pettigrew along the platform to the far end where a small cleaner's office afforded them the availability of an internal phone within, enabling them to summon non-urgent uniform assistance in the form of a prisoner van to the local nick.

As they sat around a desk in the cramped confines awaiting the 'cavalry', Pettigrew, feeling a little brave in his cheap 'Man at C&A' clothing, said, "OK then, what am I nicked for?"

Al responded, "Just being you, and oh yes, attempt theft from the person."

"You can't do that, I ain't done nothing."

Dave said, "Look Arthur, you're a thief, we know it, you know it, there's only one reason you're here and that's thieving. It's what you do, and you know that when we catch you down here you're going to get nicked. And one way or another you're going to court. Look at your previous, it's all for thieving, mostly on the Underground. Who's going to doubt what we say? You're at it, as you always are down here, you've got no other reason for being here."

Pettigrew tried standing but was firmly planted back on the chair by Dave. "I ain't done nothing. You ain't seen me nicking anything."

Al leant across to a wooden broom propped against the wall to the side of Pettigrew.

He took hold of it and standing above Pettigrew he said, "Hold this a minute will you, Arthur?" Not thinking or realising he took hold of the greasy shaft of the broom, immediately finding that the engrained filth of the broom had transferred to his hand.

"There you are, Arthur, theft of the station broom. That'll do for starters, I don't give a fuck how stupid it is. You've got grease on your hands, I'll swab you at the nick. Forensics will prove your possession. It'll appear on your previous, your reputation," said Al.

"You fucking bastards, I ain't done nothing, theft of a broom? Fuck off, I ain't having it," Pettigrew remonstrated as he realised these two meant business and were going to fit him up whatever. His shouting woke a tabby cat which had been fast asleep next to a hot pipe under the table that Arthur was sitting at. It first stretched its front legs then rose on all fours before looking around at the three humans who had invaded its space, not knowing if they were friend or foe.

Dave seized the animal and in one swift move, rubbed the cat up and down the front of Pettigrew's top. "There you go, fibre transference, look at all that fur on you, theft of the station cat!"

"You fucking nutters, you come at me in fancy fucking dress, tell me I'm nicked for nothing, cos you ain't seen me doing nothing and now you fit me up with theft of a fucking broom and a cat. I ain't having it. You can just fuck off. I've been stitched up too many times by you lot. No!" Pettigrew was incandescent with rage.

"All right, Arthur, you are nicked but—" and before Al could finish,

"What for?" Pettigrew shouted.

"For attempted theft from that woman who fucked you off as she got on the train. That'll do. But at the moment I might load it up with another one, don't know yet," as Al thought about the script with the Chief Super as the 'victim'.

Arthur, realising life was not good on this occasion, although he'd had a nice touch earlier which the boys didn't know about, resigned himself to being nicked and said, "Not happy, you leave that cat out of it."

With that, the door opened and two burly uniformed officers confirmed that their 'chariot' awaited upstairs. The cat, seeing his chance to escape the previous melodrama, made a bolt for it out along the platform and into an adjoining subway. "There you are, Arthur, the cat's got bail."

The uniformed boys reverted to type, firmly taking Arthur in handcuffs upstairs to the waiting police van. His protests at being manacled fell on deaf ears. Dave and Al said nothing of what was about to befall Pettigrew on their arrival, simply ensuring the transport was taking them to Bow Street nick, a familiar haunt of theirs, and not Vine Street just off Piccadilly, as the boys had learnt it was one of a couple of police stations that were trialling newly acquired tape recording facilities for interviews. *Sod that*, they both thought, although nothing was said. Their arrival in the yard found it full of Territorial Support Group or TSG carriers, long wheelbase vans having the benefit of around ten thugs or uniformed 'robust' response officers together with their flameproof kit and circular shields reminiscent of classical Greek gladiators, and a veritable cornucopia of other devices for exacting pain, all in the cause of keeping the Queen's peace.

The escorting officers, realising this was a very popular place, simply unloaded Pettigrew, Dave, and Al at the charge room door and decamped. As the trio entered, it was obvious that the place was busy as two harassed sergeants sat at their desks waiting for the next customer. Al quickly established there had been a street fight near Trafalgar Square with quite a number of the protagonists having been deprived of their liberty and who were now residing in the various sumptuous cells adjacent to the 'hotel reception'. The only place left for this sad excuse for a criminal was the Divisional Surgeon's room, utilised when a doctor was called to examine a prisoner to establish whether he or she was fit to be detained, and not requiring removal to a hospital or other medical institution.

Dave reassured one of the sergeants that Pettigrew was not violent or an escapee and that either he or Al would always be in the room with him until time of charging. He briefly went through the facts of the arrest, without mentioning their cunning disguises leading to apprehension, or the stunts with the broom or the cat. The sergeant, knowing the two officers, was quite content to let them get on with their paperwork.

On opening the door, Al saw that aside from the doctor's couch, a couple of chairs and a small table, in the corner was a giant coffin of a cream-coloured photocopying machine. Again he got the devil inside him. He pulled out a piece of A4 paper from the hopper on the side of the machine, quickly wrote on it and placed it on the glass under the flap as if ready for copying.

He beckoned Dave and Pettigrew to join him in the room and said, "Sit down, Arthur. Now I thought it might be an idea just to have a quick word with you about the reason for you being here. Now I know my colleague has searched you and found about three hundred quid on you. Before I ask you anything about it, see that over there in the corner? That's something new the police are trying out to see if it helps with getting to the truth in interviews of suspects, it's called a polygraph or a lie detector, OK?"

Pettigrew, not being the sharpest knife in the box, agreed, thinking it might stop his money being kept by the police. Besides, he thought, he could make allegations about the two officers!

Al positioned himself next to the photocopier; Pettigrew sat with Dave at the table, as Al sounded as if what was about to take place was a formal interview.

He said, "Right, Arthur you're under arrest for attempted theft from the person and you have been cautioned." Before he had a chance to respond, Al continued, "Now when you were arrested you had £305 on you, correct?"

Arthur, believing he was now in an interview said, "Yes sir, it's my money, I won it on the dogs last night."

Al said, "We both know that isn't true, you've nicked it this morning, and before you answer, remember the polygraph is monitoring your answers."

Pettigrew, "No, I didn't nick it, it's my money."

Without showing he was touching the photocopier, he ran his finger across the print button, sparking it into life. It quickly issued an A4 sheet of paper, which Pettigrew to his horror watched as it fell into the hopper with the word 'LIAR' printed on it.

Arthur reacted, "No, no, no, this ain't right, the machine's wrong. Get someone in to fix it."

Dave tumbled what Al had done and said, "Sorry Arthur, the machine is a new one, it can't be wrong. Tell you what, I'll ask you a question. Is your name Arthur Peter Pettigrew?"

Quick as a flash, Arthur answered, "Yes."

The photocopier did nothing, little surprise really as Al didn't touch the print button.

Dave said, "OK, let's ask something else. When we saw you on the platform earlier you tried stealing from a woman's bag, didn't you?"

Pettigrew said, "No, I was just confused where I was, I thought I was on the other platform. You didn't see me do nothing."

The photocopier buzzed into life again. 'LIAR' – out fell another sheet of paper.

Pettigrew looked incredulously at it, shook his head and said, "I don't understand, how did you see me? I would've seen you with those stupid noses and wigs. First thing I knew was when you started singing 'Happy Birthday' to me."

The two of them just smiled knowingly at each other and at Arthur.

They continued asking questions about the two attempted thefts, even the theft of the station broom and the cat, and with each denial dropped another sheet of paper from the 'polygraph' declaring Pettigrew a liar.

Dave finally said, "Arthur, the machine has shown you to be a liar, you're a thief, you were trying to steal when we saw you, the three hundred odd quid you have didn't come from the dogs, they were rained off last night, I know cos I was going to go. That money is from an earlier theft, isn't it?"

Arthur was weakening, not really comprehending how this new lie detector worked, but he continued to maintain his innocence. 'LIAR' – out it popped again.

With an air of defeat he just leant back in his chair and declared "This is a fit-up, I ain't done nuffink like what you said. I ain't talking no more." At last there was some truth to this charade.

Dave left the room and spoke with the sergeant who had by now become a regular conduit of the squad when it came to charging dips. He confirmed he was ready to charge Pettigrew with the two attempt thefts and a dishonest handling of stolen goods, the unexplained cash he had on him.

Al wheeled Arthur back out to face the music. "Stand in front of the sergeant and listen to what he has to say," said Al with a rather authoritative air.

The skipper rattled it off, and asked Arthur if he had anything to say in response. Pettigrew simply asked why two detectives looking like clowns tried to nick him for theft of a cat and a broom and then fitted him up. The sergeant looked quizzically at the two who in turn shrugged their shoulders and in unison claimed they didn't know what the hell he was on about. But Arthur did have a settled address, in other words one where he could prove he lived, and so by way of softening the trauma he was bailed to appear at the Magistrates' Court next door.

It was late in the evening and having met up with the chaps I declared it was now beer o'clock and refreshment was required after a long and arduous search for thieves. To find the only thief was a petty thief was unfortunate, but hey, a prisoner is a prisoner! Never let the truth cloud a good story. Maple Leaf it is then.

14

HOT CHILLI DIP

I believe I've mentioned to you before, albeit briefly, about the South American pickpockets invariably from Chile or Columbia who visit our green and pleasant land, at the height of London's tourist season, somewhere around June and July. They arrive like a bout of thrush, making life uncomfortable for their victims, destroying the public's happiness and causing havoc and misery of stolen monies, cards or sentimental attachments, then depart these shores with equal speed to descend on some other poor unsuspecting European capital as with an unannounced tornado. They are bastards of the highest order; but they're bloody good at it!

Paul and the guvnor had a 10am appointment with the victim of a robbery gone wrong, which had obviously started as a dipping, but had escalated for one reason or another, whether the thief was spooked by the victim's resistance or a member of the public was too close, they wouldn't know until they spoke with her. All they knew from the brief report at hand was that she had alighted at Borough tube station, and seemingly was tailed off, then assaulted by the would-be thief who demanded her purse. Their meeting, at her suggestion, was at a tourist pub almost opposite one of the cobbled roads into Borough Market, a mid-Victorian fruit and veg market south of Southwark Cathedral with its roots going right back to the thirteenth century when its site was nearer to London Bridge. Her chosen venue was the George public house, a favoured haunt of Charles Dickens in his time, but with its beams, low ceilings and old-world charm, it had become a magnet for American and Japanese tourists seeking British authenticity.

The two of them entered the end bar which led into a coffee bar area in the middle. Miss Pike was seated at a round table sipping her Americano, almost in unison with other upwardly mobile types doing likewise. The two vacant chairs adjacent to her beckoned the officers to her side. Bob introduced himself to Valerie, a willowy blonde, about 5'6" Bob thought, wearing a smart two-piece blue suit, the skirt riding halfway up her thighs as she sat smiling at their approach. Paul's eyes were on stalks, hoping to believe what he thought, trying to disguise his obvious attraction to the dark area at the top of her legs. His mind was racing – was she or wasn't she wearing any? – as he strategically sat opposite her in an effort to satisfy his curiosity without seeming like a dirty old man. Bob opened the conversation with the victim, having sent Paul for the coffees, returning in record-breaking time back to the strategically placed chair. They ran through the details of how she had travelled from the City, where she rather unusually worked as a broker in that male-dominated arena known as the Stock Exchange, late in the evening and as she left the station via the lifts she was aware of a short-arsed skinny black lad walking too close behind her as she exited the tube station on to The Borough.

When he clumsily failed to open the zip on the top of her shoulder bag, he backed off, walking a measured distance behind her until he was obviously content she was now isolated, as Valerie continued to walk towards her home. He dashed round in front of her, produced a small blade in his left hand, at the same time demanding her purse. Realising she was unable to escape, she readily handed it over to him as her only alternative option, she thought, to being stabbed. He snatched his quarry and ran off as Valerie shouted "Bastard" after him.

They ran through the circumstances of the robbery, trying to glean as much as they could from her, but despite her enthusiastic efforts to assist with identifying the culprit, it was quite apparent they were flogging a dead horse. Not wishing to dampen her ardour, Bob asked Valerie, or Val as she was at pains to prefer, if she would have a look at some suspect photographs of possible contenders for the robbery. The boys knew this would probably be a waste of time but Bob sensed that Paul was making progress on the sympathy front and Val seemed to be responding to the touch of the 'common man'. In conclusion, with Bob feeling a little excluded from this love-in, he confirmed Val's contact details. She showed off a new pager she had, which unlike the simple bleep ones such as Bob's, actually showed a short message from the person wanting to speak on the phone. Typical of the job, always behind the curve, but he resolved in his mind he was going to make a case with the Commander to get one issued to himself. As expected, Paul made a careful note of her contact details, assuring her they'd be in touch in the next couple of days. Paul took a last swig of coffee as they rose to walk the short distance towards London Bridge tube station, where Val told them she fancied a walk across the bridge back to the Stock Exchange.

As they parted company she turned to Paul and with a wry grin said, "No I'm not wearing any! Don't worry, the boys in the office are always asking as well. At least you didn't, Paul. See you soon."

And she skipped off towards the bridge.

The two detectives looked at each other quizzically, agreeing that she was definitely up for it, Paul laying claim to her. With a new spring in his step they descended into the bowels of the station. As they did, Paul drew Bob's attention to some graffiti on the over-bridge that just said, 'Swimming to France'. Neither got the significance of what they determined was a stupid slogan, but Paul thought he might be able to use it as a bet to get into evidence at some later stage. Going north on the Northern line they turned their attention west as they got off at Bank for the long boring walk to the westbound Central line platform, trawling through the middle of London looking for their next prey. This didn't take long; having boarded the tube, their next stop was Chancery Lane. They got off, Bob leaving via the set of double doors while Paul left from the single rear door, which in days gone by would have been where the guard stood watching over his flock boarding the train. Due to 'progress efficiencies', much to the chagrin of the unions, this was no longer the case. The detectives stepped onto the platform when their suspicion emerged in the form of a short Spanish-looking man with a beige bomber jacket draped over his left arm, appearing confused and moving in and out of the boarding passengers just ten yards from where they were.

He didn't seem to approach anyone too closely, but his demeanour, as far as they were concerned, put him in the category of being 'well at it' and therefore worthy of a further view from a discreet distance. Bob indicated to Paul he would use a little booth channelled into the platform wall, where he could call the Information Room to see if the little guy they were watching had been sighted earlier as being involved in thefts or attempts. He stepped into a dingy phone box-sized cupboard, dimly lit by a forty-watt bulb suspended under one of one of those 'coolie' style lampshades, which had obviously been there since the last war when so many of the Underground stations were used as community air-raid shelters. On a small paint-chipped shelf at about chest height was a black Bakelite telephone, which also seemed to have been there since the beginning of time. Bob lifted the receiver, which to his astonishment had a dialling tone. So he began winding round the dial to get in touch with the dedicated Information Room dealing with crime and public order matters on the Underground network. As he waited for what seemed like forever to be connected, his attention was drawn to all the pale green electrical junction boxes humming the tune of raw power passing through them. He mused how dangerous it might be to be near so much potent electric power.

"Hello, Police Information Room, how can I help?"

Bob refocused; introducing himself, he enquired whether the current 'flavour of the month' had been propped up as a suspect in any earlier theft reports. The response was negative but he was asked to hang on while he was passed through to the Area Commander. The line clicked as he waited, once again giving the electrics the once-over, without touching them of course.

"Is that you, Detective Inspector Trebor?" said the stern voice immediately familiar to Bob.

"Yes, guv how are you?"

The voice said, "Now remember, this conversation is taped for future reference. Is DC Clarke one of your officers?"

Bob was comfortable in answering that he wasn't, knowing that Andrew Clarke was Divisional CID and so would only rarely have contact with him as his chain of command would be through a Divisional Detective Inspector.

"Did you authorise DC Clarke to take a CID car home with him yesterday?"

Bob enquired if there was a problem with his authorisation and the voice repeated his question. Bob, after a pause said, "Yes, guv, I did, he asked to take it as he had an enquiry and statement to take on his way into work. It seemed nonsensical for him to come into work simply to go back out on the enquiry, not the best use of a resource, so I authorised it. I think he was going to be in the office later today."

The Commander gave no further clue as to the nature of his enquiry and Bob didn't think it wise to ask further. With that, the phone clicked dead and he slowly replaced the receiver, thoughtful about the conversation he'd just had.

Deep in ponderous thought he re-emerged from the kiosk on to a crowded platform, Paul some five yards to the left of him. The little 'Spaniard' was wandering back and forth from the rear to the front of the platform, as if he was focusing on the map on the far wall displaying the route of the tube.

Paul sidled up to Bob and whispered, "He's well at it, guv. He needs a tug."

Bob suggested they wait until the next train arrived and take him out in the confusion of people alighting and boarding the train. They parted to a discreet distance either side of the suspect and waited, blending with the busy platform as if they were intending passengers. As Bob looked up to the right, a new dot matrix train indicator proudly announced the next train's arrival in one minute. It felt like forever as the seconds ticked away, until they heard the imminent arrival of the train preceded by the familiar rush of ozone wind as it entered the platform, signalling their strike on the suspect.

As the passengers alighted and the crowd moved towards the double doors, the 'Spaniard' jostled in using his jacket over his left forearm as he tried to get up tight to the city gent just in front him. This was the cue they'd been waiting for as with one movement they intercepted him, Bob taking his right arm as Paul tried to take hold of his left forearm only to find it was what some might have called a withered arm.

"You're nicked, attempted theft," said Paul as they spun him out of the back of the crowd.

He said nothing, as if it was an occupational hazard to him. The city gent, who was obviously unaware of what was going on behind him, had gone deep inside the carriage making it impossible to recover him to speak to.

As the platform emptied, the 'Spaniard' found himself pinned against the back wall furthest from the rails. He obviously believed that he was in some kind of trouble when he heard the word 'police' used; he didn't resist but invited through gestures for Paul to check the zipped inside jacket pocket of the jacket he had draped over his arm in his act of preparation. He spoke no English but kept smiling and saying, "*Passaporte, passaporte.*" Bob and Paul agreed it was pointless trying to talk to him, so they resolved to take him upstairs to street level to await police transport to the local police station. A quick phone call from the Underground station manager's office prompted the arrival of a uniformed van driver to take them to Bob's favourite port of call, Bow Street nick. Again, a familiar-looking sergeant greeted them in the charge room, and after the briefest of chats the 'Spaniard' was put in the cells.

Bob phoned the squad office from the Divisional Surgeon's room, while Paul closely examined the seized passport.

Bob re-emerged saying to Paul, "Conroy speaks Spanish, he's on his way down to us. I'm not bothering interviewing him, he can just tell the twat what we've nicked him for."

Paul said, "The passport's bent, guv. Look at the way the photo has been stuck down. It belongs to someone else, it's not his. Even the ink where he's tried to overwrite the original seal on the paper and photo is poor."

Bob replied, "OK, so we need to know who he is, anything in the rest of his property that might give us a clue? While you're about it, just check with Crime Bureau, and the Spanish embassy to see if they've had a report of this passport being stolen. I reckon we've got one of our Chileans, just doing a bit of lone thieving."

Paul concurred and went off to make few phone calls trying to bottom out the passport conundrum. Bob, in the meantime, put the skipper in the picture. He didn't expect to be too long, trying to establish the true identity of the prisoner. As he sifted through the property bag he found a Chilean identity card, carefully tucked inside a loose flap in a small leather wallet, and the bonus was it had the prisoner's photograph on it. Bingo! Identified. A bit more work and he could be charged, kept in custody and would appear in court tomorrow, happy days.

An unshaven John Conroy arrived, having done it in first thing on account of a lager frenzy with a few of his old work mates from a time before he was on the squad. His eyes still red, not from crying, but the effects of the many pints of 'Nigerian lager', a cockney reference, or Guinness as you may know it, first apologised to Bob for the lateness of his appearance and reassured him that he would speak to the prisoner in his native tongue. Seemingly, John, prior to joining the job, had spent some three years in the Irish Army, which, clearly recognising 'talent', transferred him double quick to a NATO occupation force serving out of a base in Andalusia in Spain. Bob got the 'Spaniard' released from his cell to a little side detention room, usually used for those little treasures called juvenile offenders.

Whilst Bob was present, he didn't have a clue what John was saying to their little friend, but it seemed OK as the prisoner had a smile on his face and clearly understood what John was saying. It finished with John declaring that the pickpocket understood completely why he had been arrested, didn't mean to cause any problems, and if they looked in the hollowed-out heel of his left shoe there was a little something in the form of five one hundred US dollar notes for their trouble. Bob took the cash from his shoe and saying "*Gracias*," reflected on earlier pickpocket squads before he was in charge. Armed with the knowledge of five hundred dollars which they could 'tax' the dip, in other words steal it from him knowing that he was in no position to bleat, would ensure they could have a nice little earner amongst themselves. It sickened him to think of it being so routine back in the day, whether it was his earlier squad, Met crime squads or the supposedly elite Flying Squad's own little dip team.

Having cut through the crap of the bent passport, using the ID card and a quick call to the Chilean embassy, Paul established his true identity as Jorge Gallegos, originally from the capital, Santiago. Bob sealed the prisoner's property bag, including the five hundred dollars, placing it on the cheap laminated table where the sergeant sat waiting to know what the boys wanted to do next. A brief chat with Bob led to Paul pushing Jorge forward to hear that he was being charged with an attempted theft from persons unknown, a conspiracy with persons unknown to steal, from persons unknown within the jurisdiction of the Central Criminal Court, otherwise known as the Old Bailey, and theft/handling of the Spanish passport. Conroy put Jorge at ease telling him he'd stay in custody until he appeared in front of the Magistrate in the court next door in the afternoon that day. It was a bit of a pain but Bob knew it would only be a quick remand for further enquiries about the passport and trying to get evidence together for the other charges, he'd object to bail with about three weeks being enough to get the statements sorted out for a quick committal to Crown Court. Bob, Paul and John left the charge room allowing Jorge the opportunity to sample the delights of a prisoner's lunch, served on a plastic plate complete with the finest plastic cutlery while they went to the first-floor canteen for a late full English!

As I sit here sipping my tea while the boys negotiate with the canteen staff as to who would fund my grub, I can hear you say, what was all that about with the Commander? Simple. Detective Constable Andrew Clarke pulled a stunt, but he didn't do his homework and now he's in shit creek. Remember what I said, failing to plan is planning to fail. He asked me yesterday if he could take a car home to do an enquiry today and I gave him permission. What I didn't know was that the Vauxhall Astra he took home was the same as his own car. He had a quandary, in that the MOT on his car was due and he needed four new tyres on it. So he switched them from the 'job' car to his own and, surprise, surprise, his car passed! Here's his problem: he did the swop in the street outside his house, and not in his garage out of the way. Now I knew he was a wanker, and a bit of an acquired taste, but what I didn't know was he'd had some sort of row with his neighbour. I needn't join the dots, I'm sure you can. He grassed him up on three nines, which meant uniformed officers turned up as he returned from the MOT. So now he's nicked for fraud, theft, albeit temporary, and plenty of other little troubles for him. Fortunately for me, I had my pocketbook with me, which meant I could record my authorisation for the CID car before I started my notes on Jorge today. Never did like the effeminate twat anyway. Always thought he was a bit a 'Uriah Heep'. If he'd approached me differently, maybe I could have helped, but he took me for a mug, and that's not happening. So I say fuck him. You might call me Machiavellian, maybe, but I'm still standing, and he's not. Happy days!

John left Bob and Paul kicking their heels waiting for bully-off for the afternoon sitting in Court One at Bow Street. Jorge had been transferred via the back door at the nick into the gaoler's custody in the cells of the court where his duty solicitor, the old foe Luca Zengretti, using his broad grasp of South American Spanish, diligently took his instructions. Stipendiary magistrate Sir Gordon Bennet MC, in recognition of his brave pursuits in the Second World War, burst through the door just to the left, and dropped into the sumptuous armchair more befitting a monarch than a magistrate with an air of 'here we go again'. The oak-panelled courtroom exuded a grand solemnity – this was a place of serious consequence, the defendants ever aware that the magistrates held their fate in the palms of their hands. Luca felt no such trepidation as he wafted into court, sharp double-breasted suit, buttons released, billowing behind, firmly in the belief he'd been overlooked for a Hollywood role, but making an 'honest' living from representing the poor oppressed.

A grand bow towards the 'stipe' announced that he appeared on behalf of the man with the withered arm, being marched into the dock by the court officer. Bob knew Luca of old, and given that he was starting to lose his own hair, he was quietly pissed off with his opposition's long flowing shoulder-length black hair, and no bloody grey ones! Bob, having been acknowledged by the magistrate as a regular in his court, outlined his need for a remand in custody for three weeks for further enquiries regarding further crimes, connected suspects and of course the mystery surrounding the passport. In a note of optimism he felt he would be ready for a Section One committal, being simply the original statements and typed copies, to Crown Court on the next hearing.

Luca burst into life, "Officer, now that you have the defendant's identification card, the means by which he entered this country, if a suitable settled address can be found for him, do you still object to him being granted bail by the learned magistrate? You see I have made some enquiries and have found a bail hostel in Clapham, south London. As you are aware he has a deformed arm, and does actually require regular medical attention, something which the hostel I'm assured can arrange."

Bob responded by telling him that firstly he was in possession of a stolen passport which it appeared had been stolen in the UK, which would lead him to suspect he could acquire another, and flee the country; secondly, the prison service could assist regarding medical needs.

Luca interjected saying, "Officer, he also has some mental difficulties, were you aware when he was in his home country of Chile, he had been diagnosed as being schizophrenic?"

Bob wasn't, but he couldn't resist the temptation to observe he thought the defendant was in two minds whether to steal from the man in front of him. 'And some fell on stony ground.'

Bennet MC warmed to the idea of the bail hostel, particularly as the courts had all received a missive from the Lord Chancellor's office advising where possible to grant bail, the prisons being close to overflowing. His look of disdain at Bob resulted in the little South American getting bail to the hostel, and as a side swipe he told Bob to get his enquiries completed within two weeks not three!

And here's what happened: two weeks later I was at court with Zengretti, but no defendant. I was right, the sod absconded within twenty-four hours of being at the bail hostel. I was ready for a committal even though that idiot Conroy wrote his entire statement top to bottom in Spanish delivering it the morning of the hearing. When I challenged his 'undoubted Spanish expertise', he said, but that's what I said, so I told him without translation no other fucker would understand it. He even called himself Juan. It was too late to do anything about it, so I dumped it on Zengretti without comment. He tried not to be fazed, saying he didn't think he needed to call his evidence. I gloated that we were still a defendant light, and I would be asking for a no-bail warrant for his arrest. Bennet MC looked at me and was just about to speak when Zengretti stood to say he had some news of the defendant. "Sir, I understand a telephone call from Jorge has been received at the court." Bennet MC asked if he was on his way, to which Luca said, he feared not as the defendant was phoning from Madrid asking how the trial was going! Bennet MC said, "Looks like I should have listened to you, officer." "Yes, sir, can I have a warrant now?" I said. He granted it there and then, but sadly we never saw the one-armed bandit again!

15

TRIAL RUN

"I want to dance with somebody, I want to feel the heat from somebody," blasted at close to full volume from the clock radio on the cabinet on Janet Flynn's side of the bed. The music prompted her arousal from a deep sleep encouraged by a number of gin and tonics the previous evening. The big red button on the top received a slap from her as she threw her legs out of the bed. Janet continued to sing the lyrics as her feet found the floor and she twisted to sit up. She was in something of a foul mood reflecting on her husband's decision: it was more important he go on a rugby tour with his mates instead of keeping her company and supporting her at Southwark Crown Court, leaving her alone two days before. She left the half-decorated bedroom, which he had promised he'd get round to before he went on the tour. Staggering into the bathroom, she set about getting herself ready for Al to pick her up at 9am. *He's so kind and thoughtful*, she concluded as she smiled back at herself in the mirror, resolving to wear something special for herself, and possibly him.

*

"Another one bites the dust, and another one's gone and another one's gone, another one bites the dust," sang Freddie as Al wiped his two slices of toast with some Marmite, in the little galley kitchen of his flat, after his split from his missus. He mused at a tabby cat outside the small window about to launch itself onto a corpulent wood pigeon who hadn't grasped how much danger he was in. His mind drifted back to the night before when he met up with the lovely Janet, simply to put her mind at rest at the trial about to start today. Despite his low animal cunning, he played 'the perfect gent' card, dropping her off at home after a couple of drinks at Jack Straw's Castle on Hampstead Heath. The dark car park to the rear allowed Al to kiss and play with her erect nipples as she groaned in eager anticipation; he resolved to leave her wanting more. *Weird*, he thought, as they overlooked the undulating hillside known locally as 'gobblers' gulch', given this was a renowned haunt frequented by homosexuals. Finishing his toast, he double-locked the front door and drove off in the CID car, scene of their romantic embrace the night before.

*

Bob left home at about seven, driving a short distance to the local railway station where he dumped the old Ford Escort estate in the station car park. He had an arrangement with the car park attendant not to be charged for parking in return for him turning a blind eye to him pocketing some of the loose change from the punters and regular information on car park thieves preying on cars left there for many hours of the day and night. His morning had started with a row with the other half, less than understanding why he had to work such long hours. It didn't seem to matter how much he explained that 'the job' was a cruel mistress and demanding, with little room for negotiation, and frankly all she was interested in was the money at the end of the month. He loved his kids but she was intent on arguing with him, whereas he wouldn't do so in front of them. To him they were most important, and he was resolute in never exposing them to upheaval, his mantra being adults can mess up their lives as much as they liked, but you don't mess with kids' heads risking them being messed up as well. He jumped on the fast train to London, sitting in first class, where his daydreaming out of the window drifted into a light sleep, in which he dreamt of his 'legal dalliance', resolving to ring her on his arrival at court.

*

John Innes stood stripped to the waist; the bathroom mirror beckoned. He had a shave for the most important appointment of his short police career, for today was the day he would be required to face his assailant across the courtroom – the first time he'd seen him since picking him out as he alighted the escalator at Brixton tube station. The time before that was when Jackson redesigned his face right down to the cheekbone, resulting in massive blood loss and nerve damage – that side of his face was beginning to sag. He now had an uneven scar the length of his face, which if looked at in profile would resemble the rolling hills of southern England. He sighed, realising this particular 'badge of honour' would be with him for the rest of his life. He toyed with idea of a beard to conceal the initial visual impact, not least so it didn't cause his two little girls any more distress than had already been caused, but he felt it important that a jury of twelve good men and true should see the magnitude of what he had to bear.

*

Judge Salter rose from his lodgings bed, this being the second week of his sitting at Southwark weighing up the evidence in a variety of cases placed before him. Today would be the start, as he understood it, of a not-guilty trial, after he'd weighed off a couple of guilty pleas for burglary from repeat offenders, or recidivists, being the posh word. Vivaldi's *Four Seasons* provided a calming introduction to his day; the dulcet tones of 'Spring' emanated at low volume from the in-house music system as it pursued his progress towards the dining room. There he indulged in his usual favourite of two poached eggs on toast and some coffee, which in these 'austere' times he had to pour himself. His indignant sense of rough justice at having to do so, then pay for the privilege, begged the question why he was paying so bloody much to the judiciary for a service they weren't providing!

*

Detective Sergeant Jim Hunt pulled up outside the Innes house in the grey Peugeot 205 GTi on loan to the squad for assessment as a covert surveillance vehicle. Jim was a former class-one driver and trusted to evaluate its suitability for those tasks. Fortunately, he'd seen the light and was no longer excited at the prospect of a defective exhaust pipe and was now more interested in who'd nicked the car! John led him into the kitchen where they chatted casually over a cup of tea. His wife had wished him well for the day, leaving for school with kids before Jim's arrival. Looking out of the window, seeing the heavy grey clouds rolling across a windy sky, John resolved to wear a mac over his suit, not uniform, as the assault had occurred when he was engaged in plain clothes enquiries. He was comfortable that his dress code was the same as the others involved in the case, as he felt incredibly self-conscious about the very noticeable, as he felt, scar across his face.

Jim invited John into the car, off they went for the thirty-minute journey to Southwark Crown Court. The radio greeted them with 'Relax' as Holly Johnson's lyrics seemingly implored acts which ensured the record was banned from BBC radio, not the case on Capital. John said very little on the way there, his head racing as to what his evidence for Jackson would be, the inexperience of his youth in service causing his heart to race at the impending challenge to his credibility. His quietness betrayed his apprehension, noticed by Jim but not commented on, not wishing to add to John's thoughts. As they turned left off Tooley Street by London Bridge the giant five-storey red-brick box that is Southwark Crown Court came into view. Having then swung round to the right, leaving Hayes Wharfe behind, Jim turned left and down the slope following the route of the prison vans, and curiously the judges, into the underground car park, away from the mounting press interest congregating outside the front doors of the court. From here he was able to take John in the secure lift up to the police room and out of public sight. Plying him with a mug of tea and a comfortable chair, Jim left him with the instruction to wait there while he went looking for Bob.

*

Morning to you, just taking a shortcut through Hayes Galleria past the pseudo pirate ship going to Southwark Crown for the long-awaited trial of that shit Michael Jackson for the GBH on my PC John Innes. Between you and me, I'm not sure it will be all that long. Two witnesses, John and the lovely Janet, who to my mind is my trump card, evidence of my short interview, obvious allegations of a fit-up then jury out for a decision. Three or four days max I would've thought. Fuck me, the press — damn, they've just clocked me, I'll just walk past dignified and aloof. I'll speak to you later.

*

Janet opened the door excitedly to see Al suited and booted and smiling at his latest 'skirmish'.

"Ready?" he said.

She nodded, selecting the Yale key from the bunch in her hand, turning to double-lock the door as Al turned, walking back down the Minton-tiled front path to the waiting car. She remarked whether it was the same one as the night before, when she had succumbed to a few gins and Al's smooth advances. She skipped lightly behind him, forgetting her impending appearance where she had been told she would receive a less-than-easy ride in the witness box. The radio burst into life: "Should've known better than to cheat a friend, and waste the chance that I'd been given…"

She smiled at Al and said, "I've got this album, he's got a lovely voice hasn't he?"

Al nodded and smiled; the car burst into excited life as it accelerated away for their journey across London. Boy George was next, followed by any number of New Romantics serenading these two apprentice lovers through the city, over London Bridge turning left past the London Dungeon to the court. Al had cleared it with the court staff: he could drive down into the bowels of the building, avoiding any public or press attention. The security gate rolled down announcing its closure with a loud metallic clunk as it hit the floor, sealing the pair inside the court building. Her knight in shining armour escorted her up to the public canteen on the second floor away from John Innes, although in truth there was no real legal reason why they couldn't see each other. Al just thought it might be better to play safe until Bob had seen how things shaped up. Janet was quite content with a cup of coffee looking out over the Thames and HMS Belfast moored right outside.

*

Bob was found chatting with Steve who had run the two escalator identification parades at Brixton tube station.

Following a tannoy announcement, they had gone to the reception on the ground floor to meet with their counsel for the trial. On arrival, Bob recognised an old 'friend', a skinny, chain-smoking man by the name of Ian Playton, someone who Bob had requested on previous trials to represent the prosecution case. He was someone who he could essentially 'do business with' – he got it, he understood. Buoyed by this, the three of them opened up their negotiations and strategy for the trial. As Ian confirmed a batting order for the witnesses, they were joined by Ernie Monee QC, counsel for the defence, a gap-toothed individual with a monocle who in Bob's experience was one of the most obnoxious briefs he'd ever come across. He was someone who firmly believed that 'all coppers are bastards', corrupt, in that they not only fitted poor criminals up, but also that many were on the take. From the first meeting of the counsel it was obvious to Bob and Steve it wasn't going to be the kind of trial that would simply be an academic exercise of two great minds jousting for supremacy of their case. This was going to be dirty; Monee was going to go for the jugular. Al approached the group deep in conversation, and without interrupting, quietly told Bob that both Janet and John were safely ensconced in the building at separate locations and safe. Monee swung round on seeing Al whispering and said, "Ah, I see we're in the presence of a very fishy individual."

He knew Al from an earlier trial, which he lost, his client screaming all the way to the cells that he was innocent and had been fitted up.

"Oh. Hello sir, how are you? Here's a good one for you:

how many policeman does it take to throw a prisoner down the stairs?"

Monee shrugged his shoulders.

"None, he fell!"

Having delivered his message, as he walked away, Al quietly directed his comment to Monee saying, "Everyone likes a bit of arse, but nobody likes a smart arse."

Monee exploded, "What did you say?"

Al sauntered off saying, "You fucking heard, dickhead."

Monee screamed for Al to be investigated for insubordination or contempt of court, basically anything. With great 'sadness', Bob said that nobody else heard him say it, they were too engrossed with prosecution counsel on the case. Steve took the opportunity to escape the dubious pleasure of Monee's company thinking he wasn't surprised he was known as 'Earning Money' as he'd turned representing dips on legal aid into an art form. He'd made a fortune, he thought, as he entered the comparative safety of the police room. Summoning a mug of tea he joined John Innes in the next easy chair while Steve buried his head in the delights of the *Daily Mail*.

*

Judge Salter strode back to his chambers from Court Seven where he had just 'weighed off' a recidivist burglar with two pages of form for dishonesty with four years' porridge. He slumped back into a large green captain's chair, its ample upholstery cuddling and caressing him as he settled. His clerk followed him into the room, and observing protocol waited before being invited by Salter to take the weight off his feet on the matching green Chesterfield adjacent to him. The judge casually pulled the irritating horsehair wig from his balding head, dropping it on the green blotter in front of him.

"Right, a coffee I think. What's next?" he enquired from his clerk.

Thomas, his clerk, phoned the canteen organising the drink before outlining the trial of Jackson, next on his agenda.

"Ian Playton, yes I know him, chambers in Lamb Building, Middle Temple, plays with a straight bat; and for the defence that old war horse Monee, from 6 Kings Bench walk. OK, that's fine, is there anything they want to address me on before we start or ask for a jury?" The clerk told him there didn't appear so, and with that left Salter to enjoy his coffee in one of those brief moments of peace, asking if ten minutes would do.

*

Janet's eyes lit up as Al re-entered the canteen, relieving her boredom of looking at the World War Two warship and wondering what life must have been like on D-Day, the last time the ship engaged in direct bombardment, a bit like she hoped her first and last day at court would be. Al sat next to her on the fixed seats attached to each of the tables, specifically placed in the canteen should some defendant on bail or a witness get a little agitated and believe the only way to ease their tension was to send the furniture airborne.

His left hand drifted across to her right thigh unseen by passing traffic as he sought to reassure her of the menu for the day. She would be the second witness into court after John Innes; he gave her copies of her statements, one relating to the incident, and a second one for the subsequent identification at Brixton tube station. She felt at ease with Al as he described the geography of the courtroom, where the defendant would be, the barristers, and the witness box where she would give her evidence from. For Fish, this was all 'old hat', second nature, like a season ticket holder, but for Janet, well, she just wanted to get it over with. She told him that his advice was very much appreciated and wanted to thank him in some way. Al feigned embarrassment thinking to himself that this was early days but he reckoned to himself he was on the scent.

*

Bob sat behind Ian Playton to the right of the benches facing where the judge would preside from an elevated position in front of them. Monee sat to the far left, as far away from his fellow barrister as was possible, as if fearing he'd be infected by some communicable disease, supported behind by Bob's regular opponent, that 'rodent' Charlie Dickson.

A loud knock on the door to the side of the bench. "Court rise," bellowed the judge's clerk as Salter wafted in and sat in the centre of three chairs, below the Royal crest, signalling the rest were now allowed to retire to their seated positions.

Look at that little shit over there. How the fuck does he

sleep at night? More to the point, how is he still practising? I was hoping the soppy Sicilian would be here, instead we're lumbered with the 'used car dealer', Dickson. Never mind, he'll try pulling stunts if he sees it going against Jackson. I don't think he liked it when I served a notice of additional evidence which had that short contemporaneous note interview in which he made admissions, but which his client refused to sign. Fuck him, as I've said before, more than one way to skin a cat. Quiet now, we've got the jury to swear in. As officer in the case I'm allowed to remain in court as the witnesses give their evidence then succumb to a form of slaughter by the defence. So here we go.

16
OPENING SALVOS

Salter introduced himself to the jury consisting of eight women and four men, outlining his function and their role in the proceedings. Fairly standard stuff for all trials, which then led into Ian Playton opening up for the prosecution. PC John Innes slipped from the edge of the bench on hearing his name called by the court usher at the doorway to Court Seven. He gathered his composure, mindful of the briefing he'd received from Jim; the contents of his two statements were swimming round his head as he tried to second-guess where the defence would attack. A deep breath and he strode towards the door then purposefully to the witness box, the jury following his every stride and clearly focusing on the huge scar to his face. Playton, still on his feet from his opening address to the jury, watched as the usher enquired as to John's religion, then offered the Bible to him for the oath. John stood erect and with the Bible held aloft in his right hand and a card with the oath in his left hand, delivered his declaration to tell the truth, the whole truth and nothing but the truth with the solemnity of someone delivering a eulogy.

Allowing John a moment of composure, Ian Playton commenced, outlining John's evidence of who he was, establishing he was a married man with two young children and young in police service. He'd successfully completed his probation of two years and was keen to pursue his career as a plain clothes enquiry officer, which he'd been engaged in for the past six months. His duties revolved around interviewing witnesses and victims of minor crimes, some of which may be thefts or minor assaults. John confirmed it was work he enjoyed doing, he felt he was contributing to a better community, actually making a difference in people's lives. His persona came over as someone who was quietly spoken, conscientious and an obvious asset to the police per se. Ian, by way of invitation, asked John to relate what happened on the day in question.

"I had booked on duty that day at Baker Street police station at 0800 hours. Eight o'clock in the morning. I then was making enquiries on the phone and writing up some crime reports. I spoke on the phone to an elderly man who had been assaulted as he got on a train a couple of days earlier. I had arranged to meet him at his flat in White City at one o'clock, so I left Baker Street at just after twelve."

Ian was content to allow John to continue without interruption.

"I went down on to the tube and after a couple of minutes a southbound Jubilee train arrived and I got on about halfway along its length. The journey to Bond Street was only one stop and took about five minutes. As I got off I remember looking at the platform clock and saw it was twenty past twelve and I thought to myself I had enough time to get to the appointment, just needed to go to the westbound Central line."

Ian quizzed John on what clothing he was wearing to which he responded that he was wearing a dark two-piece suit, a three-quarter length jacket and was carrying a small portfolio case under his left arm.

John paused as he related the incident. "I walked into the interconnecting tunnel between the Central lines. As I did so I saw the defendant only a yard in front of me with his left hand and forearm fully inside a young girl's shoulder bag as she walked, oblivious to him immediately behind her. He looked about himself as he did so and he saw me looking straight at him. I said, 'Police'. He swung round and all I saw was a flash of something in his right hand as it caught the light from the tunnel illumination. I felt a searing pain across my face as I pulled away. I knew I was bleeding badly as I dropped to my knees. I didn't see where he went, and I don't think the girl with the bag even realised what had happened. Another lady came to my assistance, trying to hold my face together and stemming the blood. After a while an ambulance took me to the hospital."

Ian enquired if he remembered DI Trebor being at the hospital, which he did.

"If it please Your Honour, I have a set of photographs in an album here, there are copies for the jury, one between two, would Your Honour wish to see them first?"

Salter beckoned them to him as Ian explained that, with the court's permission, he would next show them to the officer for him to identify them as an exhibit in the case. The court usher ferried the album from Ian across to the judge leaving the bundle of albums on the bench in front of Playton.

Salter lifted the outer folder, recoiled in his chair and said, "Oh my goodness. I can't let these go to the jury in this form. I think I'd better speak to both counsel."

The jury looked surprised and bemused as to the judge's reaction at seeing the photograph album, but in line with the judge's comment the clerk rose, awaiting Salter to advise the jury to retire whilst he spoke to counsel on some legal matters. The usher opened an adjoining door from the courtroom and ferried the jury through, closing the door behind.

Lovely, just the reaction I wanted. The first photograph is of John's face with the wound open, like in a horror movie, before he was cleaned up and stitches applied. The rest of the photos are taken after medical attention and then monthly until the time of this trial. I wanted to get them all to the jury, but Salter's reaction has conveyed to the jury how vicious the injury was. He'll direct the open wound photo is removed but the message has got over to the twelve good men and true. Deep joy!

Salter directed the jury to return and, once comfortable, he explained that they could now have the edited photograph albums at the conclusion of the officer's evidence. John confirmed he was off sick for some three months while the wound healed and he underwent a course of facial physiotherapy. The jury, hanging on his every word, listened intently as he related the identification of Jackson as he emerged from the escalator at Brixton tube station. Ian asked John to remain in the witness box, in expectation of Jackson's brief wanting to cross-examine his evidence.

Monee rose to his feet and shrugged his robe forward; with both hands he pulled his wig forward and with great theatre leant forward on his portable lectern and leafed through what were obviously pages of a statement, the contents of which, he endeavoured to convey to the jury, he was intimately aware.

"Now then, officer, I represent this defendant, Mr Jackson. I want to ask you a few questions about the incident. Now I don't seek to allege that you are not telling the truth, quite the opposite. My instructions are that you are mistaken. Do you understand, officer?"

He then asked John if he agreed that on that day, the station was very crowded with intending passengers who consequently impaired a clear view any distance in front of him. John confirmed that it was very busy, but he had a clear view of events occurring in front of him.

Monee then ran through all the earlier points prior to the apprehension of his client upon which he said, "Do you recall another black man wearing casual clothing just like Mr Jackson's walking with my client as you entered that connecting passageway? In fact he was a casual friend of Mr Jackson, did you know that ?"

He didn't. Monee then went on to quiz John as to whether he was mistaken in identifying Jackson as the assailant, as it could have been his casual friend who was responsible. He suggested that John was typical of many white policeman who thought that all black men looked the same. John, trying to contain his frustration at this suggestion, remembering what Jim Hunt had told him in keeping his replies brief, simply told Monee that he was wrong, but flippantly then suggested the casual friend might be available to give that evidence in the court. Monee ignored

John's reply, moving on to the identification at Brixton and suggesting that it was little wonder John picked him out, as he had wrongly identified him from the time of the assault. Again, John refused to accept any of Monee's suggestions.

"No further questions," said Monee, and sat down with a flourish, his gown landing around him as he eyed the various members of the jury as if determining whether they had grasped the points he was making. Ian rose to re-examine whether John was in any doubt as to who had assaulted him, and if he was certain the person he picked out was in fact Jackson, the assailant. John felt comfortable in confirming he had no doubt who assaulted him and that he was in the dock today. With that, Ian was content he'd recovered the salient points before asking His Honour whether he had anything to ask. He quietly, just discernibly, said no and a half-hearted smile was offered as he appeared to carefully study the injury to John's face. Ian thanked him, confirming he was released but requested he remain within the confines of the court building. John rejoined Jim Hunt in the police room for a much-needed cup of tea and lunch perhaps at a nearby café in the arches near London Bridge.

Ian then took the requisite number of photograph albums from Bob and offered them up to the clerk via the usher for distribution to Salter and the jury. The rodent leant across and asked for two for the defence team, which Bob duly supplied.

Salter leant towards the twelve good men and true saying, "Members of the jury, the time of the hour would seem to be appropriate to break for lunch, will you be back at two sharp please?"

The pronouncement prompted the clerk of the court to stand and bellow, "Court rise." Salter stood then swept out via the side door held by the court usher.

Well, that seemed to go OK. The jury have got the photos now, to keep throughout the trial. The open wound one has been removed but I'm happy with the effect it's had. Although the ones they've got are pretty gory, they'll be wondering how bad the one that's been removed was. So all good. That prick Charlie Dickson has just asked me for two sets of up-to-date antecedents, that's Jackson's background, and also a list of his previous convictions. Just like his brothers, he's a dishonest little shit with form for thieving, handling, robbery and drugs going into two pages. Not bad for someone in their early twenties! I'll take this opportunity to give two sets to the clerk and a set to Mr Playton. Excuse me, I just need to have a quick chat with Janet to make sure she's read her statements and try to put her at her ease as she's kicking off at two o'clock.

17

THE FAILED STUNT

A knock on the judge's door and the court usher bellowing, "Court rise" announced the start of proceedings for the afternoon. Salter swept in and sat at his chair prompting both counsel and those supporting them to likewise return to their benches. He enquired whether there was anything either counsel wanted to address him on before the jury were recalled. Neither had any points to raise prompting the court usher to return them to their seats from the jury room, unaware of who would be called next while Janet paced up and down outside the double doors leading to the courtroom oblivious to various barristers and officers 'horse trading', or doing deals for other impending cases, in the corridor as she tried to compose herself. Al winked and smiled at her as she was summoned into the courtroom.

The clerk clarified her religion while the usher offered up the Bible to her. Ian rose to his feet and with a wry smile established who Janet was, that she was a mature student studying human biology, living in London, albeit her West Country accent was still discernible. She was then invited to run through what happened to her on the date in question. Apparently, she was on her way to the Guy's Hospital museum for a lecture from her north-west London home, when she was changing trains to reach her destination. She had got herself disoriented and realising she needed to double-back found herself walking towards the flow of passenger traffic and the defendant. Her first awareness that an incident of some sort was occurring in front of her was as she saw a white man in a suit take hold of the defendant's arm; the defendant was really close to a woman in front of him.

She heard the white man say the word 'police' by which time she was only a couple of yards from the group. Her voice faltered as she told the jury how she saw Jackson spin round quickly obviously trying to escape the officer's grip. She paused, taking a sip of water from the glass in front her, then said she couldn't be certain where the knife came from, but she could see it in his hand, it seemed about five inches long, and he swung it towards John's head. Janet, breathing deeply as if struggling for breath, described how she saw blood flying from the officer's face as he let out a yelp, falling to the floor. She didn't see where Jackson went in the confusion of the crowd but her concern was to help John rendering first aid using a thin scarf she had to try and stem the flow of blood by now forming a large pool beside John.

Salter, sensing Janet recounting the events was taking its toll on her, declared a ten-minute break so she could regain her composure before going on to finish her evidence-in-chief. Once the court had cleared, Bob followed her back out of the courtroom, meeting Al just outside. Mindful of the judge's direction not to speak to anyone, she resisted the temptation to run to Alan's embrace; she walk away down the corridor towards the ladies' cloakroom. Bob followed her out and told Al to make sure he got her back home safely at the end of her evidence as she was showing signs of strain at telling her story. Al, in his mind rubbing his hands with glee at the prospect, assured the guvnor he would, as he wandered back to the police room humming Annie Lennox, "Some of them want to abuse you, some of them want to be abused, sweet dreams are made of this…"

Janet returned to the bench and sat pensively outside the courtroom while Bob and the barristers re-entered to await Salter's return. The rodent Dickson remained in the court while the short adjournment passed, Bob not attaching any importance or thought to it at that time, just watching as he tried a sort of 'ever so 'umble' Uriah Heap kind of smile in his direction. Bob just assumed, *He's a lowlife, so he must be up to something, not a person to be trusted.* A knock on the side door announced the re-entry of the judge to get proceedings under way again. Salter sat rearranging his red diary in which he was making his notes of the evidence in the trial although there was a stenographer, taking a shorthand note of everything said, who sat adjacent to the clerk. Having enquired with both counsel whether they were ready to continue, their confirmation led to Janet being recalled by the usher to the witness box.

Janet confirmed she appreciated she was still under oath as Ian continued, leading her through her evidence, confirming that an ambulance crew arrived together with two uniformed constables who recorded her details. She told the court she was thanked by the emergency crews for her prompt action. John had wanted to record his gratitude as well but was frustratingly unable to, due to the large wads of gauze and lint holding his face together. Having given descriptions of the female victim and more importantly the suspect, she left, shaken, to continue on her journey.

Ian said, "Were you contacted by the police subsequently?"

Janet said that Al Fish called her, she thinks, the following day to arrange to get a full statement from her and the next day Al did so. He then ran her through the details of the day she attended Brixton tube station for the informal escalator identity parade. Janet sensed it was very important to sound forthright in the evidence she was about to give, and so it came to the scenario at the top of the escalators.

She said, "I was positioned just to the left at the top of the escalator coming up. I stood there with a police inspector who was to my right and there was a lawyer who I understood was there to observe the proceedings and ensure fairness. I would describe the inspector as slim, balding, quite debonair, whereas the lawyer, although smart in his suit, gave me the impression he was a bit in love with himself as he kept on throwing back his hair and looking at himself in the mirror glass by him. I understood perfectly from the inspector what I had to do, and that I may or may not see the man I had described in my earlier statement. I waited for what seemed like three or four minutes when I saw that man appear carrying a young child with a baby buggy and talking to a woman who I guess was the child's mother. I told the inspector that he was the one I'd seen assault the officer. Then a couple of other officers took him away and I didn't see him again. His lawyer was writing something down on a clipboard but he didn't object to anything I said or did."

Ian Playton thanked Janet for her account and asked her to wait there in case defence counsel had any questions. Monee rose to his feet, adjusting his robes and wig as he had done earlier, before explaining that he represented the man in the dock, Jackson. He then went on to question Janet's certainty about what she had seen at the time of the assault, alleging that the scene was crowded and confused, which meant she couldn't possibly have seen what she says she did. He fell short of calling her a liar, as he didn't want to run the risk of having to introduce Jackson's history of bad character and previous convictions, preferring to suggest that, in all that confusion, she hadn't seen the real assailant next to his client, and that she had been duped into the description of Jackson by the officers. The imputation was that somehow they already knew who had committed the assault, and that she as a member of the public would give their version of events some credibility in the eyes of the jury. Bob was impressed with the way she batted back the allegations, confirming that she was in no doubt that she saw Jackson commit the assault and that he had tried to evade identification at Brixton by using a stooge to conceal his appearance and demeanour. She concealed her trembling hands beneath the front ledge as she stoically stood her ground. Monee, seeing he was getting nowhere, fell back down onto the bench pronouncing he had no further questions. Salter declared a comfort break for the jury as he thanked Janet for giving her evidence. Feeling much lighter on her feet, she walked past Bob and out through the double doors at the rear of the court, not feeling brave enough to give Jackson a glance in the dock as she exited. The jury rose in concert with the court usher who escorted them to their room, leaving their notes and photographs on the benches in front of them as they did so.

The rodent left Monee and went to his client in the dock to try and give him a few words of encouragement that all was well and if he wanted to, he could give his account either from either dock or, if he was comfortable with being cross-examined, from the witness box. Bob, having returned from thanking Janet for her efforts and leaving her with Al, strained his hearing trying to garner the content of Jackson's chat, without success. He sat back down behind Ian with an air of confidence as if the trial was simply procedural and ultimately the defendant would be 'potted'. Once again a knock on the side door signalled the judge's re-entry to the command "Court rise," as he wafted across to his seat.

"Right gentlemen, before I bring the jury back in, is there anything you wish to address me on?" Ian rose to his feet to explain that he and Monee had agreed a few of the procedural statements such as Steve's 'street' identification procedures, the officers who attended the scene, the officer who went with Bob to the hospital when Jackson had been nicked and the officers who arrested him after his bid to escape. He emphasised the saving of court time and saving of the public purse because just their statements would be read to the jury after Bob had given his evidence.

The jury re-entered, returning to the same seats they had occupied from the start of the trial. The elderly woman, with her blue-rinse hair, wearing a twin set and sensible brogues, on the bottom right of the twelve, wrote a short note on a piece of paper summoning the court usher as he passed. She carefully folded it and handed it to him. He didn't look at its content but walked it to the clerk, who sat just beneath Salter. The clerk simply turned to the judge and advised His Honour a note from a jury member had been received, passing the folded paper to him. The silence was almost deafening as Salter opened then carefully studied its content.

He looked to the jury and said, "I have received a note from one of your number which I need to deal with now. Before I do so would the jury member concerned please raise their hand?" The blue rinse complied, hesitantly raising her right hand.

Salter thanked her and said, "Members of the jury, I now want you to rise and leave the courtroom, all of you except you, madam, please as I need to ask you more in the absence of your fellow jurors."

The usher led them out to the jury members' room, closing the door behind them. "Now madam, I intend reading out the note in court for the benefit of both prosecution and defence counsel. 'I just got back to my seat and was just tidying my notes and the photograph album when I found what looks like a previous convictions form'. Usher will you retrieve that from the jury member, thank you."

Salter again read the note then looked at the previous convictions form. There was no doubt they were Jackson's.

"Now madam, I see your note. Can you tell me when you found this?"

She said, "Just now, sir, when we came back into court. It was tucked inside the rear cover of the photograph album."

Salter said, "And having found it, has any other member of the jury seen it or even become aware of its existence?"

Blue rinse immediately replied, "No sir, I didn't think it right. Nobody's seen it except you."

He declared, "I'm afraid I'm going to have to ask you to stand down from this trial. This is no reflection on you. Can I thank you for your efforts and for bringing this to my attention? The usher will retrieve anything you may have left in the jury room. He will assist you outside court. You are excused from any further jury service at this time. Thank you."

She had to walk the long way round the jury box to exit then walked quickly past Jackson and out of the court.

Salter turned to both counsel. "Now then, it's very unfortunate and I do not know how this has happened, but we still have eleven members of a jury."

Ian Playton rose and told the judge that in view of how far the trial had progressed he thought perhaps the trial should continue. Monee rose saying that he was concerned that such a thing could occur; he wanted to emphasise that neither his client nor his team had anything to do with its appearance in the jury box. He hoped this wouldn't adversely affect his client and on that basis he was content to let the matter rest there.

The judge said, "Right then, let's get on with it." He signalled to the usher to recall the jury.

Now I'll let you in on a little secret. You remember when we had a break earlier? That little shit Dickson could obviously see the trial wasn't going well for him and his client. John and Janet gave good evidence, they stuck to their scripts, and wouldn't be swayed by Monee. Sensing this, he tried to ambush the trial by distributing copies of Jackson's pre-cons surreptitiously to the jury, which in all probability would cause a retrial with a new jury. You recall I walked back in on him, which prevented him going any further than blue rinse. Don't know how he did it but he got some more photocopied, so if he was challenged he still had the ones I'd supplied to him. I know he did it, he knows I know he did it, that's why he had the two in his hand and was overtly waving them around for me to see. If he'd succeeded, it would've been a retrial, and who knows where that would've gone. Luckily, the judge I think tumbled what was going on, although he couldn't say so. Still, we can still do a majority verdict if it gets that far!

As the jury returned to tell them that the trial would continue with just eleven of their number, and Bob was to commence his evidence, Janet was seeking the 'attention' of Al Fish in a locked witness waiting room that he had found on the first floor. Her hands slipped down the front of his suit trousers as he pulled in his stomach muscles to assist. She felt a firm cock in her hand as he returned the pleasure, lifting her dress to reveal stockings and a small G-string covering her neatly trimmed bush. His fingers explored her garden, the wetness encouraging his every move as their tongues danced in an extended kiss.

"Good news," he said, "I've had a word with Bill, one of the court police officers here. They're having a little cheese and wine do here in the police room at the close of play. Do you fancy it for a while, until the traffic's died down when I take you home?"

She said she'd love to, as long as it was OK with the rest of them. Al reassured her that Bob, the guvnor, had arranged it, he knew the court staff very well. There'd probably be a few court clerks, maybe even a couple of the judges who enjoy a bit of a party. With that she felt comfortable saying yes.

Bob got as far as giving his evidence-in-chief, including ensuring Michael didn't escape from the hospital ward, the identifications at Brixton and his vague admission in contemporaneous notes, which he 'refused' to sign, that he had been passing through the tube station at the time of the incident but that he wasn't responsible, claiming that he was on his way to see a film in Leicester Square. Salter, looking up at the clock above the dock, declared the hearing over; the case would continue the next sitting day. The judge went one way, the jury the other and Bob retired to the police room where old George, one of the court constables, was setting out the bottles of wine. He was a bit of an expert when it came to cheeses. Bob chipped in with a twenty-pound note expecting Al and Jim, not John, would do likewise. Needless to say Janet, as a guest, would not be obliged to donate. Al told her he'd cover her cost. George, who had previously got pissed with Bob in the wardroom on HMS Belfast, was perfectly happy with the donations; any not used on this occasion would go to the next one, which of course Bob and his cohorts would be invited to. As George poured him a large one, he reminded him of the great evening they'd had on the Belfast when HMS Glamorgan was alongside. That time they were in the operating theatre, Bob thought it amusing that two small doors on the theatre wall were opened, revealing two beer taps, one lager and one bitter. Deep joy.

18

JUST DESSERTS

She let out a groan as Al slipped his cock inside her as they leant across the table in the witness waiting room across the corridor from the police room. He felt beneath her blouse as her ample breasts were pressed firmly against the tabletop. He overbalanced as the effects of the wine took a hold of both of them. He fell forward; they both collapsed with laughter as they came to an agreement that possibly Her Majesty's court building was not the best place to have carnal gymnastics, particularly as others might notice them missing for too long. He lifted her upright and she adjusted her clothing to make herself presentable once more. With that, they returned to the semi-drunken soirée unnoticed.

Jim turned to John and suggested that, as it was just after six in the evening, having avoided the rush hour, maybe it was a good time to leave. John, feeling a little better following his court appearance and aided by the alcohol, was content to excuse himself having thanked Bob for all his continued efforts in nicking and potting Jackson. Bob waived the thanks away saying it was what the job does, looking after each other, because no other bastard will do it. They rescued their crumpled coats from underneath one of the other officers who been invited and was sitting across them. They left the room unnoticed, descending the main stairs, past the glorious 'waste of money' painting high on the vestibule wall and were intercepted by a security officer who was in the process of double-locking the front doors to the court building. He'd just set the alarms and so he led them out via the shutters where the prison vans deliver their 'customers'. He wasn't impressed to learn that George's little cheese and wine tasting was still in full flight in the police room, knowing he'd have to be the party pooper very shortly.

"Where have you two been?" asked Bob as Janet and Al came back into blurred view while he necked another glass of George's recommendation. In an effort to conceal Janet's guilty blushes, Al told the guvnor that he'd been giving her a guided tour of the building, showing her some of the other courtrooms, and encouraging her to feel that sense of power by sitting in the judge's chair. She said it gave her a better idea of the isolation maybe a judge feels by sitting up there, as the buck stops with him or her. She now appreciated how they have to get it right for all parties concerned.

Bob, sensing the seriousness of her comments, played up to it with a knowing and thoughtful nod. "Quite so," he said.

And the clerk from another courtroom chipped in how important it was they have their finger on the pulse and have an almost encyclopaedic knowledge of the law, not knowing earlier she'd had her fingers on Al's pulse!

"Time, gentleman, please," said the security officer as his seven o'clock entrance into the police room signalled the end of the wine-tasting process.

Some checking of watches made them realise they probably ought to wrap up and go home. The only way now to escape the building was to exit via the basement. Al, convinced he was more sober than was actually the case, escorted Janet to the car as the security officer released the gates and he drove out at a sedate pace, not wishing to draw attention to his glazed condition. Janet slunk back into her seat, discreetly hitching up her coat and skirt to reveal her stockings.

With a smile she said, "Are you driving me all the way home?"

Fish laughed and said, "I think it's my duty to take you all the way, don't you? I wouldn't want you to feel insecure with your husband being away, and you going back to any empty home."

"I'd better do as the nice policeman tells me," she said suggestively.

He smiled and carried on driving with a self-assurance she'd come up with the 'goods'.

Bob wandered along Tooley Street towards London Bridge for a prearranged meet outside the National Westminster Bank with his secret assignation. As was so often the case, he'd kept her waiting for ages, prompting a profuse apology again for his lateness. She drove across the bridge, knowing this was to be just a quick drink at Dirty Dick's in Bishopsgate before they went their separate ways. She enquired how he'd got on that day at Southwark Crown Court, sensing that he'd already had a few beers with his cohorts. He was indifferent in his reply, not really wanting to count his chickens, but he thought the jury were with him so far, despite Ernie Monee doing his best, together with that slimy shit Dickson, to derail the trial. He told her about the stunt he pulled with the pre-cons but the judge just dismissed the juror and continued to run the trial with eleven jurors. She then told Bob a tale about Monee.

She couldn't believe I hadn't heard the story. I'd known Monee from earlier trials over the last year or so. He was an objectionable arse who had a great deal of difficulty in not having a go at police at every opportunity, invariably alleging some sort of corruption or collusion for nefarious reasons.

*

She leant across the counter of Dixon's wondering if the day could get any better than the first hour of boredom; her reflection in the glass counter confirmed she needed to apply a bit more red lipstick. Her blonde hair fell forward as Geraldine, or Gerry, retrieved the 'Red Passion' from her clutch bag just below the counter. As she came back up from behind it, a well-groomed man, slightly balding and dressed in a suit, smiled revealing a small gap between his front teeth. She thought it looked kind of cute, as he then took a monocle from his inside jacket pocket, placing on his left eye. She'd never seen someone making such a statement of 'class' before, having been used to the usual punter, middle-aged, greasy hair, casual scruffy dress and often trying to tap her up for either her phone number or a drink after work. He was different, slightly older than her, she thought, but she was divorced in her early forties, no kids any more (they'd grown up and flown the coop), slim and available for a meal or whatever with the right man.

"Hi, I wonder if you can help me, I'm looking for a dictaphone to use for work, could you show what you have?" he said smiling wryly.

Sensing his cheeky enquiry she said, "Is it for the office desk, sir, or do you prefer to hold your dictaphone?"

They both fell into fits of laughter, after which she regained composure and said, "That's a nice belt, is it a sort of cowboy hat on the buckle?"

Justin confirmed it was, going on to tell her he had an interest in the Wild West, cowboy outfits and that sort of thing. She found him fascinating in an attractive way. He was different from the usual customer; the cowboy boots covered by his flared jeans told a tale. A few minutes had passed in social chat neither of them remembering what the original question was. Finally he bought the dictaphone and the insurance for it as well, knowing she'd get a kickback for selling it to him. He wasn't bothered; he'd just put the bill through chambers, reclaiming the expenses.

He danced out of the shop having won her over with his tales of being a slick criminal defence barrister, usually found frequenting the Old Bailey representing some poor unfortunate, stitched up by plod, and sharp of mind and wit. She was intrigued to learn he had an interest in the American West and was a regular at his local line-dancing club, but most importantly for him, he now had her phone number. She indicated she'd look forward to him phoning, only knowing his name from his credit card: Justin Thyme. She thought it a little odd he didn't give her his phone number, but in her naivety she thought maybe it was a security issue for him.

She made her way home late afternoon catching the usual

bus to her little two-up, two-down house in a not-so-affluent part of town. She sighed to herself as she walked up the short front path, seeing that the next-door neighbours still hadn't got rid of the discarded fridge from their front garden. She unlocked the double-locked Yale, coinciding with hearing the phone in the hallway spring to life. Dropping her bag she picked up the receiver answering with a casual "Hello." She was delighted, although tried not to sound too excited, to recognise the male voice at the other end, as it was immediately familiar as Justin from the shop. He was a smooth operator, for within a few minutes of chat, she'd agreed to meet him the following night for a drink in a local wine bar.

Over the next couple of months their relationship grew in intensity, with sex always occurring at her place whether that was after a quick drink at lunchtime or post the line-dancing, which she'd grown to enjoy. It gave him a great buzz to regale the clerks in chambers about his exploits with the girl from Dixons, how they'd fucked in every room in her house. They knew he was married, his wife was a family law solicitor in a firm which required her to be away some nights of the week at hearings up and down the country, giving him both time and opportunity to execute his indulgences. But he made a big mistake. He complained to one of the clerks over an outstanding case which he was yet to be paid for, and shortly after, Mrs Thyme became aware of his secret tryst via an anonymous tip-off. Mindful of the expression 'don't get mad, get even', she didn't tackle her wayward narcissistic husband head on, preferring to employ the expertise of a private detective.

Two short weeks later, she had all the ammunition

she needed. Her mindset was to ultimately divorce him, but she wanted to exert maximum pain and regret on the pair beforehand, so this 'woman scorned' sent a letter to the unsuspecting Dixons employee both to her home and her work address for the attention of her boss. The communications weren't so much blackmail notes, as stating knowledge of what she was up to, who her husband was, and that she wasn't the first to fuck her sterile husband. He'd had a vasectomy before he and the current Mrs Thyme had got together and didn't think it important to tell her that the fact might be an impediment to their marriage. He'd never wanted children, preferring to focus on his career to get to the top of the judicial tree, whereas she had been duped into believing one day they might hear the patter of tiny feet, so she resented his deception from the date at the altar.

Gerry fell back devastated in her armchair having received the second of the two letters at her home. Dozens of emotions raced through her mind from betrayal, to violation, to outright embarrassment that she had been so foolish to give herself so freely to the man in cowboy boots. Unaware of his wife's letters, Justin strolled up the garden path eagerly anticipating another round of carnal gymnastics. The door released Gerry into a full tirade of abuse declaring the affair to be over, and that his wife knew much more than he'd ever imagined. Despite his pleading that there had been a misunderstanding, she told him to go forth and multiply and die there and then. No more contact. He was incandescent with rage; he needed to be in control, manipulative, it was in his nature, so he stormed off to have it out with his wife. In the meantime, he promised he'd be back.

After the next few days of constant pestering, Gerry sought legal advice and now had a restraining order against both Mr and Mrs Thyme. This didn't seem to stop the now warring pair – she received letters from her and unannounced visits from him, until she dialled three nines for the police. He was arrested for an indecent assault on her and public order offences, she for sending malicious communications. Sensing the whole situation was getting out of control, they both made full and frank admissions. At the Magistrates' Court he received three months' imprisonment suspended for a year while she received a conditional discharge and pay compensation of three hundred pounds.

Unbelievably, Justin, thinking he would be disbarred from ever practising again, was given a year's suspension from the bench; the Law Society appeared to understand her strained relationship, suspended her for six months and to leave her law firm where she was a partner! When he restarted his career he'd changed his name by deed poll to Ernie Monee, she reverted to her maiden name and the house was sold. Licking their wounds still, they recommenced their 'illustrious' careers. As for Gerry, she moved to Spain to start a new life and was never heard of again.

*

That's some story isn't it? Seems like at the end of the day he had all of the reputation but ended with none of the pleasure! All I know is, if it had been a member of the blue serge he would've been hung out to dry. Not a chance of staying in the job. Just shows, one rule for some, and so on and so on.

19
DOUBLE VISION

Day two. Bob woke to find his promise of a quick drink with his 'legal adviser' and home had changed into a night of unbridled passion at her place. He raised an eye to see her beautifully formed arse disappear into the kitchen to make the tea and wondered if time allowed for a few more strokes of the *bleistift* before he had to set sail back to court. As he looked around the bedroom at all the feline trinkets and decor, he resolved that he needed to sort out his married life. It was crap, he never felt valued, his function just seemed to be as a meal ticket. His only concern was his kids who, it might be difficult to believe, he really cared for. They hadn't asked to be born, they were simply two recipients and observers of a turbulent relationship. He tried hard to make their lives as tolerable as he could, ensuring an enthusiastic interest in all they did, whether in schooling or their own sports and hobbies. He just didn't seem to have the tools to make it right for them all the time. His wife was so negative towards him, as if he was an encumbrance to her lifestyle, his presence was a pain, hence his weakness for a relationship giving him a feeling of being needed.

Not enough time, she pronounced on her way through to the bathroom. *That's OK, I can take rejection,* Bob thought to himself as he tried his best to convince her. No luck. They shared the facilities each doing their best to keep their hands off each other. Bob's resistance was low as he played with her breasts as she tried to apply mascara with a steady hand. Giving in, she dropped to her knees and in one fluid action gave a token suck on his hardening cock. "Now that will have to do until later," she told him. Realising he was pushing it a bit he did the right thing, as he thought, and got washed and dressed ready for another battle at Southwark palace of variety. Grabbing a quick bit of toast and a gulp of tea they left together, she off to defend the indefensible at Camberwell Green Magistrates' Court, while Bob returned to the Jackson trial.

DS Jim Hunt changed from the Bakerloo line to the southbound Piccadilly line wending his weary way to Knightsbridge Crown Court for two trials in the list requiring his and Basil's appearance to give evidence. As he emerged into the bright sunlight from the stairway feeding the early morning eager shoppers into the Harrods halls of expensive merchandise, he couldn't get 'Oops Upside Your Head' out of his mind, and remembered sitting on the floor in the middle of Stringfellow's doing some stupid rowing routine with the rest of the lads late into the night. He wandered along Hans Crescent turning right into the main doorway of the one-time Hans Crescent Hotel, now a house of correction for those miscreants in need of incarceration or some other form of judicial resolution.

Things are coming a bit on top at the moment. We've got this trial of Jackson here at Southwark which I'm covering with the assistance of Fish, whose cock seems to be ruling his head at present, two trials at Knightsbridge, luckily involving just Jim and Basil, and three or four magistrates' courts to cover for remands with each of those requiring an officer to attend to ask for remands or commit for trial if we're ready. To cap it all, as I sit here in the police room, Conroy has just called me to tell me that he's nicked a white dip on his way to Bow Street Court and now he's asking me to come to Snow Hill police station because he thinks he's a dip called Freddie Cutler, but that's not the name he's giving. Now I know Freddie, hence John wants a lift on identification. He'll have to wait until lunchtime. I can't get away until then, so I've told him to explain to the custody sergeant that he has to cover the bloody remand first while his arrest is banged up then get back to continue dealing with his body. Any problems, tell the sergeant to call me. So business is brisk!

DS Hunt descended the main staircase down to the police room to book on, meet up with Basil, and find out the state of the trials. His junior officer immediately invested in two coffees from the 'tea club' operated by one of the PCs on the court staff. Jim established the first trial of Terry Barrett was due to start at eleven o'clock after Judge Cousins had weighed off a couple for sentencing beforehand. The second was what's known in the trade as a 'floater', in other words, it's going to start in one of the courts probably that day but at that time it hadn't been allocated a trial judge – a bit of a lucky dip which court will cop for it. Their brief chat and run-through of the evidence was interrupted by a tannoy announcement declaring that their prosecution counsel was waiting at reception on the ground floor to meet with the officer in the case. Basil continued rehearsing the 'facts' of the case having been to the scene of the alleged dipping at South Kensington tube station, the female 'victim' being the description of someone they both knew well. They both agreed it was about time Terry be nicked again; he'd had a good run for a few months so it was only right that it was his turn, so to speak.

Jim danced up the wide carpeted staircase two at a time, not easy on such a grand structure designed for a more elegant ascent, arriving to see his barrister for this particular extravaganza, Paul Crawford, sporting what looked like a newly acquired black eye, who was apparently a distant relative and perhaps heir to a frozen food empire, hence shedloads of money in the family meaning that his advancement in the legal profession was more a pursuit of a hobby than a need to earn a living. Jim and Paul knew each other from earlier dip trials. Jim's view was that Paul was a half reasonable journeyman, not necessarily the sharpest knife in the box, but fairly aggressive when necessary. Paul viewed the case as just another run-through of familiar facts, the modus operandi strikingly similar, but then he conceded they probably would be. They ran through the case ensuring both were happy and how it was going to run. It was a straightforward dipping: Terry, a white dip from Islington, known to both officers, approached a young student-looking girl, just going towards the ticket barrier when he rummaged around in her shoulder bag. He saw the officers approaching him and so he did a runner out of the station towards the Natural History Museum and was arrested just by Exhibition Road. Needless to say, by the time they returned to the station there was no trace of the girl. Terry has plenty of form, running into two pages, about twelve pre-cons, but at this stage Paul hadn't met the defence brief so he didn't know if it was a case of mistake or whether a fit-up allegation would flow.

"So what's with the black eye?" said Jim.

Paul took Jim across to a corner away from the court traffic in the reception and in hushed tones said, "You remember the last time I prosecuted for you against that Colombian pickpocket and there was that beautiful interpreter, you know the one with the long dark hair?"

Jim just nodded, knowing exactly who he was on about, the gorgeous one looking like Sophia Loren.

"Well I don't know if you remember but at the conclusion we went across the road to 'Briefs' wine bar opposite Inner London Crown Court. Cut a long story short, after a few glasses she was quite taken with me and I with her. She lived just down the road near the Imperial War Museum, and she invited me back for coffee. Her husband was away and so being the gentleman I am, I couldn't let her run the risk of being accosted on the way home so I went back in the cab. We were getting on very well and I felt a bit tired so we decided before I left we would grab some shut-eye. Well, bugger me if her husband didn't decide to surprise her by coming back from a business trip in New York a day early! This is the result of him not understanding my entirely innocent presence in their love nest. Needless to say, I haven't heard from her since!"

Jim, trying to contain his laughter and resultant derision, changed the subject saying he had to go back to the police room to make a phone call.

Basil, who had been leafing through Terry's file, looked up to see Jim walk in with a grin on his face.

"What's up, sarge, you look like the cat that's just got the cream?"

Jim beckoned Basil away from being overheard and said, "Do you want a laugh? Crawford has just fessed up to me. The Colombian dip the other month at Inner London when we had that gorgeous interpreter, think I told you about her. Fucking hell, she was beautiful. Well Crawford, being the ageing incurable romantic he is, took her for a little wine tasting in Briefs bar opposite and after a few gargles of Pinot Grigio she succumbed to his advances. Then, fortified with a rush of blood and courage that her husband was still in New York, she invited him back to her place – she doesn't live far from there. And just as they were getting down to the slippery bits, hubby returned. Now he's a bit of a lump, whereas Crawford, although schoolboy-attractive to the fairer sex, isn't. Hence the physical recognition that he was a bit pissed off!"

Basil's face alternated between astonishment and hysterical laughter, much to the bemusement of the other occupants of the police room.

Focusing back on the case, Jim said he'd go in the witness box first to be 'roasted' by the defence brief; fairly straightforward, he reassured Basil, who was still settling in to the concept of complete works of fiction requiring their attendance at court simply because the aforementioned dip was obviously 'well at it' at the time of his arrest. He had no visible means of support and yet had several hundred pounds and no credible reason for its possession other that the usual 'I won it on the horses'. Jim enlightened Basil on the peculiar but distinctive trait of the judge. Any officers whom he addressed when they gave evidence he would call 'Mr Policeman', not Detective Constable Chakrabarti, as in Basil's case. Why? Nobody knew. Cousins was just odd that way, but Basil was grateful for the tip-off, nevertheless.

Almost on time the trial kicked off in Court Six, as Jim went into bat first. In the meantime, Bob at Southwark launched into his cross-examination by Ernie Monee who released a tirade of bile about Bob's reputation as an honest police officer. It was nothing less than he expected so he stood his ground and remained calm and composed, particularly when Ernie suggested the unsigned contemporaneous notes were a work of fictional vision containing little half-truths and partial admissions of guilt by his client. Bob denied it, of course, citing Jackson's identification by the victim and also by the member of the public. Ernie had difficulty in challenging those aspects as the identifications occurred in the presence of Luca Zengretti, his solicitor.

Next in the witness box, in a change of Ernie strategy, was Steve whose evidence of the escalator identification was simply procedural with Ernie not wanting to challenge it too much, raising the positive aspects to the jury. Instead of accepting it as read, as originally agreed, he called him to give live evidence and tried making the point that this kind of identification parade was not the most ideal, getting Steve to admit that a formal parade or line-up is always the best form of test. So essentially this was second best, in an effort to convince the jury that perhaps Steve could have tried harder to form a formal parade. After fifteen short minutes,

Steve was released, with no further questions from Ernie or the judge. Ian read out the doctor's statement together with the surgeon's, who attended to John's wound, and closed the evidence for the prosecution. Ernie rose to his feet and pronounced that his client would not be giving evidence and he didn't intend calling any other witnesses, giving way to closing speeches and the judge's summing up.

Basil checked his newly acquired Swatch watch, waiting with a combination of nerves and impatience as the big hand brushed with twelve indicating a break for lunch as Jim swept into the police room.

"No sweat, textbook, no monsters," said Jim in reassuring tones to his 'sorcerer's apprentice', whereupon they emerged into sunlight at the front of the building turning left and left again round the back of Harrods, walking determinedly towards a 'greasy spoon' on Walton Street. The all-day breakfast did the trick and saw the two of them returning to the grand building playing host to the scrotes of the parish, no not the lawyers, or indeed the coppers!

The trial kicked off promptly at two with neither knowing if their second floater case had yet been allocated a court. Basil went into bat next while Jim sampled the questionable delights of the cheap coffee granules in the police room. In no time Basil was back with Jim having had an easy ride in the witness box, the brief confining cross-examination to whether Basil was mistaken in what he saw, therefore removing the spectre of revealing his client's, the defendant's, previous convictions as a balance for calling the officer a liar. Jim told Basil to sit tight in the police room while he returned to court to see both counsel doing their closing speeches before the judge did his final directions to the jury. On his way back Jim called into the List Office to see what was happening to the floater.

To his horror he learnt the second trial was going to follow in the same court, in front of the same judge! A major problem now presented itself in the form of the victim's description being the same as in the previous trial! Now while the method of the dipping could reasonably be described as similar, in that dips operated in a similar way to achieve their theft, a victim description that mirrors that of the first trial was just impossible to overcome. Jim resolved something had to be done, he needed to get the second trial put off and away from the judge to avoid him smelling a rat. In a panicked phone call to the guvnor, who was still at Southwark wading his way towards the jury being sent out to deliberate their verdict in the Jackson trial, he tried sharing the problem with him in the vague hope of some inspirational solution. Bob gave him very short shrift, including giving him a blast, doubting his parentage, for using what might be a taped phone line.

I don't fucking believe it! I've just had DS James Hunt on the phone, and yes he is a James Hunt. The two trials at Knightsbridge Crown feature an anonymous female victim with the same description, the bloody female DC, both trials coming before the same fucking judge! This is what happens when you trust your DS to do his homework before the day of the damn trials. If he had, he could've fixed it with our tame contact in the List Office to ensure the trials came up on different days or even weeks. The second one was a floater for Christ's sake. Now he's put a junior officer on offer because of his complacency, I'm so damn annoyed. It makes us look stupid, to say nothing of inviting a bloody internal criminal enquiry from 'Complaints and Discipline' who would delight in shafting a couple of 'bent' coppers, starting a trawl through loads of our other forthcoming trials. I've left it to him to figure it out otherwise it could come on top for me as well. I can't be seen to be directing the 'get out of jail free' card. What if he suddenly went wobbly on me and he found God or Jesus? To say nothing about the less-than-experienced Basil. What a twat! His only real option is for some reason the second one can't go ahead because of sickness, like a sudden migraine or something, just anything to drop it out of the list.

20

A RASH DECISION!

Ernie was getting nowhere with trying to break Bob's intransigence to his suggestions that somehow Michael had been fitted up by the scurrilous Detective Inspector, so much so that his exasperation was beginning to become evident to some members of the jury. He turned to look at the rodent Dickson behind him, hoping for some divine inspiration from him, but to no avail. He simply looked back at Ernie with a resigned expression as if to say, they'd been beaten by a better team and with that Ernie sat down on his bench knocking several of his papers and his brief's notebook to the floor just behind his portable lectern. As with previous trials, the closings speeches would now start. Fortunately, Al Fish turned up to see how the trial was going, and much to Bob's relief it meant he could get away to the Snow Hill nick to see who Conroy had arrested, giving him the chance then to nip over to Bow Street Court to cover the long overdue remand. This kind of court juggling had become more commonplace in recent times because of the squad's increased arrest rates and enviable success in ridding London of the scourge of pickpockets.

Prior to Al putting in a 'cameo' appearance for the guvnor, he'd gone to University College Hospital, or to those more familiar, UCH, for a rather difficult enquiry of his own. Nothing to do with seeing a doctor or nursing staff or even a victim of a crime. He entered the hospital on Gower Street descending down the stairs immediately to his left having negotiated two sets of double doors. He couldn't help thinking this was a part of the hospital that hadn't seen a lick of paint or modernisation since its Victorian opening, unlike the imposing modern edifice more recently completed. It was as if he was being subjected to some kind of vilification for his current plight. In the basement, he turned right presenting himself at the counter. A nurse, obviously failing to keep to her diet, directed him to a ticket machine which spewed out the next number implying he had to wait his turn, removing any last sense of dignity he thought he had. Al was handed a clipboard to record his details – who his GP was, and declarations of agreement to using penicillin. Like a naughty schoolboy, he sat on one of the neatly arranged chairs around three of the walls along with four or five other seemingly shamefaced males in their twenties, maybe thirties, each clutching their ticket waiting their turn. His dilemma was how much truth he should tell on the hospital form, particularly as he was unsure where the information was going. The last thing he wanted was for some official letter landing on the family doormat and his not-so-understanding wife celebrating the fact that his medical treatment for the 'clap' had worked! So he opted for a work of pure fiction, calling himself John Smith and a mysterious doctor who ordinarily looks after his piles and annoying ingrown toenail. Handing the clipboard back, the nurse greeted his recorded details with a wave of indifference, and he resumed his seat, apprehensive for the next stage.

Al nervously waited for about ten minutes, seeing another of the young hesitant men arrive, taking their tickets and assuming their seat.

"John Smith," called the male nurse from the doorway to his right. Two other waiting men also acknowledged the name. Who would've thought! Al, seeing that his ticket number was lower than theirs, stood to own the next appointment.

"Yes, that's me," said Al as he passed through and into a cubicle. He lay there on a bench similar to those in the Divisional Surgeon's room back at the nick, with his boxer shorts flying at half-mast on his thighs, as instructed by the effeminate-sounding nurse. A stainless-steel trolley sporting dishes, wipes and what looked like very long cotton buds pushed past the drawn curtain, eagerly followed by the nurse. Al pensively acknowledged his grand entrance; the nurse, like a matador, threw the cubicle curtain back and forth, closing out prying eyes from the waiting room. Without a word, just a smile, the nurse gently caressed Al's meat and two veg while Al looked down towards his gentleman's vegetables quizzically assessing what he was up to as he continued to regularly rub him up and down.

"What is it you're doing? Aren't you going to take a sample and check it?"

Breaking the distraction the nurse said, "I'm just trying to make it a bit more erect so I can put the probe down your penis, otherwise it might hurt more."

Al, thinking the nurse was getting bit too personal, indignantly said, "Let it fucking hurt mate, just do the test."

Having got his sample, as Al registered that it was excruciatingly painful, he told him to re-dress and go back to the waiting room.

It seemed like an age before Al was called into an adjacent room where the doctor gave him the good news that he didn't have the clap but did have an infection which man's best friend, a course of penicillin capsules, would solve. Now with a lightness in his step, and with his 'get well soon' medication, he stepped back out into the diesel exhaust-filled air of Gower Street. Knowing he was now pushing his luck with the guvnor, he dived down on to the Underground arriving at Southwark Crown in record-breaking time. He ran up the main staircase two at a time finding Bob fuming at his lateness.

"Where the fuck have you been? Conroy's got a body in at Snow Hill, he still hasn't got Bow Street to cover the bloody remand."

Al felt like a scalded cat, but desperate not to enlighten Bob on the real reason he'd be delayed, with a light air he said, "I'm really sorry, guv, but I got stopped for speeding by a black rat. I left home and I realised I was going to be late for me train so I put me foot down, thirty, forty, fifty, then I saw him in my mirror. I thought I'd better pull over and he came up to me and said he was on his way back to the traffic garage for breakfast. He said he wouldn't do me if I gave a good reason for speeding. So told him my wife had an affair with a traffic copper and had run off with him, I was speeding because I thought he was bringing her back."

"Twat! Stay here, the jury's going to be sent out soon. I'm off to see Conroy." Although Bob knew Fish was hiding something as to why he was late, he couldn't be bothered with the speculation. He'd turned up, that was it, so he rushed out of the court building for his meet at Snow Hill.

Somehow the gods were looking down on the boys at Knightsbridge as the judge had a couple of sentencing matters to deal with, which took him up to just after four o'clock, and so the floater wouldn't kick off until the following morning. Basil pulled open the heavy mahogany front door of the court building unaware of Jim's cunning plan to avoid the potentially criminal embarrassment of the second trial, as they passed out turning left heading towards the tube station entrance next to Harrods. The late afternoon sun cast long shadows across Hans Crescent as they walked purposefully towards the staircase leading to their transport back to the nick.

This better be worth my bloody effort of leaving the Jackson trial to come and look at a dip that Conroy's nicked. The walk from Farringdon is not just around the corner, but it's probably the nearest to Snow Hill. Allow me to be your tour guide, pain in the arse Conroy; mustn't be too harsh if he's nicked another dip. Still, here are the sights of Smithfield market, and that excellent watering hole, the Cock Tavern, underneath – the only place I know of selling Red Stripe lager, a West Indian medicine, on draught; the underground NCP car park, which many years ago was the way they used to herd cattle to market for slaughter; and finally St Barts hospital; now, turning left into Snow Hill, the road opposite where the Old Bailey is. Right, now in the front door, down to the cells for my wicket gate ID parade.

Bob gave a cordial greeting to the custody sergeant, explaining he'd only come to look at the dip for Conroy who thought he was Freddie Cutler. The skipper showed him he'd been booked in under the name Trevor Sutton, not as what John thought was his true identity. John reappeared in the charge room having taken a leak in the cell next to the suspect.

"Hello guv, he reckons his name is Trevor David Sutton, but remember that team of white dips we had off the bus, top on Walworth Road near the Elephant and Castle the other month? Well, you know I wasn't there for the actual arrest, but fancy it's Cutler. The age and description is right, but I dunno, I just thought a second opinion would be good. The name he's given, his form comes back with only a couple for thieving and it's motors, not our game."

Bob said, "Right then, let's have a look," they strolled purposefully towards the cell door, Bob undoing the bolted wicket gate. The sound of the bolt reluctantly giving up its firm grip caused its occupant to look up as Bob peered through at the mystery within. He beckoned him to come to the door, where the forty-watt bulb, illuminating the cell from above through thick glass, might shed some light on his identity. But to no avail.

Bob said, "No, John, I don't know who you've got there but it's not Cutler."

Closing the wicket once more, they turned, walking towards the charge room as Bob said in hushed tones, "How's your evidence. Got a victim?"

John confirmed that he hadn't. Bob, knowing Paul Hazel was at the Guildhall Magistrates' Court in the City, phoned the gaoler's office there, and having found him, told him to get his arse over to Snow Hill to help out John so he could get away to Bow Street to deal with the remand that he had originally been on his way to do when this 'inconsiderate thief' delayed his journey. Bob had a quick word with the sergeant who was quite happy to keep Sutton banged up for the time being pending 'further enquiries', meaning his incarceration would continue until his identity could be verified if possible. He then left, content that John had squared things up on his delay with the court staff at Bow Street and to await the arrival of Paul.

"All right, John, what have you got here, mate?" Paul asked as he settled himself into a seat opposite Conroy down in the basement canteen.

Nursing a cup of tea, slowly stirring it, he said, "White dip working on his own. I was on my way to covering the remand at Bow Street when he performed bang in front of me. I don't know though, Paul, the name he's given doesn't seem right. CRO confirm he's known in that name but it's not for dipping. The way he shaped up, I can't believe it's the first time he's done it, you know what I mean? Where you been?"

Paul responded, likewise stirring, "I was at Guildhall mags with that bustler Starling, you know Oswald Washington, fucking perv."

"Not for bustling a bird, surely?" asked John.

"No, fuck off, attempted theft from a female unknown. You know what he's like. He taps up a bird and gets his jollies, but whenever he's nicked he begs you to do him for 'attempted theft person', cos if he goes inside he don't want to be treated like a nonce! And guess what, this was one of those times. I didn't nick him, one of the plain clothes crime squad lads did, but I managed to get to the nick at

Bishopsgate just before they were gonna give their facts. Luckily they got the message and gave the 'right' facts to the skipper charging. You know he's still wearing those smeg-stained black tracky bottoms with the white piping? Dirty fucker. So what have we got? Any complainant?"

John shook his head and said, "No, he shaped up behind a woman but backed off at the last minute. I gave him a chance to go back in but something spooked him, and I thought he was going to get away from me and get on, so as the carriage doors closed with her on board I jumped him. He gave up pretty much straight away, so I pulled him back telling him he was nicked."

"What time was it?" enquired Paul.

"Why's that?" said John.

"I'm just trying to figure out if I could've been there but just a few feet away, but he didn't see me."

The pair then went through the sequence of events and to John's relief, to say nothing of surprise, they realised that Paul could've been there, seen the events and then had to rush off to Guildhall to cover Starling's remand. Double-checking the script they found it could work, so now it was two on one. Better odds, they agreed.

*

Up the three steps where all the press boys hang around, through to revolving doors and back up to the police room on the first floor, passing that fantastic waste of taxpayers' money I told you about, three blobs of colour pretending to be modern art. Fish can wait for me now while I have myself a nice cup of tea.

"A note from the jury, guv," said Fish using his detective acumen as he found Bob relaxing in an armchair chatting to the court sergeant, arranging a little get-together on HMS Belfast.

"What now? Find out what it is, Al, will you? It's almost the end of the day," said Bob determined to finish his tea.

"I know what it was, guv, they asked if it mattered that we hadn't recovered the knife that caused the injury. He told them it didn't and sent them back out. The clerk said he's going to give them ten more minutes for a verdict otherwise he'll send them home overnight."

Bob took in the meaning of the message sending Al back to the courtroom for close of play. Just after four, he returned telling Bob they'd be back in the morning.

Bob took a call from Conroy, still telling him that he wasn't happy with the details given by Sutton, but the address seemed to check out so the sergeant was going to give him bail after charging him with the attempted theft, by 'good fortune' Paul having 'seen' everything, stepped forward to go witness to the offence. Apparently Sutton, when he was charged, claimed he had a fiver more in his personal property when he had been arrested and it hadn't been recorded on the list of property on the charge sheet. The sergeant gave him very short shrift saying he must have been mistaken but he was not happy about being five quid down or being nicked. Neither Conroy, Hazel nor the guvnor appreciated how much shit this would stir later on. At this stage, it was just a gobshite dip laying grounds for allegations of corruption or theft at his later trial date, nothing more, nothing less.

21

PLAN B

Detective Sergeant Hunt emerged from the shower to the dulcet tones of Frankie goes to Hollywood booming out 'Two Tribes' on the radio, resolving his mind that whatever happened, the second trial cannot go ahead in front of the same judge at Knightsbridge today otherwise he and Baz would be in serious difficulties, allegations of corruption, perjury and everything that comes with it. He had decided on a plan: he was going to fake a migraine when he got to court, which hopefully would get the case dropped out of the list. His only worry was that the judge might insist on it coming back in front of him as soon as Jim had recovered. He was mindful of Bob berating him for such a cock-up and the mantra of piss-poor planning leading to poor performance.

Basil wasn't privy to Jim's plan at this stage when he agreed to meet him in the booking hall at Piccadilly Circus. Coming in from different parts of London's suburbia, they met by the Barclays Bank 'hole in the wall' adjacent to the ticket booths at eight thirty, and seeing as they had some time before the start of the day's events, they went upstairs to the coffee shop at the bottom end of Regent Street near to the Café de Paris. Once seated Jim offered up his plan to Basil who hesitatingly agreed adding that he hoped it would work. Jim canvassed Baz for a better plan but none came forward, Jim sensing he was not entirely convinced. Thoughts raced through his mind that if it all went wrong Basil might have a rush of blood, discover God or whoever he held in high esteem and grass him up to the powers that be. But at this stage he felt he didn't have a better plan. They polished off their coffees, with Basil bending forward on the corner of the bench seat, pretending to tie his shoelaces, meaning Jim had to pay!

The misty rain greeted them as they stepped out into the remainder of the rush hour busily going to and fro, oblivious to their presence on the pavement. Jim led the way against the tide of pedestrians towards Lillywhite's on the corner opposite Eros where they descended the rain-soaked steps leading to the booking hall. *What's with the brass treads on the leading edge, bloody dangerous*, Jim thought. Their journey took them down an old wooden escalator, the treads again proving slippery underfoot, as Jim's leather-soled shoes illustrated and he responsed, "Fuck me I nearly went then!" They descended into the bowels of the Piccadilly line, Basil reassured that Jim had come up with a plan ensuring the second trial wouldn't go ahead, Jim preoccupied in thoughts as to whether the migraine ploy would work. If only there could be something a little more definite which would knock the case out of the court list for a couple of weeks.

Their journey proceeded to Knightsbridge station with little conversation other than speculation whether it would still be raining as they emerged for the short walk to the court in Hans Crescent. The novel British preoccupation with weather was something that had always mystified Basil, as the only time he thought about it was when there was a risk of it spoiling a good day's cricket! They followed the crowd of obviously excited punters making their way to donate their money into the coffers of Harrods, doubtless much to the pleasure of Al Fayed's family. Slowly they made progress step by step up the escalator towards the exit barrier.

"Shit! There's Errol Heath by the ticket box, Baz," whispered Jim behind his hand so as not to been seen.

"Got him," said Basil acknowledging he'd seen him but not wishing to raise his profile.

"He's got bail conditions not to come within fifty yards of any Underground station," said Jim referring to a recent hearing the guvnor had ensured was imposed on him at Horseferry Road Magistrates' Court for a series of dippings and a knife-point robbery.

"Are you sure, sarge?" enquired Basil not really doubting Jim, more a case of needing reassurance as he knew they'd be challenging him and nicking him for breach of bail conditions. He knew what a violent individual he was; he deliberated in his mind how they'd take him out, drag him back to the floor by his dreadlocks, the surprise giving them enough time to hold him to the ground while they tried to 'cuff' him. Maybe a good kick in the shins, dropping him to his knees – he'd heard blacks were weak there and couldn't withstand that pain. One thing he did know was that he could hit him as hard as he liked, even with his 'stick', aka truncheon, on his head, and he'd just shake it off.

"Errol!" shouted Jim, as Heath swung round to see his familiar face. He first barged past the exiting travellers at the top of the escalator prompting Basil and Jim to spin round and chase him themselves. Heath quickly realised his escape was hampered by the crowds disgorging from below, and so he turned again barging past his pursuers, charging towards the exit. Catching the pair of them off balance, Heath bounded up the stairs towards the street, two at a time like a gazelle fleeing from a hungry lion intent on taking it down and enjoying a long-awaited meal.

Realising they were never going to catch him, Jim shouted, "Police stop," as he saw Heath's heels disappear out of view. With a rush of blood, combined with the obvious failure of catching the dip, and his panic in the surrounding melee about the imminent need to dump the second trial, Jim saw his opportunity. He barged Basil down the escalator. He let out a yell, losing his footing, and tumbled from the top to the bottom arriving in a heap, his fingers dangerously close to being caught in the metal comb at the base of the escalator designed to capture discarded fag ends from the moving treads. Unfortunately, in his concussed state his face met with their cold steel and the hard tile floor. A passenger about to ascend adjacent to him managed to drag Basil free, pulling him across to the left-hand wall of the subway while looking up the shaft to search for a reason for such a dreadful and obviously painful fall.

"Police, mate," shouted Jim down to the Samaritan giving rudimentary first aid to Basil, who was dazed but confused as to how he had sustained cuts and bruises to his legs, his suit jacket ripped up the centre stitching at the back, both knees of his trousers torn, the blood of his wounds knitting with the mesh of the material providing an improvised bandage stemming the flow of blood from the wounds. His back was killing him as if he'd been kicked by a mule, and his face was a mass of cuts and bruises as if he'd suffered at the hands of Henry Cooper.

"Look after him, is he OK? I'll call for help," said Jim as he disappeared from the view of the first aider. He dived into an adjacent phone kiosk next to the ticket barrier.

"We've just tried to arrest Errol Heath for breach of bail conditions at Knightsbridge tube. He violently resisted, and escaped from us into the street, but he pushed DC Chakrabarti down the escalators. He's injured, I'm just going to him now. We need urgent assistance and an ambulance for one injured officer." Jim's storyline was accepted without question with the Information Room operator ensuring they wouldn't be alone for long. DS Hunt bounded down the escalator to his colleague, immediately thanking the attentive passenger for his help. Confirming he hadn't actually seen who had pushed Basil to his fate, he recorded his details as a witness.

"I'm really sorry Baz this happened to you mate, we'll get Heath," said Jim as he assessed his visible injuries hoping he didn't tumble who had really been responsible, while Basil slipped in and out of consciousness. Unable to speak, he simply tried to make himself comfortable while the ambulance beat a speedy path to their location. The echo of the 'cavalry' arriving in the form of two tones could be faintly discerned by the two officers, Jim not daring to move Basil in case of further injury. His moral compass had gone into meltdown as he tried to conceal his guilt, continuing the storyline that the escaping dip had caused all this, while he vowed he would get the bastard who had done this to his colleague. His half-hearted assertion that, by way of compensation, every cloud has a silver lining as the second trial couldn't now go ahead, rang hollow to Basil as he lay propped up against the wall, the blood now drying on the plethora of wounds he had sustained.

A rush of noise and several uniformed officers arrived at the foot of the escalators, leaving the remainder sealing off the various entrances and exits from the tube, until further updates from those arriving at the scene would dictate further action. Almost immediately, as a result of Jim's account, the hunt was called off in the immediate vicinity after they learned the suspect had made good his escape from the scene. Those on the surface jumped back into their response vehicles and left like a bomb burst outside Harrods, commencing searching the surrounding streets armed with only a scant description given by Jim. He of course knew Heath and what he was wearing, but he couldn't afford for him to be arrested too soon as his version of events might be compromised by the escaping dip, who might very well add to Basil's vague suspicion of who was responsible.

As the two ambulance crew arrived, listening intently to Jim's account while judiciously attending to obvious wounds and assessing the risk of Basil's removal from the scene, one of them disappeared back to his vehicle from where he returned carrying a fold-away wheelchair. Within a few moments he was once again mobile and being conveyed up the escalator, covered in the mandatory red blanket, something to do with keeping him warm to negate shock, Jim thought, or maybe to hide the blood, his black humour kicking in!

You know when you're told something and you're just not

sure about it? Well, I've just had that feeling. DS Hunt, you'll recall, the one I bollocked over his quality of evidence, has just phoned me here as I wait for the result on Jackson. It seems he and Basil were on their way to Knightsbridge Crown for the second trial, with a female victim description the same as their first trial and to cap it all, in front of the same fucking trial judge, when they saw Errol Heath on the Underground, despite him having bail conditions not to stray anywhere near! Originally Jim's plan to avoid it going ahead was to feign a serious migraine, probably with all the drama he could muster. But he says they tried to arrest Heath but he was too quick for them and in his effort to escape, he pushed Basil down the escalators. So now I have an officer badly injured, concussed at St Thomas' Hospital awaiting examination. The one saving grace is that Hunt has been along to court and having told them of the story, succeeded in getting the trial taken out of the list. Added to which a member of the List Office court staff was passing through the station at the material time and saw everything, she's willing to make a statement! So maybe my suspicions are unfounded, it just seemed a bit too rehearsed.

The arrival of the ambulance was announced with its two-tone horns as it swept across Westminster Bridge going south towards St Thomas' Hospital, turning right and up the slope to Accident and Emergency, where the paramedic attending to Basil's plight was relieved by an army of pre-warned doctors and nurses keen to admit him to assess his condition. The officer had been drifting in and out of consciousness, not really making any sense, but being told to relax and rest while the team went about their triage routines. To cut a long story short, the hospital staff were briefed by the paramedic attending the scene, their only source of information. Basil was in no condition to give any reliable account of how he came to be so badly battered. They were now advised in a short telephone call to reception that Jim would be arriving shortly to give the full picture.

"Hello mate," said Jim as he pulled back the curtain to the side of Basil. A look of concern etched his face as he looked down at the result of his efforts at avoiding the trial. He tried to conceal his shock as his fellow officer tried to speak through a swollen mouth and intravenous painkillers now pumping around his traumatised body, giving him some relief from the pain, but making his responses less than coherent. Jim took the opportunity to remind him of how he came to fall from top to bottom of the escalator, stressing how it was that Heath, in all the fighting and confusion near the ticket barrier, had committed the ultimate coup de grâce. Over the next thirty minutes he continued to reinforce the storyline until he was ejected by nursing staff when Basil was whisked off for X-rays and scans.

"I'm going to get back to the office now, Baz, and I'll update the guvnor. Your missus has been told by one of the uniform lads and they're picking her up. So she should be here later this afternoon, mate."

Basil thanked him for all his help, feeling content about the reason he at present was in so much bloody pain!

*

"What's keeping them, Al? They've been out for bloody ages. I want to get down to Tommy's to see how Baz is," said

Bob as he checked his watch looking up at the clock in the police room.

"I can cover this if you like, guv, so you can get on your way," said Al obligingly.

"It's tempting, but I think I need to be here for the result. Nip up to the court see if there's anything going on."

As they rose from their chairs, the court officer came in, telling them both it looked like they had a result. The jury was being called back in to deliver Bob's desired result.

"Hi sir, I hear we've got a result?" said Bob enquiringly with his counsel for the prosecution.

"Yes, have you got the up-to-date previous convictions and antecedent history on the 609s and 402s? Is there anything else I should know? I rather suspect if we have a finding of guilt on the Section 18, he'll probably remand him in custody for reports. Still, let's not count our chickens."

Bob nodded knowingly with his barrister.

"Court rise," bellowed the clerk as the door at the end of the bench disgorged the judge back into the courtroom. He directed the jury to be called in, the occupants of the court remaining silent as they filed in. Bob couldn't discern from any of the jury which way their thoughts were directed. The clerk enquired and confirmed that the spokesman for the jury was seated bottom left, nearest to the judge.

"Will the defendant please stand?" said the clerk now standing just below the judge. Jackson pulled himself to his feet from his slouched position on the bench. The prison officers also stood either side of him, conveying the unmistakable message that should he have a sudden desire to 'play up' or even dare to try escaping, his efforts would be very quickly curtailed in a robust manner!

"Members of the jury, have you reached a decision on which all of you are agreed?"

"Yes," said the jury foreman standing nearest to him while the others remained seated and expressionless, looking across at Bob.

"To the count of causing grievous bodily harm with intent, do you find the defendant Jackson, guilty or not guilty?"

"Guilty," came the response.

"And is that the verdict of you all?" enquired the clerk. The reply came back loud and clear that it was, reinforced by the rest of them nodding their heads.

Judge Salter turned towards the eleven jury members and thanked them for their time taken in reaching their decision and their obvious conscientious deliberations.

Ernie was straight to his feet but before he could utter a word, Playton stood to address the judge, almost second-guessing what the judge was about to say. Neither was right.

Salter said, "Stand up, Jackson. Now before I go any further in this case and hear from those representing you, I intend to rise for a few minutes. Members of the jury, your function is now complete but if you wish to remain to witness the conclusion of this case you are welcome to remain when we resume in a few minutes."

Not one of them moved, each deciding they wanted to see the right punishment meted out to the defendant.

"Court rise," bellowed the court usher, calling all to stand as the judge swept out through his 'trap door'.

Dickson rushed to his client in an effort to console a bitter Jackson, who had believed he was going to get a not-guilty verdict despite everyone else in the courtroom, including Ernie Monee, realising his inevitable fate. Bob's face couldn't conceal the wry smile of satisfaction as he glanced across at the jury experiencing for the first time the procedure after their verdict. Catching the eye of several members in the back row he mouthed "Thank you" for their unanimous decision, knowing such a verdict would make it difficult for Jackson to appeal against it. Some of them made no response while others mouthed "OK" or just smiled and nodded back.

A knock on the door interrupted Bob's enquiry of Al's mystery movements prompting his lateness at court, disbelieving the original version of being stopped for speeding. *Leave until later*, Bob thought, as the judge assumed his position in the big chair. Monee prepared his notes to address the judge, endeavouring to mitigate the unfortunate circumstances his client now found himself in. Bob went back into the witness box and, being led by Ian Playton, he went through Jackson's previous convictions for theft, robbery, and assault, galvanising the attentive jury that they had obviously made the right decision. Ernie had only the one question and that was to ask Bob if his client had used a knife in any of his previous convictions. Bob wasn't able to say, but it didn't seem to be the case. He pressed further: did he know that Jackson's life had been threatened only a few days before the incident, and hence the reason for him carrying a knife? The officer knew nothing of this, dismissing it as a last-ditch ruse to reduce whatever penalty the judge had in mind, and by way of observation perhaps he should have raised it during the course of the trial. Salter immediately interjected thanking Bob, telling him he could now stand down, avoiding a tit-for-tat spat between Ernie and him.

Monee next launched into a tirade of mitigation for his client, pulling out all the stops, including that he had two older brothers both of whom had vast criminal careers, thereby causing a retrograde effect on such a young impressionable man leading to an early life of crime, etcetera, etcetera. He cheerfully danced past the fact that an older sister of his had a very good career, and was always in work, so clearly it was in his gift not to go down the same path as his brothers! Sadly then he played the race card, emphasising colour, housing, poor schooling, negative influences of his peer group, unemployment, and so droning on for about five minutes. His biggest error was to try to trivialise the injury as somehow accidental and not the vicious predetermined assault that it was. Bob thought any minute he'd add that someone stole his teddy bear when he was young. Why not? Everything else had been thrown in the mix. Next he addressed the judge on sentencing, emphasising that although he faced a serious conviction, he was young, desperately remorseful for his actions and somehow if a suspended sentence could be considered this would give him the opportunity to start life afresh. With that last plea for clemency, Ernie sat down.

The clerk turned to look at Judge Salter anticipating his final few words before issuing sentence. Both counsel, Dickson the rodent, Bob and Al were in unison transfixed by the judge's every move, who with a half-smile and a nod caused the clerk to swing back around and stand.

"Will the defendant stand," he said, as Jackson drew himself to his feet from his familiar slouched position.

Salter gave him an icy stare as if staring down the twin barrels of a shotgun about to be discharged when he launched into his sentencing speech. "Jackson, you have been found guilty of a most heinous assault, vicious in its commission and devastating in its result. You are a career criminal who set out that day to steal or rob from innocent members of the public. To assist you in that quest you carried a knife, one which I am given to understand was of the type carried by members of a group known as 'Yardies', nothing of course to do with Scotland Yard. By some good fortune, a plain clothes officer, going about his duties, ever vigilant, spotted you attempting to steal and prevented you from achieving your purpose. Frustrated at him stepping in and in an effort to escape arrest you sliced his face open in a most appalling manner, causing severe injury and blood loss requiring urgent surgery, and leaving him with a lifelong visible memory of your indiscriminate use of your knife. Having been arrested whilst on the run you then deployed every ruse possible to avoid identification to no avail. You came and pleaded not guilty, causing the officer and indeed a female member of the public to relive the ordeal at your hands. No credit can be given to you in this case to you or those you instruct. You will go to prison for seven years. Take him down."

The dock officers standing either side of him took hold of Jackson firmly, and as they led him out he shouted, "Seven years for a fucking Mars Bar?" (Slang for scar.) The door slammed shut and he was gone, on his way to commence his incarceration. No family there, no friends to witness the event, just an isolated individual whom the state had little time for.

Ian Playton turned to Bob and in a brief chat agreed it was the right result. He asked that Innes receive his best wishes for the future and hoped he had conducted a fair but firm prosecution. Bob shook his hand, thanked him, confirmed he would be speaking with the officer, and left the courtroom to head over to the hospital to see Basil. Dickson scuttled off to speak with his client knowing there was little he could say to soften the blow he'd just received. As for Monee, he shuffled his papers together, and swung out of the court, intent on contacting his chambers to enquire what his next lost cause would be.

That's a good result, I hear you say. Well, I thought so. We had a good rinse afterwards on the strength of it, pleased that we wouldn't see that arrogant little shit's face for some time. We had done a good job of culling the less desirable members of the Jackson family, so happy days. One problem: he appealed! I couldn't believe it, but he did. Not against the conviction, because frankly he'd been roundly fucked on that. Our evidence was tight and compelling. No, by virtue of his age, in other words a young man in his twenties, seven years seemed to be a bit strong if he was to stand a chance of reforming his character and rehabilitate himself. So it was that a couple of months after we had weighed him off sending him away for an 'HM' holiday, I found myself sitting at the Royal Courts of Justice in Court Two, listening to some sponsored hack of a barrister setting out why poor little Michael wasn't up for doing all of his porridge. I just sat there alone boiling inside at the tilt being put on the facts of our case, my 'rent a barrister' for the day already capitulating before we'd even taken a step inside the courtroom. I was reminded of the Irish comedian Frank Carson who after every gag would say, "It's the way I tell 'em." I didn't have the heart to let John Innes know about the appeal. Least said, soonest mended, so I watched and listened to three 'learned' Appeal Court judges decide that in order to give Jackson a chance in life they would reduce his sentence to five years! What the fuck!

22

FURTHER ENQUIRIES

"Hello, Mrs Chakrabarti, I'm Basil's boss, I'm Detective Inspector Trebor, but please call me Bob, won't you? I'm sorry we meet under such unfortunate circumstances, but let me assure you we believe we know the identity of the assailant and we'll do everything in our power to get him."

She looked up at Bob, her eyes searching his face for reassurance that her husband was going to pull through, still holding his hand, careful not to disturb the drip taped to his arm.

Bob squeezed past her to the left side of the bed and, leaning forward, he left Basil in no doubt the squad would very quickly get who did this to him. As he left, Al met up with him at the Accident and Emergency reception and told him to ensure that all members of the squad be in the office for 9am sharp to be briefed on tracking down Heath. The only ones excused would be those engaged in court appearances. His chat on the phone during one of the earlier interminable delays waiting for the jury to come back with an answer held a very attractive proposition for Bob that evening. A phone call home to the mother of his children dictated he should really put in an appearance on the home front and forego an evening and probably a night of undiluted pleasure with a woman he had grown so fond of.

Truth is, I'm growing sick of her at home moaning that I'm never there, but in the next breath moaning she hasn't got enough money to go out shopping for designer clothes, berating me that the children are forgetting what I look like, but I have to do the hours otherwise this detective doesn't get paid! Her choice, quite frankly, so I'm heading home to see the kids, whom I love dearly, but these days it doesn't extend to her. One of them is training at the local swimming club and the other is at a gymnastics class about the same time, both of which are at the sports centre, so I can kill two birds with one stone and watch the pair of them. Then take them to the upmarket burger restaurant 'Back in Time' for a treat while she's sat at home festering and plotting my downfall!

*

Bob had barely made it into the office at eight thirty when his phone rang.

"What happened to you last night, I thought you were coming over?" He recognised her beguiling voice, as she made her enquiry so disarmingly casual, but from bitter experience when he'd tried lame excuses in the past, he sensed he was in for a hard time from her.

"I… erm had to cut away, I'm really sorry but one of the kids was sick and had to go to the doctor's. She didn't have a car as it was in for a service so I had to take mine home to do the trip."

Silence. Then an appeal that he could have let her know as she'd cooked a nice meal for them both and was 'dressed to kill', knowing that he would know exactly what she meant, but she accepted the reason this time, conditional on better notice should something like that happen again. He replaced the receiver, pledging he'd see her before the weekend, she accepting their complicated relationship meant he had all the balls in the air at the same time.

A hesitant knock on the door announced the entry of DS Hunt, dressed in jeans and an open-necked shirt hanging over the waistband as now had become the fashion, Bob noting it for next time.

"All right, Jim?" asked Bob as Hunt planted himself in a chair the other side of Bob's desk. "So what happened?" he continued.

Hunt unveiled his tale of woe as to how he and Basil were at Knightsbridge tube in the booking hall when they spotted Heath who was on conditional bail from the Magistrates' Court not to enter the Underground network because of his form for dipping or more violently robbing punters innocently using the services of the tube. A confrontation then took place between them, although he claimed he didn't directly see it, resulting in Basil being pushed and taking a fall down the escalators. The first thing he knew was Basil near the bottom having gone head over heels down the stairs. Heath by this time had turned and made good his escape. Bob sat staring at Hunt, his hands resting as if praying with his elbows firmly resting on his desk in front of him, waiting see if that was the end of his account. A pregnant pause was broken with Bob giving direction.

"Right, brief the boys and send them out looking for Heath. I want you to go to Knightsbridge Crown and see the witness to this. I believe they're in the List Office. In the meantime, send Hazel into me will you?"

"OK, guv." Hunt left, believing his account of Basil's rapid descent to injury had been accepted by the guvnor.

Bob shuffled some paperwork on his desk, signing off a number of crimes with no hope of ever resulting in a successful arrest or prosecution – a constant frustration to him that so many victims of this hideous crime saw no positive end result, so much so that in many cases the absolute minimum of enquiry by police, consisting of a phone call, a bit of 'tea and sympathy', was the best many could hope for. His thoughts were broken with Paul knocking and entering the guvnor's office.

"Hello, boss, good result for John Innes," said Paul.

"Yeah Paul, I'd like to catch up with him soonest, can I leave it to you to arrange? I want to get his CICB claim in, I'll do it for him; he deserves a decent payout from the Criminal Injuries Compensation Board, poor bastard. Meantime, we're going to see Raul Darby, see if he can shed any light on Heath's whereabouts. We need to nick him damn quick."

Paul concurred with Bob's declaration, and left to get a car from the pool, realising he'd be the driver to Darby's address in Deptford.

"It means nothing to me, oh Vienna."

'Click', as Bob turned his office radio off. *Right let's go,* he thought to himself, checking he had his wallet, his brief, aka warrant card, and his loose change. Happy that his day's papers were up to speed, he strolled down the six flights of stairs from his third-floor office to the station yard where Paul waited, the car on tick-over.

"OK, Paul," he said as he dropped into the front passenger seat. "Do you know where we're going?"

Paul knew the address in Shelduck Court in Deptford; confirming with the guvnor, he asked, "Is there any chance he can help us then, guv?"

Bob filled in Paul on Raul's background: he'd been a snout of his for a couple of years, in return for getting a 'life', as he perceived, and not getting nicked, or in his mind fitted up for a non-existent attempted theft offence adding to his extensive previous convictions for previous offences. From the nick they went east through the Angel Islington, down to Old Street, then to Houndsditch, over Tower Bridge – something the United States thought they'd bought when they actually purchased the old London Bridge – then Old Kent Road to Deptford.

"Will the car be alright here, guv?" asked Paul as they parked up in an area below Darby's address looking more like a war zone in the Middle East than a place where on return you wouldn't find the car on bricks! Bob laughed and said he'd been there many times without incident; of course, there was always a first time but it was a job car, not their own.

*

Hunt, dressed casually, carrying a small black leather portfolio, acquired as a present from his peers when he was first promoted to sergeant, walked purposefully along Hans

Crescent towards his appointment with the young lady in the List Office, who it seemed had seen everything when Basil met his demise. In his mind he ran through how he would approach the witness statement he was about to commit to paper, if she really did see Jim's 'shove'. In his mind, what he needed to ensure was that, in the confusion, she might not have seen what she thought she had. The List Office was on the same level as the front doors to the building and was one of those new modern ways of using office space with everyone in together, no walls, just room dividers. Hunt realised he'd have to find somewhere more private with the witness if he was going to succeed in convincing her what she 'really saw'. Penny's face drained as she saw DS Hunt enter.

*

Paul followed like a dutiful dog behind Bob as they ascended to the first-floor maisonette via the urine-smelling staircase, something which seemed to inform anyone visiting they were entering a block of council flats. Turning left they went past two front doors before arriving at Raul Darby's reinforced metal gate at the end of the landing. Bob pressed the buzzer to the right but then saw a small wire hanging loose from the back of the bell plate. Paul shook his head, berating Raul's crap doorbell. *Typical*, Bob thought, and resorted to leaning through the gate banging hard on the dirty white-painted wooden door.

Now I've known Raul for about three years. He's a dip pure and simple, probably with the accent on the latter, but that said

*he was honest enough to put his hands up to the attempted theft
I nicked him for, without crying 'foul' as so many in his position
have, he just accepted he wasn't going to win by claiming I'd had
such a vivid imagination shall we say? He accepted his fate, did
his time – he had to with the form he had – but we got on well,
and I don't know why but I felt obliged to help him get somewhere
to live when he was released from 'the Scrubs'. It's amazing
sometimes what a little rank and authority can do! Since then
he's been a useful source of information, particularly when I was
looking for members of the same ethnic group, you get my drift?
Today I'm hoping he might tell me where I can find Errol Heath.
The boys have already been to the home address he gave when he
was charged and last remanded and as King Charles I said, 'it
seems the bird has flown'. So now we're on a hunt for the shit!*

"Who is it?" came the voice from behind the closed
door. Raul, not anticipating visitors at the unearthly hour
of eleven o'clock, had just staggered to his kitchen inside his
maisonette to get a glass of water.

"Raul, it's me, DI Trebor, open up will you for fuck's
sake, before one of us gets a bad reputation."

Two bolts were slid open and a key in the middle
Chubb lock enabled Raul to free the door from its security.
Slowly it opened revealing a bleary-eyed Raul, seeking visual
confirmation of the voice he thought he recognised. His
buck teeth started a smile across his face as he was happy he
was right in his assumption. Without saying a word he then
unlocked the deadlock on the gate, beckoning Bob and Paul
into the hallway.

"Hello boss, sorry about that but you can't be too
careful round here. I've just got up, want some tea for you

and DC Hazel, isn't it?" he said as Bob and Paul followed him into a sparsely appointed lounge, where they sat on a brown corduroy sofa facing the lounge door. Raul left them and after a desperate search for two mugs, which he hastily washed out, the kettle whistled to announce it was ready to disgorge its contents on two 'Happy Shopper' teabags. To his surprise he found a new carton of long-life milk in his fridge, courtesy of his mate still sleeping upstairs. Having wrung the life out of the teabags he returned to the lounge with the mugs and milk, placing them on an upturned orange box doubling as a coffee table, apologising for an absence of sugar. His humbleness was now beginning to irritate Bob.

"Raul, sit down on the beanbag. You probably realise why I've come to see you."

A quizzical look adorned Raul's face indicating he obviously didn't have a clue what Bob was referring to, but then he'd often deployed such a look when being interrogated by the police over some crime which he claimed he did know about. He waited for the officer to divulge more before he'd commit himself.

"You see, Raul, you know I've always been straight with you, I've let you run when I could've nicked you, you've had a 'life' or two off the boys. Why? Because I've told them to leave you alone, not to cause you hassle, and that's because of the… what I'd like to call friendship between us. You know?"

Darby sat, still mystified as to why the guvnor of the Dip Squad was in his lounge and smiled to himself about the unthinkable proposition of getting fitted up by Bob.

Friends? He wasn't quite sure about that, but he could give Bob some old nonsense he'd believe, then maybe he'd just piss off out of his flat. His mate John was upstairs and he definitely didn't want him getting even a whiff he might be a snout for the 'old bill', especially Trebor!

"I bet you know about one of my officers being thrown down the escalators at Knightsbridge, don't you? Now don't say anything. I know who's done it, I just want to know where he's living. The last address he gave is crap. I want to get to him before his next court appearance, Raul."

Darby wondered to himself, *What the fuck is he on about? I haven't heard nothing at all.* But he nodded as if he was an all-knowing Buddha, waiting to impart his pearls of wisdom.

With that, there was loud thumping as someone descended the stairs two at a time, and a roar of anger as the lounge door burst open and Darby's massively built mate stood, filling out the doorway, wearing camouflage jeans and jacket and holding a large carving knife in his right hand poised and ready to use. There stood Sean Vivian Crawley, a violent black pickpocket, the whites of his bloodshot eyes glazed against his dark skin, nostrils flared, his growl revealing the two bright gold teeth at the front of his snarling mouth.

Darby spun round, "No Sean, no, they're sweet, man, they're sweet." Bob and Paul remained seated, creating the impression they were unaffected by some gobshite hell bent on filleting the pair of them.

"Hello Sean, wondered where the fuck you were living these days, now I know. So now you have a problem. As

Dirty Harry said, 'Do you feel lucky?' Are you going to try and get both of us, in which case a fight will happen, and I guarantee you'll get fucking done. You're wanted on warrant at the moment, and even if you're not, you know a script will mean you stay banged up until your trial, and you know Raul is sensible enough not to get involved, or you fuck off while we carry on extending our hand of friendship to Mr Darby."

Crawley said nothing but threw the knife to the ground with such force that it dug into the chipboard floor and quivered like a spent arrow, turned, slamming the door behind him, and a second slam of the front door announced that he had indeed left the flat.

"Now Raul, where was I before I was so rudely interrupted? Yes, my officer lies injured in hospital, recovering from being thrown down the escalator. I know who did it and I want to know where he is."

"Honestly, Mr Trebor, I haven't heard anything. I will ask around for you."

"Errol Heath," said Bob, "that's the fucker that did it and I want him. Soonest."

Darby was honest in his declaration, he knew nothing, but he knew Heath; it didn't really sound like a thing he would do, but he'd try to find him, and tell Bob.

With that assurance, Bob and Paul left Darby to recover the knife still stuck in the floor.

I'm on my way back to the 'dream factory' to see how Jim got on with the young lady in the List Office. With any luck her statement will put beyond doubt that Heath is the man and I can charge him with a good GBH or better still attempted murder with the right verbals. Must say I'm a bit surprised Darby didn't know anything, usually the old jungle drums beat very quickly on something like this, especially when a copper has taken a fall. Still, there it is.

*

Paul drove back through the busy rush hour traffic of central London to the nick, cursing the endless procession of buses causing, as he thought, more gridlock and aggravation than they're worth. Bob, tiring of Paul's whinging, was relieved to get back, and as punishment he told him to make the tea and bring him a cup. Jim picked up the case history folder on Basil's assault, gathering together a sheaf of papers together with the much-awaited statement from the List Office witness. He knocked and entered Bob's office to find the guvnor leaning back in his chair listening to Kenny Loggins declaring, "I went through the danger zone."

Bob beckoned him in. "Sit down, Jim, let's have a look at this statement."

Hunt pulled out the totality of her statement, which went into three pages. Bob studied its content, reading each page slowly, conscious this was the only independent view of Basil's assault.

"What the fuck is this, Jim? She's given a detailed account of how she came to be there in the first place and she tells us a lot of how she went to the court. But when it comes to witnessing Heath pushing Basil down the escalator she gets all vague. Didn't you try and pin her down on what is obviously the crucial bit of her evidence? What happened?"

Hunt realised he was going to have to confess all, because sooner or later the boss would find out or the witness might drop him in it anyway.

"Basically, guv, she swears she saw me push Basil down the escalator. To be honest, guv, I think I might have done, I just don't remember. Because of that I thought I'd leave it a bit up in the air. I didn't want her thinking I was trying to get her to tell lies, I honestly didn't know what to do. I'm sorry, guv, I just panicked."

Bob stared at Hunt. "Shut up, you tart."

He picked up the statement and slowly read through it again. Hunt didn't dare say a word; he figured he'd wait for the guvnor's response to the monster of a problem he'd created. *If only she hadn't come forward*, Bob thought, *he'd be able to mask his actions with Basil, nick Heath for the offence and fit him up.* Who's going to argue with the story of a violent black dip, breaching his conditions of bail, trying to escape, and in the process throwing a plain clothes copper down the stairs. Not only that, the Asian-looking copper could have just been a member of the public. So the defence could dress it up that maybe it was an accident he fell, in which case Heath would just be facing the breach of bail conditions, and maybe an attempted theft allegation, better still, attempted theft from Basil not realising he was in 'the job'!

"Right, here's what you are going to do. You are going to be the officer in charge of trying to catch Heath, and for putting the file together to nick and charge him, not only for the breach of bail but also the assault on Chakrabarti. Also you are going to have to get together with him to write up

Heath and that it was as a result of Basil discovering he was being dipped that Heath pushed him down the escalators. You sit on that statement you've got from the bird at the court. Better still, give it to me; I'll put it in my safe, so no one else sees it. I assume nobody else has seen it?"

"No guv, I haven't spoken to anyone in the office; I just came back and seen you."

"So you put it about that she wasn't really that helpful on the actual time of the assault so basically the whole case revolves around you and Basil. I'm going to leave it to you to get your storylines tight and together with him. When's he going to be discharged from hospital?"

"I think probably tomorrow, guv. He's a bit bashed about but he'll be all right. I'll speak to him, he's still a bit vague about what happened."

"You'd better straighten him out for this otherwise we're all in shit creek. You hang on to the case, and don't be so quick at getting Heath circulated as wanted for this. It needs a bit of distance put into it, which also gives you a chance to run through the script with Basil a few times to make sure you have it right! Do a recce on the location to get some idea of measurements for the scene, see if Heath could've lunged at you as you ducked and he connected with Baz pushing him in the back to his fall. I think that's the safest scenario, don't you?"

"Yes guv. I'm really sorry for this. I'll make sure Basil is well briefed on what happened."

"Not half as sorry as Basil, he's still licking his wounds! Now fuck off and get it sorted. But you tell me if any problems arise otherwise I can't help you. OK?"

Hunt left the guvnor to get on with a huge pile of crime reports he had to sign off.

I knew it, I bloody knew it! That prick Hunt, rhymes with... He's causing all sorts of aggro for me. First he fails to do his homework on two jobs where all he had to do was have two different descriptions of victims in each of the attempted theft cases and he would have been home and dry. But no, he gets sloppy, uses the same victim description and both trials follow one after the other in front of the same judge. The same judge for God's sake! The judges already know what's going on, they know the dips need 'taking out' regularly, what they don't want is to be put in an embarrassing position like that caused by the efforts of Hunt. You might think his stunt to avoid the second trial a tad extreme. So do I. What panicked him into throwing Basil down the escalator is anybody's guess. Luckily, from what I hear, Basil is going to be all right. But fuck me, it now means he's got to con Basil into believing Heath did it. That would be all right if it was only me who knew, but we've got a female witness who honestly believes Hunt did it. So now he's got to reframe the whole story again and somehow lose the witness! I wouldn't mind but this isn't the first time he's done it. Before, he stabbed a DC in the arse to avoid a repeat like those on the fucking BBC! I'll let you in on a secret, someone stabbed in the arse will survive, it's soft tissue, no vital organs or arteries, so no risk to life. A good GBH, and just unable to sit down for a while, but a very good excuse for getting out of a difficult situation. And, so my DS Hunt has form. There's me trying to show that we're clean, good thief takers, good reputation, pillars of society, not on the take like my predecessors, and I get an idiot of a sergeant who wants to dramatise every damn incident he's involved in!

23

SET THE TRAP

"I'm telling you, boss, they're on the take, all of them, even their guvnor. He's probably the worst," said an ageing Trevor David Jones, also known by some as Sutton, leaning back on his chair secured to the floor in the prison interview room. Pentonville Prison had played host to the hanging of many notorious criminals, including Dr Crippen, arrested as a result of the first telegraph request to a ship as he attempted to escape with his girlfriend Ethel le Neve to America. More recently Timothy Evans, for murder of his wife implicated by John Christie at 10 Rillington Place. Both were buried in the confines of the prison with little ceremony. Now it had the 'pleasure' of providing food and a bed for many nights to a sly professional pickpocket whose dishonesty knew no boundaries, using any advantage Jones could to ease his incarceration. A thoroughly disreputable individual.

Detective Chief Superintendent Maurice Branch and his 'bagman', Detective Sergeant Greg Dennison, paid a visit to Jones on the strength of a prison officer contacting the CID believing Jones might have some information on police corruption, which he had knowledge of. Branch had responsibility and supervision of all CID officers throughout the London area together with all dedicated squads such as crime squads, robbery squads, and the Central London pickpocket squad. He had known of allegations of corruption against some of his officers before; it was sometimes utilised by the dip as a first line of defence when he came to trial. But in this case he was led to believe this was a corruption on an industrial scale, where officers of the Dip Squad were routinely stealing any monies or 'taxing' the suspects in exchange for a 'life' or not getting nicked. His bagman, Dennison, was well aware of the nature of the allegation as in past years he had been head of an ad hoc team of detectives hunting dips and gaining a considerable revenue from them. Needless to say, Branch had no idea of Greg's earlier involvement in this lucrative 'business' but he did know by virtue of his reputation that he had a considerable knowledge of the pickpocket fraternity. When Maurice canvassed the general CID office from another location, Dennison, who had moved on as a result of promotion to sergeant, saw an opportunity to 'kill two birds with one stone'. Jones made a short written statement, recorded by Dennison, while Branch asked the questions sufficient to warrant further investigation, albeit as far as Maurice could discern Jones hadn't been nicked by the current incumbent or his team. So why now? Coincidence, or something more?

*

The music boomed loud in Heaven, a gay nightclub underneath Charing Cross railway station, the dance floor jammed with young men writhing and randomly dancing with complete strangers in many cases, to Dusty Springfield and the Pet Shop boys, asking "What had they done to deserve this?" Andrew McMurray found a two-seater red leather sofa away from the heat generated by the dance floor's occupants near to the bar. His white singlet glowed in the ultraviolet light almost silhouetting his dark skin. Greg Dennison, like Andrew, was no stranger to the club, approached him, he smiled, the light catching his grin in the dimly lit club. They exchanged high fives as Greg enquired what drink he wanted, after a few minutes returning with orange juices for both of them. They had been casual lovers in the past, having met as a result of Greg nicking him for attempted theft a couple of years previously. You could say it was love at first sight, but of course their liaison had to be kept quiet in a less-than-tolerant society, to say nothing of the fact that one was a law breaker whist the other was supposedly an upholder of the law. Greg gave Andrew a 'life' on that occasion in return for taxing him the two hundred and twenty pounds he had concealed in his socks and trainers.

Greg needed to talk to Andrew, who thought maybe tonight his luck was in. As they left the club into the cold evening air, Greg made it clear their meeting was only going to be business this evening but there could be a promise of more in the future. Much depended on him listening to what he had to say. They turned right into Villiers Street and walked closely down towards Embankment tube station where they sat at a table in the window of a late-night coffee bar. McMurray left no time in telling Dennison how pissed off he was with the current Dip Squad who, not two weeks ago, had nicked him for the usual, as he saw it, attempted theft from a person unknown, a female of course. He went on to tell him how Trebor, along with Hazel and Fish, simply walked up to him while he was sat on a bench on the Central line, then Trebor sat down one side, Fish on the other and Hazel stood right in front of him so he couldn't do a runner. Hazel told him he was nicked and when he asked why, expecting the usual old bollocks of a woman who had just lost her purse and he was nicked for 'sus' or something, Hazel just said he was nicked on a bench warrant, then all three of them laughed. It was only when they got to Holborn police station that he found out he was going to be charged with an attempted theft; not only that, they verballed him up as well, saying that he admitted the offence in questions and answers in the back of the van on the way to the nick.

"Do you know what they did?"

Greg stayed silent but was interested in Andrew's every word.

"They sat me on a bench in the room where you get charged. Then that cunt Fish over the other side shouted, 'Oi catch,' and I saw something flying towards me. As I reacted I just held my hands out and almost immediately I caught a soppy little plastic purse! 'Lovely,' said Fish. 'Now we've got your prints on that purse. There you go, a second offence of theft from a person unknown.' Bastards! That ain't right, is it?"

Dennison, laughing inside, tried to show his concern for McMurray's plight. But he conceded to himself that Fish's ingenuity was nothing if not a smart move, putting his 'lover' under pressure, probably resulting in a plea to at least one count on the indictment when he eventually appeared at Crown Court.

"It's not like when you ran the squad, Greg, at least we could do a deal with you. We got off with you just takin' our dosh! At least we never got nicked each time."

Dennison smiled and held Andrew's hand across the table, hidden from view by his shoulder bag. He tried to reassure him that he might be able to help; of course it wouldn't be easy, but it could lead to the charges he currently faced being kicked into the long grass, in return for a favour. He confirmed Andrew still lived in the block of flats round the back of Brixton nick, not far from Monk, the white dip.

"I'll be in touch, give me a few days, you're not at court for a couple more weeks are you, so I've got time to make a few enquiries, OK?"

McMurray said nothing, simply nodding as Dennison tried to console him. They hugged as they parted outside Embankment station, McMurray disappearing into the station watched by Greg who turned and sauntered back up Villiers Street, catching a cab out to his east London flat.

*

"Morning sir, a lovely morning isn't it?" said Greg in the hope of engaging Detective Inspector Secrett a 'Little Napoleon' of a man, sitting deep in thought as he studied a prosecution file sprawled out across his desk in the central CID office.

Secrett looked up and acknowledged Dennison saying, "Get the coffees in will you, Greg, and pull up a chair. We've got work to do."

Dennison returned to the guvnor's office, which still smelt of recently decorated shell-pink emulsion; apparently the 'big boss' had read somewhere that the colour pink had a calming effect on those who worked within it. All that Secrett knew was the aroma of paint really pissed him off, reinforcing his belief that those who had the brilliant idea ought to live in it, then perhaps they wouldn't be so quick to impose it on the people who actually do the work!

"Thanks Greg, what I'm going to talk to you about now remains between you and me. You speak to no one else about this. I turned this file over so that it couldn't be read. What I've got is two full statements from Trevor David Jones, the first I know you took at Pentonville, but Mr Branch made another visit to him and believe me, it's heavy stuff. You're going to know more about the general running of the Pickpocket Squad so we've got the task of doing all the background stuff on the job. I expect we'll have to speak to a few of the dips they've had dealings with; probably you'll know a few of them anyway, so that'll be helpful."

As Dennison sat down to read through the two statements his blood ran cold at some of the content, outlining the way various dips were either arrested and fitted up or taxed by members of the squad. He tried not to express great concern although he knew sooner or later he'd be identified as one of the bent coppers before Trebor's promotion had led to a clear-out and the team operating with a different purpose. A more utilitarian approach!

As he reread the second statement of Jones he saw that he was only mentioning white dips, and while he knew some of them he'd taxed or taken money from in the past he quickly realised he'd have to change the tack of Secrett's investigation to avoid scrutiny of his own previous behaviour. It was mainly black dips and a few of the South Americans that were his currency. Why? His rationale: who's going to believe a black thief or a foreigner that they've been rolled by the old bill? Easy pickings.

"I'll start working on this straight away, guv, I can think of a couple I talk to, they'll know what's going on."

"Good, Greg, we've got to keep this tight, just you and me and I'll report to Branch on our progress."

Dennison felt he'd done enough to con Secrett into believing him. He knew from past experience that Secrett was an irritating little shit, who thought of himself as an ace detective and because he'd managed to get a 2.2 degree, known as a 'Desmond' in the trade, from the Open University in anthropology and a Masters in criminology, he believed he was more intelligent, more astute and generally a right smart arse when it came to his peers. This made him universally loathed by his contemporaries, but he was so arrogant, so convinced of his own pissing importance, he really didn't give a toss what others thought. In fact he pretty much revelled in it! The downside of course was that not many people wanted to work with him. He knew Trebor back when Bob was just a Detective Sergeant and Bob had the dubious pleasure of working with him. He was mindful of the time he'd just been putting his sergeant more and more under pressure on a conspiracy job when Bob was banging away on the Imperial typewriter, trying to get all the corroborating statements typed up for a number of the officers in what was quite a complex 'robbery and handling' case with multiple defendants. Secrett made the mistake of badgering Bob's thought processes so much as he was typing with a succession of questions to which he demanded answers there and then. Bob let out a roar of "Why don't you just fuck off and die somewhere?" and picking up the heavily cast typewriter, he threw it across the room, some fifteen foot, at Secrett. Had he not been quite so nimble on his dancers he would have been wearing it across his face! Secrett learnt from that day not to ride Trebor if he valued his health.

*

Hunt has just been in to see me; Heath has been nicked. Fuck it. Really needed him to be running a bit longer. Still, not much you can do about a couple of 'eagle-eyed' uniform lads who just happened to see him standing at the bus stop outside Baker Street tube on the Marylebone Road. I wouldn't mind betting he was shaping up to dip the bus queue, but I can't try and convince the two youngsters what they might have seen. That would be a bit much, wouldn't it? None of the squad know them, so it'll just have to be the arrest for Hunt and Basil's job. Speaking of which, I hear he's still in hospital, which I find a bit of a surprise. Thought he'd be out and at home on sick leave, but apparently he's got sepsis or something – I know, I've never heard of it before – so they're keeping him in for a while longer.

*

Hunt made his way to Paddington Green police station on the corner of Marylebone Road and Edgware Road, this being the start of the A5, an old Roman road running straight out from London to Edgware and beyond. The nick is a high-security police building which provides accommodating cells for those lovely IRA terrorists nicked anywhere in the capital, usually after yet another explosion atrocity where members of the public have either been killed or dreadfully maimed, losing sight or limbs or both. Hunt left it until just after eleven in the morning, knowing the early turn custody sergeant would by now have had his 'full English' or whatever.

He went in through the station yard at the back of the building negotiating three or four challenges to his identity before opening the charge room door, noticing only the one handle on the outside, the inner one removed so that the door could only be opened remotely by the gaoler as a final security barrier. The skipper was understandably twitchy as he had three Irish terrorists in the cells brought in overnight after they had slung a nail bomb through the window of a West End restaurant, nicked courtesy of the Special Patrol Group who, after a long car chase, nicked them at gunpoint in Park Lane near Marble Arch. This meant that the phones were now ringing off the wall, with various legal representatives each claiming they were representing each or all of the miscreants, so a casually dressed Hunt's appearance at the sergeant's desk was something of a relief.

"Yes, DS Hunt, how can I help you? Tell me it's an easy problem, will you? This fucking lot are driving me mad, no bloody Bomb Squad team here yet. Still having their breakfast I expect."

Hunt outlined why Heath was languishing in cell four, courtesy of Paddington nick. The skipper looked about the same age as Hunt, so they reminisced about being in the police cadets for a couple of years before joining the job proper at the other end of the police station complex where the recruitment centre was, then getting a single room in the section house tower block above where they were chatting. The custody skipper noted everything that Hunt told him about Heath without question – there was an affinity between them borne out of their similar starts in police life – and he made reassuring noises that whilst in his custody, Heath would be in for a rough ride for badly assaulting Basil.

"Here you are, just been given a note from the reserve in comms. I'm told that none other than Commander George Churchill-Coleman is coming down to sort these paddies out—"

Before he could finish Hunt said, "No problem, I'll nip up the canteen for a cuppa, I'll come back down in half an hour."

"That's great, then I'll sort your bloke out. I take it you don't need to see him. I'll just go ahead and charge him with the GBH and breach of bail, anything else?"

Hunt said, "Yeah, and attempted theft, person unknown. Be a nice surprise when I see him." He laughed out loud, leaving the charge room just as the head of the anti-terrorist branch swept past him followed by his bag carrier hanging on his coat-tails, a pompous-looking, obviously ineffectual Detective Constable announcing himself.

"I'm DC Robert Brace, I'm with the guvnor," he said, as if expecting people to fall at his feet.

And I'm an alcoholic, thought Hunt as he remembered the AA adverts. *What a dick*, Hunt thought, *clearly trying to have a champagne lifestyle on beer money, ideas above his station in life, doubtless poncing every hour of overtime he could*, as Hunt bounced up the stairs two at a time to the welcoming arms of a brew.

*

He sat at the window overlooking the dross of Paddington stirring from the cheap hotels around there, the toms or 'ladies of the night' of Praed Street long gone to recover for the next night's trade as the morning bustle resumed in the more legal trades of shops and market stalls. As he nursed his cup of tea, the canteen phone rang – the custom was that one of the young uniform officers would answer.

"Is DS Hunt here?"

Jim acknowledged, sauntering over, not wanting to show out that anyone knew where he was.

"Oh hello guv, I'm just waiting to sort out Heath, bit of a delay cos the bomb squad have got bodies in."

There had been a problem, he was told. Basil wasn't looking too good, still conscious, but the sepsis infection was beginning to take hold. He was told to get his arse over there quick as possible after sorting Heath to find out what was happening. Hunt tried to reassure the guvnor there wouldn't be a problem with the case. He'd done his statement and had it typed up and he'd got Basil's script for him, so all he had to do was sign it. Then on the next hearing, which would probably be at Horseferry Road Magistrates' Court, he would be in a position to commit the case to Crown Court. Bob seemed satisfied with Jim's explanation. The phone went dead and Jim returned to his table, removing the saucer from the top of his half-finished cup of tea. He had just sat down when the phone rang again, summoning Hunt back down to the charge room to get Heath charged.

*

Bob's phone rang, interrupting his killing off a pile of crime reports, and he heard the horny sound of his dalliance.

"Hello DI Trebor, I just wondered if you remembered me. I haven't heard from you for a few days so thought I'd better make sure you're still alive."

"I am and all the better for hearing your lovely voice. How's things, are we going to meet up later?"

She lowered her speech to a whisper saying, "I do hope so. I've got something special for you. I've just been at a remand at Deptford Court and thought I'd do it without any knickers on, just stockings and suspenders. I was so wet thinking of you pumping inside me while you bend me over the table."

Bob chuckled, "That sounds just dandy. What else have you got in mind seeing as we're on the subject?"

"Bit of oral?" They fell about laughing at either end of the phone, agreeing to rendezvous later. Bob fell back in his chair, having never heard her talk in such graphic terms before.

"OK, I can't wait, I think I'm getting a bit of a beat on just thinking about it. You've not been with someone else have you? It's just I've never heard you be so upfront before."

She said, "No, silly, it's just what I've got in mind."

The call finished with them agreeing to meet at six that evening. Bob smiled to himself, knowing he was in for a very enthusiastic encounter. Best he have a shower in the basement changing rooms before dressing to kill. Needless to say, he made another phone call home to say that a serious job had come up that he would have to deal with before making it home, and the usual 'don't wait up' message. Not that she cared anyway. In the morning once the kids had gone off to school she was off down the stables for a bit of saucy exercise of her own with the boss, who had taught her to drive his horsebox.

Bloody hell, my phone's busy. Just finished speaking with my daft detective Hunt. He tells me he's charged Heath now with the GBH, breach of bail conditions and an attempted theft. Apparently, Heath went ballistic on the GBH and theft, he thought he was just there for the breach, and so he started lashing out in all directions. The gaoler tried restraining him along with Hunt and got bitten on the arm for his troubles so now he had an additional ABH charge to contend with. He's in custody until his appearance tomorrow at Marylebone Magistrates' Court. Anyway, Hunt has just slipped in to see Basil. Apparently, he's now in a coma, and heavily sedated with two drips fighting the infection. It's not looking good, just hoping he makes a recovery otherwise there's bound to be some kind of shit storm enquiry, and then we're all under the microscope.

*

"Baz, Baz, can you hear me mate?" Hunt, on a promise to the blonde nurse that he wouldn't be long, slipped behind the curtains in the side room off the main ward, after swapping phone numbers with her first, of course. *It's like raising the dead*, he thought to himself. *Oh fuck, I hope to Christ that it's not that*, his panicked mind raced. Again he tried to rouse Basil who, with one eye open, acknowledged his presence.

"How's it going, mate? Blimey, you're going through the mill, aren't you? This is a bit of a surprise, I thought you'd be out by now; still, you've got the best help there is, mate. I expect the antibiotics will take a while to kick in then you'll be up and about again, mate. Heath has been nicked, I charged him earlier today, he's up at court tomorrow so I'll cover the remand. Can you do me a favour if you're up to it? I've knocked out your typed statement, if you could sign it, then I can commit the bastard in custody to Crown Court on first appearance."

Basil nodded, which Hunt took as agreement. He fished out a sheaf of papers just as the nurse entered telling Hunt he should leave now, as Basil needed his rest. Despite his pleas just to get the statement signed the nurse was having none of it and turned him out of the room. He complied, not wishing to annoy her and decrease his chances of taking her for a drink. She was having none of that either!

*

"Greg, I can't take no more of dis. Them Dip Squad on my case again. I told you if you don't sort it, I'm telling the feds about you and me."

Greg leant back unconcerned in the brown velour armchair in McMurray's flat. His Doberman wandered in from the hallway having had a crap on the cheap lino and nuzzled into Greg's hand looking for some affection, never shown by its owner. Dennison was unimpressed with Andrew's veiled threat, asking what had happened since he last saw him.

"Andrew Keith McMurray, we've got a warrant to search this flat for stolen property from a number of recent dippings on the London Underground." Three plain clothes officers, one of whom looked familiar, barged into what could only be described as a 'Third World' establishment, while the Doberman snarled and growled at them. McMurray ran into the sitting room closely followed by a dog, thinking it was playing kiss chase, and two of the officers, both skidding on the randomly distributed dog turds on the hallway floor. A yell of "Oh fuck" indicated they had nearly been wearing the dog's gift as they pursued him.

They each took hold of Andrew as a precursor to the search when a loud thud could be heard emanating from the doorway outside as the third officer let out, "I've got shit all over my arse, what the fuck?" as he joined the others with a face like thunder.

McMurray trying to soften the blow and with obvious embarrassment said, "Yeah I know, I did that."

"You dirty fucking twat," said the officer, now exhibiting a less-than-exotic fragrance, and punched McMurray about the head with such force he fell back, together with the two officers, onto the tired sofa, which struggled with the weight of three lumps suddenly testing its robustness, closely followed by the dog, still believing it was playtime. His protests and vain attempt at explaining that he'd also slipped curried no favour with an officer just seeing red, who continued to hit him about the head until the other two called time out. Finally, a degree of calm returned with the search of the flat. Still embarrassed and fuming at his cheap suit being involuntarily damaged probably beyond economic repair, the officer waited downstairs near the CID car, imagining how the journey back to the nick could be negotiated, given that he was probably the least favourite of the car's occupants. He resolved that the discarded Tesco bags in the boot might go some way to smothering the aroma whilst at the same time protecting the 'fine cloth interior' in the bottom-of-the-range car.

The remaining two declared they had completed their search. McMurray was relieved they hadn't found his stash of drugs in the paint tin behind the bath panel, but he was left in no uncertain doubt they would be paying regular visits. He was a shit and he needed to understand where he was in the great scheme of things. Nowhere!

Greg continued to reassure McMurray that he had it all under control. He arranged to meet in the café beside the entrance to Russell Square tube station in two days' time. He then outlined what he wanted him to do, which would take the heat off him once and for all.

24

BAD TO WORSE

DS Hunt sauntered into the squad office carrying the case history folder for Heath. The guvnor leant back in the chair unperturbed at his arrival; he continued chatting to Fish about Arsenal's chances of doing the double this season.

Seeing as he was keen to have some kind of audience with the boss Bob said, "All right, Jim, how's Basil looking? I take it he's on the road to recovery is he?"

Jim confidently said, "Oh yes, guv, chatting to the nurse, he's probably only a couple of days away from being right as rain again. I got him to sign the typed statement I knocked out so I'm going to try to commit Heath tomorrow morning. There's bound to be a bail app but with his form and these offences I can't see him getting a result on that."

"He signed it, that's good. Well you know what to do now."

Hunt wasn't about to tell the guvnor he'd forged Basil's signature; besides, he was so out of it he'd never remember. He'd have to confirm he signed it, just to keep the evidence straight.

Bob declared he'd leave the boys to it, he was away to have a shower in the basement of the nick.

I think things are coming back on track again. The team's working well, that idiot Hunt seems to have redeemed himself, Basil's not good but according to Jim says he's going to pull through. I have an evening of carnal gymnastics with my legal eagle, then I'll get a lovely steak meal before retiring for another session of her taking control of my body. Bliss, I can't wait. Trouble is, I've got to break it to her that I'm off on a week's holiday with the kids in a couple of days' time. She won't be pleased because she'll think I'm still having it off with the wife, which couldn't be further from the truth, but it's a fact. I'm doing it for the kids, it's not their fault. I mean, adults can fuck their lives up as much as they like but you don't mess with kids' lives, so I keep up the pretence of life through rose-tinted glasses for them. In all honesty I'm just marking time until they're older, I know I'm living a lie but frankly I don't really know how to resolve this. I'm hopeful it will work out sooner or later, I know where I'd rather be, a bit like Dickens' Mr Micawber, "Something's bound to turn up." She makes me happy, what can I say?

*

Jim Hunt thanked the nursing staff for their continued efforts for Basil as he paid an early morning call on him at the hospital. He breathed in the fresh morning air as the sun gained strength rising over the Thames, leaving himself enough time to take a stroll through the streets of west London, destination Marylebone Court, for what would undoubtedly be a bit of a fight to get Heath committed to Crown Court. Hunt had been told his mate hadn't had a good night and was drifting in and out of consciousness.

He was crapping himself that the worst might happen so he went to see for himself. It wasn't good, but first he had to get the committal out of the way.

*

She dropped Bob off at Waterloo so he could get the Bakerloo line across to the nick at Baker Street. She wasn't in the mood to keep him any longer having been given the news about his annual leave; it made her feel used, but her feelings for him spurred her into believing one day they would be together. She toyed with the idea of two-timing him – another lawyer who she quite liked had made a play for her – but she couldn't see it going anywhere all the time she felt in the way she did about her copper. She did sleep with him once, but Bob was never out of her mind. It didn't make her feel any better. She didn't tell Bob; how would that make a difference? In any event she didn't want to lose the good times she had with him. So she resigned herself to seeing him when she could, just hoping there would be a time when they would always be together.

*

Bob danced up the steps from the station two at a time into the bustling streets around the nick. Oblivious to her deeper resentment, he knew she was disappointed, but he felt he'd explained it wouldn't be forever. Things would get better. He looked in on the office; a few of the squad were in with heads down, absorbed in their paperwork. Bob turned and entered his third-floor office bracing himself for more of his own paperwork, which took the form of signing off about a hundred crime reports, for which he was satisfied all necessary investigations had been explored and which could now be filed for future reference, either for the victims or any form of crime analysis. The phone disturbed Bob's determined attempt to 'clear the decks' of all his paperwork for the day. Bad news: Basil was fading fast, nothing the hospital seemed to do made any impact on his condition. He'd not heard of sepsis before and wondered if it was really that serious; surely it was just an infection that something like penicillin could take care of? Apparently not, was the response at the other end of the phone. He replaced the receiver and leant back in his chair, wondering what he should do next. He decided to join Hunt at court to satisfy himself Heath's case was committed to Crown Court without fuss. He needed to speak with Hunt to create a strategy for if the worst-case scenario were to manifest itself.

Crossing Marylebone Road towards Seymour Place, Bob walked up to the entrance facing the busy thoroughfare. Passing the signs for the disabled toilets, he thought that must be where the defence briefs were; he made his way down the long corridor to the police room at the far end. Spotting Jim finishing off a cup of tea courtesy of the court staff, he led him away to a corner where they could have a quiet chat.

"Show me what it is you're going to commit Heath on."

Jim handed the case history folder to the guvnor, without comment. Bob read through Jim's and Basil's statements.

He satisfied himself there was a prima facie case in their content, then said, "OK, there's enough there. What do we do with the bird's statement from Knightsbridge Crown, in my safe? How are we going to deal with that? Does she know anything about us nicking Heath? Because if she doesn't, it might be we can take a plea and she'll never be bothered, and I take it neither Heath nor his brief know of her existence. For fuck's sake don't serve her statement unless we absolutely have to, because it'll lead to a discipline investigation or more serious!"

Hunt reminded Bob that her statement was safely tucked out of the way in his office drawer after he took it back, and she believed the assailant wouldn't be found. Defence knew nothing. Heath was claiming foul, as was usual, but to date hadn't made a complaint against the police.

Bob left him to get on with it, with the instruction to return to his office to discuss the right strategy for the case. *No peace for the wicked*, Trebor thought, as he opened his office door to that blasted phone ringing again.

"Hello, DI Trebor, oh hello, yes… I see… my goodness what a tragedy… when? Of course, right, I understand. Can you give me time to speak to the team? My guess, they'll take it pretty hard. No I go on leave for a week tomorrow. When did he die? OK. Shall I wait for you to let me know when? OK, sometime tomorrow, yes, I'll try to get them together this afternoon. What about his family? OK. I'll leave you to take primacy on that then. How? It was a dip who was violently resisting arrest, as I understand it, who was responsible. Yes of course, it ups the ante to a murder or manslaughter at the very least. Unfortunately I can't cancel my leave, the kids have their buckets and spades packed already. I've already told DS Hunt he's covering my position while I'm away, I assume that's OK, guv? What is this sepsis, I've never really heard of it before, is it something new? I see, so some kind of super bug bacteria does it then. Can't they just boost the antibiotics? No? So sometimes that works, sometimes not. Bloody hell, what a mess. Poor bastard, poor family. OK guv, thanks, I'll be here for the rest of the day."

*

Greg Dennison looked at his stainless-steel Rolex watch, wryly smiling to himself knowing it was acquired from 'kind' donations taxing a few dips over the preceding months. The small café just to the left of Russell Square tube was doing a roaring trade mainly from foreign punters venturing out from the relative safety of the Bloomsbury and Russell hotels. He sat cupping a small cappuccino careful not to rub the nap on his light beige blouson suede jacket, his latest purchase from Harrods. He was single, yes, he had a reasonable disposable income, but his clothes showed that here was a copper living way above his pay grade. The irrebuttable presumption being that he was a thief living off the thieves. McMurray appeared at the door, saw his lover and ponce, nodded and sat opposite him at the small bench table. Greg outlined what he had in mind. They left the café and went down to the platform of the next-door station to walk through his plan to ensure McMurray would be able to make good his escape from the forthcoming prosecution.

*

Right, that's me done. Off on a week's leave; I've just said cheers to the lads in the office. They were gutted obviously with the sad news about Basil. But they've assured me, they'll go through his outstanding caseload so there are no fuck-ups looming. Hunt has committed Heath, so nothing much will happen on that until we get nearer to a date for the trial. See you in a week's time.

*

Branch wanted to know what progress DS Dennison had made since the last interview with Jones. Secrett sat in the brown vinyl armchair at right angles to the guvnor sipping his camomile tea while Branch, shouting for the knock on his door to enter, swallowed the last of his coffee. Greg minced in as if his arse was chewing a toffee, flashing a smile to Secrett before sitting on the only chair left in the boss's office. He didn't disappoint. The story he gave was one of an engrained corruption among the officers of the Central London Dip Squad. He had, according to him, spoken to a number of pickpockets who either alleged that they had been fitted up or that officers had cash taken from them. Sadly, none of them would commit to paper, a statement which would give Branch the justification for a raid on the squad and their offices.

*

"This is an interesting one," said Fred Boles, head of the Complaints and Discipline department at headquarters.

Boles, an Assistant Commissioner and head of the unit charged with investigating public complaints against the police, could barely contain his mirth, as he sensed retribution on a squad he'd loathed existed but seemed unable to do anything about. He was what is regarded as a 'uniform carrier', the one who looks busy as they carry a piece of paper around with them, very good at writing a paper on how to combat crime or catch criminals but useless at actually nicking them. They regard themselves above all that, often have degrees in management or criminology or jurisprudence, speak with authority but like an empty vessel they make the loudest noise with no professional life experience to back it up. Managers not leaders. The problem was that the Dip Squad had a formidable reputation among their peers for catching the bad guys, with many would-be detectives keen to join the team, and championed among middle and senior management for showing a higher-than-average clear-up rate with a great turnover in arrests and convictions. And of course it was in their interest to perpetuate the existence of a successful squad as it made them look good for their 'performance indicators', in the new jargon that had crept in. His comments were addressed to his 'bag carrier' or Detective Chief Inspector, by the name of Kev Spooner, whose function was the day-to-day running of the department and allocation of investigations to officers of a comparable rank for investigation.

"The letter came in this morning, guv, from the brief representing a villain Errol Heath. He's saying firstly that he's being fitted up by the Dip Squad at Baker Street but more serious he says that he saw one of the officers push another one down the escalators and then blamed him! You recall the officer allegedly killed while on duty, Basil Chakrabarti."

"Yes of course, dreadful business. Unless you have something more pressing I'd like you to take charge of the investigation. I want you to leave no stone unturned on this, and ensure those concerned know that you'll be robust in your endeavours."

Spooner confirmed he would exercise all due diligence in his enquiry, which basically meant he promised the earth, starting with an 'unannounced' visit to the squad office, a euphemism for a raid hopefully designed to destabilise Trebor and his team. He told Boles he would get a 'bagman' and start the investigation forthwith.

Nine o'clock in a rain-soaked London saw Spooner and his bagman, DS Bill Patten, meeting up at headquarters for a quick cup of tea and a bacon roll from the Italian café across the road before setting off for Baker Street nick. Bill wasn't happy working with Spooner, who had a bit of a reputation for being a bit fly. He'd been captured in the past trying to tap up a villain's wife, having put her 'dearly beloved' away for a five stretch. What he didn't realise was that she was leading him on as payback and, as she thought, perhaps an allegation of unwanted sex against the officer in the case might help her hubby get released a bit earlier. Seems it failed on both counts. The gods must have been looking after Spooner on that occasion, but it still remained, he was dodgy as hell. Bill knew he was out to prove himself to the bosses, trying to get back in their good books, so he figured he'd just give this internal discipline enquiry as much of a wide berth as he could.

They wandered out to the back of headquarters otherwise known as 'the dairy'; the building and its covered car park to the rear used to be the head office of United Dairies, before plod took it over. Finding the Escort XR3 parked next to the London taxicab used on covert operations, Bill checked round the car making sure previous drivers hadn't put mysterious dents or scratches in its bodywork, then opened it, watching Spooner easing himself into the front passenger seat, and sitting with his portfolio case on his lap. Bill adjusted his seat and turned on the main set radio, booking on with Information Room, being careful not to inform of their final location. They joined the slow-moving London traffic turning right towards Euston Road, destination Baker Street nick.

"Officer needs urgent assistance, violent robber trying to escape, Russell Square station."

At least six vehicle call signs answered the plea with more tumbling in on the 'shout' before Information Room declared sufficient were now attending, before Bill said, "Shall we go, guv, I can do a next left and come round the back of Hotel Russell?"

Spooner declined saying there were enough units going; they would continue with their journey for their 'visit' with the acting DI, Jim Hunt. Knowing the digital code, Spooner released the barrier allowing Bill to drive into the police station yard. Kev Spooner went on ahead to the back door where again he tapped in the entry code, while Bill, having found a parking bay, joined him at the door. They went to the fourth floor and as a matter of courtesy, without going into detail, appraised the Chief Inspector at that time in charge of the police station of the purpose of their visit. Five minutes later they descended one floor to Bob Trebor's office.

"Morning DS Hunt," said Spooner, surprising Jim who was deep into killing off a stack of crime reports while listening to the Clash on his Sony Walkman singing, "I fought the law and the law won," as he sang along, not aware of Spooner's unwelcome presence.

"Oh. Hello guv, what brings you here, is this a courtesy call or how can I help?"

Spooner put Hunt's naïve query to bed, telling him he was under investigation for perverting the course of justice in that a public complaint had been received from those representing Heath that he had, in common parlance, fitted him up with an attempted theft charge, and then sought to prosecute him for a GBH on Basil. He then served a Regulation 7 notice on him outlining in broad terms the alleged offences, which he countersigned. Hunt was visibly shaken by this arbitrary approach but tried holding his nerve when he handed over the case history folder on the job.

"Are these the only two statements on which Heath was committed for trial? Are there any others?" enquired Spooner as he handed over the file to Bill, instructing him to copy every sheet of paper in the file.

Hunt, looking as if he was a rabbit caught in the headlights of a car, said Spooner was holding the sum total of the trial evidence. Then came a problem.

"Right, where's your desk?"

Hunt led him to his desk in the main office; realising he'd find the Knightsbridge clerk's statement, he tried suggesting the only reason it wasn't in the committal file was because there had been a delay in getting it typed up, and in any event there was a prima facie case, hence the reason it had been committed. As it hadn't been served yet Spooner told Hunt he'd hang on to the original for further enquires. He was told to carry on with his work, and they would be in touch with view to a formal interview. Spooner and Patten left as quickly as they had appeared, leaving a panicking Hunt dwelling on the content of the Regulation 7 notice.

*

Heavy rain announced that the day of Basil's funeral at his local church would be a very damp, miserable affair. His wife didn't want a full 'police' funeral, preferring a low-key ceremony for family and friends together with those who had worked with him. A couple of senior officers dressed in full regalia insisted on being there on the day to show those watching that 'we are all one big police family', a kind of solidarity with an Asian officer. But those who knew and worked with Basil were under no illusion that this was just window dressing or bullshit by those with the power. The church service was a very short affair with the vicar alone, unaware of the reality of the incident, raising the tragedy and injustice of his untimely death.

The officers gathered outside chatting amongst themselves. They acknowledged the presence of a retired officer who had taught Basil 'beats' when he first joined the job.

"Bloody shame, a good young officer taken so early in life," said one of the group.

The pensioner agreed. "How old are you then guv?" he casually enquired.

Branch said, "I should be like you now and be retired, I'm older than I care to recall. Every morning I open my eyes, put my elbows out to the side, and if I can't feel wood, I know I'm still alive! But I do feel old."

"Little point in you going home, is there? You'll be next," the pensioner cheekily said.

"Fuck off," he responded.

Branch, seeing the two uniformed senior officers, moved away from the retired officer who no longer needed to watch his Ps and Qs, smiling as he parted company.

25

ALLEGATIONS, ALLEGATIONS

"Urgent assistance, officer being assaulted, Russell Square tube!" The cry for help reverberated through every police vehicle and each officer walking the beat in a three-mile radius of the location. The information pleaded with the officer transmitting for more detail, but none was forthcoming despite repeated requests. Greg delighted in raising the dramatic concern and needed the assistance to come running – all part of his attention-seeking. A total of six mobile units claimed to be in the vicinity, the nearest being some five minutes away. Three CID officers who were just leaving central CID on an unrelated enquiry said they could be there in less than a minute and were attending.

DCs Steve Pride and John Walton jumped out of the CID car as it screeched to a broadside halt outside the front of the station. Running into the booking hall, they quickly saw Dennison struggling with a black man trying to break free of his grip.

"Come here, you shit, you're nicked," said Pride as he and Walton twisted his arms back and applied handcuffs at his back, enabling Dennison to stand back, as they thought, to draw his breath. To their surprise, he staggered a couple of steps and collapsed to the terrazzo floor of the booking hall. The third officer rushed in from locking the car and went to his assistance. It seemed as if Dennison was going in and out of consciousness, and obviously needed urgent medical assistance.

"We're on scene and dealing, one arrest; can we have an ambulance to the location? One officer unconscious," the personal radio pleaded.

An ambulance was confirmed, as the third officer, Neil Blacklaws, continued to make Greg comfortable as best he could before its arrival. McMurray looked as if he was continuing to struggle, as tourists and the travelling public passed by oblivious to his incarceration. But a couple of digs in the ribs from Pride quickly convinced him he was well and truly nicked and was going nowhere. A whisper from Dennison to Blacklaws prompted him to contact Secrett on his radio among the busy airwaves responding to the incident. The ambulance crew arrived and quickly assessed the necessary precaution of taking Greg to hospital, at least for a check-up. Placing him in the wheelchair and covering him in a red blanket, he was removed and whisked off to the local UCH.

"The guvnor wants us to take him to the squad office. Not to the local nick," said Neil.

"What the fuck for?" enquired Steve in his own inimitable language.

"Why, what's going on Neil?" asked John. "Something's not right here. We've nicked him, he should be going to Holborn nick. Not to the squad office."

"Branch has directed it. Secrett and Spooner are going

to speak to him. I don't think we'll get a look in on this. They obviously know more than we do. Best we just do it," said Blacklaws. A suspicious Pride and Walton dumped McMurray unceremoniously into the back of the car, Blacklaws sitting with him. The journey back to the office was in silence, Steve and John not wanting to give an opinion on this peculiar decision. Blacklaws felt compromised by Dennison, and McMurray was intent on doing as much damage as he could with his allegations of corruption against the Dip Squad, on his arrival at the CID office, where he was to be interviewed by Spooner and Secrett.

McMurray remained in the care of central CID for the rest of that day, making allegation after allegation of perverting the course of justice, varying conspiracies of corruption and of theft or 'taxing' from him. Secrett and Spooner focused primarily on those involved in his latest arrest, but it was clear to their enthusiastic minds that the enquiry could be expanded if they were of a mind, and they were of a mind, to encompass a large proportion of the squad.

Pride and Walton were called in to sit with the 'prisoner' while the two glory hunters went to speak with Branch. They believed that a raid on the Dip Squad was now warranted, but they each expressed concern over the existence of Trevor Jones and his allegations. Branch brusquely told them to keep quiet about his existence as his investigations proved he had no contact with the squad and certainly hadn't been arrested by them, so their focus must be on McMurray's allegations. Spooner responded by boasting that he thought he'd unearthed another conspiracy of corruption in the

Chakrabarti case. He'd found out that there was another witness, a clerk at Knightsbridge Crown Court, who had made a statement far from supporting the content of Hunt's account, actually appearing to suggest that Hunt and not Heath had caused the fatal injuries to his colleague.

Branch told them to leave and get on with preparing for a raid on the squad at the earliest opportunity. Secrett said that he would obtain a full statement from McMurray, then consider their strategy. In the meantime he'd be lodged at a police station not connected with the location of the crime. In other words, they were hiding him away, in case of any leaks from the investigation.

*

I've just got back from my 'family holiday'. As I opened the front door I pushed back a pile of letters and junk mail, not wanting to even consider them until I'd had a cup of tea. After unpacking the bags and cases and sorting out the kids, I could put it off no longer. The usual bank statements and credit card bills were put to one side as I didn't want a lecture from them on where I'd overspent. But I'm due back into work tomorrow so I'll have to kill this lot off before then.

There's a note, I don't know the writing but it says, "Don't contact the office, your squad has been nicked and suspended for corruption. I will try to contact you later." I'm mystified. I showed it to the other half. Her only response was, "What have you done wrong? You must have done something.' Thanks for the vote of confidence, I thought. I didn't speak to her again, no point. She doesn't like me, and to be honest I don't like her either. No phone call, no surprise.

*

Rain. *That's all I need for my first day back*, thought Bob. Just then his home phone rang. He picked it up but said nothing, waiting for the caller to commit to speaking. The voice enquired if he was talking to the guvnor. Bob recognised the dulcet tones of Micky Murphy, a Detective Sergeant working on the Robbery Squad. He was concerned the call may be bugged so Bob wrote down the phone box number Mick was calling from. Bob left the house and drove two miles to a phone box to return the call. Mick tried to explain as much as he knew. While Bob was on leave, having 'quality time' with his kids, the squad was raided, lots of files were taken and those in the office were arrested for corruption and perverting the course of justice. Bob pressed him on who were in the raiding party and he was told it was a number of central CID under the direction of Secrett and Spooner. Mick thought it all a bit strange because they were taken to the headquarters of central CID for questioning, but he didn't know any more than that. He suggested DI Trebor didn't go in today but he knew he had nothing to hide, so Bob was going to make the journey.

Still raining. *Bloody great*, thought Bob as he boarded the train for the thirty-minute journey into central London. He thought it might not be inconceivable that he was being 'tailed' en route to work, so his provocative nature kicked in and he did a couple of reciprocals, or U-turns, to test. The first was to jump on the train and jump off again to see if anyone mirrored his movements. The next was to go down the Underground escalator only to return back up to look at who was also using it. Happy he wasn't being followed, he continued his journey to the office. He slipped in the back entrance to the nick unseen. His office seemed untouched as he sat and started going through the deluge of paperwork which had arrived on his desk in his absence. Resolving to crack on, he ploughed through it. *Strangely quiet*, he thought, not receiving any phone calls. Frankie Goes to Hollywood boomed out "Welcome to the pleasure dome," as Bob looked up at his clock thinking it was about time for a coffee.

The door burst open. "Detective Inspector Trebor, I am investigating allegations of corruption against you and this squad of yours. You are not obliged to say anything unless you wish to do so, and anything you say may be put into writing and given in evidence. Do you understand?" said Branch as his cohorts, in the form of Secrett and Spooner, commenced searching his office.

"This is a fit-up! And make sure you remember that. Write it down, you little twat," said Bob, directing his bile at Spooner.

*

What happened next, I hear you ask? A noble cause, a fit-up or a straight investigation? I think you know the answer. You have two choices: it's either Hunt's fuck-up or it's McMurray's allegation courtesy of that bent copper Dennison. More to come.